the artist's portrait

the artist's portrait

*A story about art, murder,
and making your place in history*

JULIE KEYS

Shortlisted for the Richell Prize for Emerging Writers

The research in *The Artist's Portrait* was supported by an Australian Government Research Training Program (RTP) Scholarship.

The quotes on page vii are fictional representations of the attitudes of the time and not genuine quotes.

Published in Australia and New Zealand in 2019
by Hachette Australia
(an imprint of Hachette Australia Pty Limited)
Level 17, 207 Kent Street, Sydney NSW 2000
www.hachette.com.au

10 9 8 7 6 5 4 3 2 1

A catalogue record for this book is available from the National Library of Australia

ISBN: 978 0 7336 4094 0 (paperback)

Cover design by Christabella Designs
Cover photographs courtesy of Trevillion, Arcangel and Shutterstock
Author photograph courtesy of Sophie Turner
Text design by Bookhouse, Sydney
Typeset in 12.2/17.8 pt Adobe Garamond Pro by Bookhouse, Sydney
Line from 'This Be the Verse' by Philip Larkin courtesy of Faber and Faber Ltd
Printed and bound in Great Britain by Clays Ltd, Elcograf S.p.A.

To my parents, Maxine and Barry Keys

Kemp's paintings have the stench of an abattoir; the flesh she depicts is lifeless, barren – a reflection of the artist, no doubt.

Norman Lindsay

I can only iterate my disgust. Kemp's pictures are vulgar and contemptible. She desecrates all men who fought for this country with her filthy smears and blobs.

Captain R.J. Henshaw

We are talking about the banal here. I'd hate to have her cook my dinner.

Xavier Herbert

If Kemp has talent, she's squandered it on these nasty depictions.

James Stuart MacDonald, Director, National Art Gallery of New South Wales 1928–1936

PART I

PART 1

1.

Tell it like it's the truth

Winter 1914

It was my father who started it. That's what I called him – not
Dad or Pa or Dada or the Old Man but my father, Lionel
Kemp. It was my father who dragged me up that flight of stairs.
I grabbed hold of the railing and refused to budge but he twisted
the lobe of my ear and caught my fist in his hand when I tried
to punch him.

'If he wants your clothes off, then he wants them off.'

The place stunk of cats, Lysol and turps, and there was the crack
of my wrist bending backwards. I wouldn't take off my clothes.
I wouldn't stay where I didn't want to be. I spat and clawed and called
him a mongrel then tripped in the dark over a loose board on the
step. My father hauled me up the last of the stairs onto the landing
by the nape of my neck then positioned his mouth close to my ear.

'*Do you understand?*' he hissed.

He opened a door and shoved me into a light-filled room. I made a holy racket falling onto the floor, followed by my father, who cursed as he stepped over the threshold and lifted his foot, aiming a kick in my direction.

'Enough. I'm working.'

I rolled onto my knees to see who'd spoken. It was an old man, outlined against a large window, frayed hair wafting across his head. I crawled backwards, putting distance between me and my father.

My father dropped his foot to the ground, pulled his hat from his head and frowned. 'Are you Max Jenner?'

The old man nodded.

'I was told to come after three. I was told you'd pay to have her sit for you.'

'No. No children.'

'She's thirteen.'

'Ten. I'm ten.'

My father glared at me. A warning. I felt behind me for the wall then slid sideways, angling myself to get a better look at the old man, dressed in his smock daubed with paint.

'I was told—'

'You were told wrong.'

There was a clear space around the door but the rest of the room was full of clutter. I crept to the left, past an easel that had a tall chair perched in front of it, then moved to the far wall where two card tables had been pushed together and stacked with paint tubes and brushes, glass jars, torn envelopes, piles of books both open and shut, bits of wood covered in skinny runnels of paint, string, knives, spatulas, three peacock feathers in a vase, an apothecary cabinet,

4

pieces of broken glass and a scattering of threepences and sixpences lurching from crevices as if someone had emptied their pockets.

My father approached the man – Max Jenner – his head jerking back and forth like a rooster's. 'I was told to bring her.' He poked Max in the ribs.

'And now you're being told to take her away.'

'Not empty-handed I won't.'

There was a fireplace opposite the window, a gramophone on a side table and canvasses everywhere, portraits: a man in uniform, a woman in a hat piled with roses, another of a woman I would come to know, Constance Mawson, but hers was a different type of painting to the others. She was naked and soft and draped across a divan with a bowl of water on the floor beside her dangling foot. The divan was covered in cushions and throws and only a step away. If I hid behind it I'd get a good view of the fight, but I figured the table was a safer bet and settled beneath it, finding cobwebs, a fallen sixpence and the raised hind legs of a pig-rooting horse drawn in pencil just above my head. A sign, I thought, and touched it for luck.

'We are not barbarians.' Max Jenner's voice brought me back to the fight.

My father, who *was* a barbarian, landed a blow, underestimating what lay beneath the smock. The punch glanced off the old man's middle. In reply Max Jenner clenched his fist, pulled it to his shoulder, then lunged forward with all his weight. My father's head snapped back. His hand rose to his nose and came away bloody. That's all it took. My father turned on his heel and left through the open door.

Max Jenner moved to the window and opened it. Sounds rose like steam from the street below, a horse pulling up short, a distant brass band on a recruitment march, a 'hi-ho rabbit-oh'.

'He's gone.'

I fingered the fallen sixpence, poked at a hardened lump of paint.

'I said he's gone.' The old man looked over his shoulder in my direction. 'And you'll be the worse for it if I have to drag you out from under that table.'

I doubted that, I could outrun an old man any day, but came out all the same and stood in front of a book opened at a diagram of a body that was split in half like a peach. A dark yellow line meandered over the figure like an unfurling vine. Only my eyes touched the page. I kept my hands behind my back as I leaned over it, pondering the workings of 'The Sympathetic Nervous System'. Max Jenner stepped in beside me and slammed the book shut. I shifted away from the table and stood beside a portrait instead. The one of the woman draped over the divan. I heard the sigh behind me, 'I'll draw you a picture,' Max Jenner said 'to take with you.'

'I can draw my own picture.'

He laughed but found a piece of charcoal and opened a sketchbook at an empty page. Crouching on the floor I sketched his head and shoulders giving him the face of a rat.

Max picked up the sketchbook and examined what I'd drawn. 'You've had lessons?'

Nan had taught me, using the soot from the stove. I could have said that but I didn't see why I should.

'But you draw?'

I looked down at the floor.

'What about home, where's that?' Max Jenner's voice was calm but his eyes were watchful like the rat in my sketch.

'Surry Hills.' The answer was automatic.

'I want you here twice a week. Tuesdays and Saturdays, after three.'

'I'm not sitting for you.' I stood.

'To clean my brushes and palettes, mix my paints, sweep the floor, clean the windows and get rid of unwanted visitors.' I waited for him to give me my drawing, but he closed the sketchbook and returned with it to the window.

'And you'll pay *me*, not my father?'

'It has nothing to do with your father.'

There was a small picture on the card table, a sketch of a dog, running as if it were on the chase. I tried to see how it was done.

'Saturday.' Max looked across the room.

I bent over the dog. It was the ears. That's what made it look fast.

'Take that and go.' He waved his hand, shooing me away like a fly.

Rolling the picture into a cylinder, I shoved it up my sleeve for safekeeping then shut the door behind me, spending unearned wages as I descended the stairs, tripping on the loose board in the dark. Bananas, peaches, a good coat for Nan, tea in a cafe, cinema tickets. Out on the street I searched for other workers, women who had a job as good as mine: typists, girls who worked in cafes, factories, haberdasheries. But it was the wrong time of the day and I was almost alone. I stopped at a shopfront to look at a display of books and stationery. The blur of a pedestrian reflected in the plate glass window as he stood beside me. A man in a dark suit whose sleeve touched my hand

'See something you like?' The cloth of his suit smelled of Christmas pudding and was soft against my skin.

I shook my head and took off, running until I reached Samuel Street, with its scabby terraces of sandstone and weatherboard and iron, and balconies that looked like eyelids slumbering above the backyard patches of dirt. And then I saw Alice Cooney, mouth open, running towards me with an outstretched hand that touched my shoulder before I could escape. 'You're it.'

Arms wide, I tried to catch bodies as they scattered along the narrow pavement in front of me, out of reach. They stood like fence posts, waiting for my next move. Dulcie's mum called for her to come inside but she stayed put until her mother pounded across the street to fetch her, hand raised, face crushed by anger. Dulcie scampered off, fast like a rabbit, wailing as if her mother's hand had already found her.

Alice Cooney's brother, Hugh, jogged past dragging his billycart, off to collect wood and fittings from a vacated tenement. We streamed in a flurry behind him, running to get there before it was picked clean, passing a barrow merchant calling, 'Turnips, potatoes, parsnips.'

'Meat pies, bullseyes, bananas,' Hugh called back, trailing his fingers along the side of the barrow.

'Oi, get off with you.' The barrowman scooped up a roll of horse dung and flung it in our direction.

At the tenement, I found a shoe, just the one. Phil wanted it. So I swapped it for a notepad that had *In the Field* and *YMCA* stamped on each page beside an inverted red triangle and a map of Australia.

I stuck the notepad down the front of my dress, put my arm across my chest so it wouldn't fall through, then ran home, stopping at the fruiterer's on the way.

Home was a three-storey tenement with a faded green door that opened onto a hall and a stairway that led to the rest of the lodgers' rooms. Nan and I were permanent tenants and lived on the ground floor. I would have liked to live in the attic room, because of the angled roof and the window which got the sun, but Nan would never have managed the stairs. I headed to the end of the hallway and our door on the right which rattled as soon as you got close to it. The door opened onto a square room that held two chairs, a side table, a tallboy and a bed behind a curtained off section.

'Muriel?' Nan heard me come in. 'Where's your father?'

I shook my head. 'Gone.' I let the notepad fall to the floor and slid it to the side with my foot, placing the picture of the dog next to it and weighing it down with the night pot to unroll the curl.

'What have you got there?' Nan asked.

'A picture. I'll show you after tea.' Nan lowered herself into her chair, eyes on my face in the dim light.

'And how'd it go with the other?'

'He said I was too young.'

Nan didn't look surprised. My father's most reliable scheme for making a quid was to turn up on pension day. Nan always gave him something.

I removed the purchase from the fruiterer's which I'd pushed up my spare sleeve. 'Which hand?' I stood in front of Nan, arms behind my back. She tapped my right elbow and I pulled both fists from behind me, opening them to reveal an orange in each hand.

'You didn't get those from your father.'

'I found sixpence.'

'They'll do for pudding.'

She got up to light the lamp then went into the kitchen to cut the damper, spreading the jam thick the way I liked it. The other lodgers mostly did their cooking on a gas ring in their rooms so we had the kitchen to ourselves, although we shared the scullery and the laundry and the dunny with its leaking cistern, and the stunted tree out in the yard. Nan said it was peach, though it never bore fruit.

After tea, I curled up in the bed next to Nan and told her about the man and his smock and the canvasses. She scratched as the bugs crawled from the ticking, which they did no matter how much we doused the mattress with kerosene.

'He paints pictures of people?'

'The room was full of them.' I thought of the woman with her leg dangling beside the water and the sketch of the dog, which I'd placed with my other keepsakes in a hatbox in the tallboy.

'And your father thought he might want to paint you?'

'For practice.'

'It sounds like he gets all the practice he needs.' She shook her head. 'But he's given you a job.'

'Cleaning his brushes and mixing his paints.'

'You'd like that – being around all those pictures?'

'Yes, and he said he'd pay me.'

'Then we won't tell your father.'

·

10

I was not uneducated, no matter what Max Jenner thought. I'd learned the basics at school, then taught myself to read on Bookstall novels when I could get them or thrown out newspapers that had been left behind or blew in scraps along the gutters.

Max piled *his* papers up against the wall and thought nothing of it. On that first day in 1914, he asked me to clean his windows using the *Herald* dipped in a bucket of metho and water. We argued about it. Not because I didn't want to do it, I knew how to work, but because he caught me shoving folded pages up the sleeve of my jumper.

'Put them back,' he roared as if I was about to steal one of his sop-eyed portraits. 'Let me make this clear, *Miss Kemp*, I will not have you scrounging from my supplies to supplement your own.'

I pulled the crumpled pages from my sleeve then looked at his pile – a good decade's worth of dusty print. I understood all right. I shoved my tongue in my cheek to stop myself from talking back and returned the bits of paper to the stack. I didn't want to give him any reason to set against me. Because of the wages, you understand. The other thing, the painting, hadn't got hold of me yet. I picked up the bucket and took it outside to empty and Max seemed all right by the time I got back.

'You can go for the day,' he said and I stuck out my hand for my money which made him laugh.

'I earned it, didn't I?' I was angrier about him laughing than I was about the newspaper.

It was dark when I left the studio. I ran in the direction of home but it was later than I thought and I had to bang on the door of the butcher's. He was closing, but let me in when I showed him the coin through the window.

'Two sausages,' I told Alice Cooney who had caught up with me under the arc of a light on Campbell Street.

'I might get a job too,' she said.

'It's all good getting one but I nearly lost mine today because I pinched a bit of newspaper from a stack the old codger never reads.'

'Like the charity women from the church.'

'At least they give you things.'

'Not even a bag of flour if there's so much as a half bottle of grog in your cupboard or anything but pious looks on everyone's faces.'

'Pious?'

'I don't know. Mum slapped me when I asked them. But we're meant to be that and reformed which means better for having met them. Why don't you try that with the old bloke?'

'Pious?'

'Reformed.'

When I returned on the Saturday, my first job was to scrape a sticky glug of a mess from the back of a chair. I tried to look reformed as I did it, but Max took no notice. As it was, he barely looked my way at all over the next few months, other than to tell me what he wanted done and to leave my money on the corner of the table. If he had a customer sitting for a portrait when I arrived he'd often send me home, then there'd be no money at all and nothing to make up for it.

After months of silence the newspapers became an issue again when Max caught me leaning over them to sneak a quick read.

'Don't think I'm unaware,' he said, 'that you're taking copies from the middle of the pile.'

Petty, Nan would have called him, to be so concerned about scraps from his cast-off dailies.

'It's not as if I'm lining my shoes with them. I bring them back as good as I found them.'

'Don't think I haven't noticed that too. You could have saved yourself a lot of trouble, Miss Kemp, if you'd explained you only wanted to read them.'

•

'I don't like him,' I told Nan when I got home.

'Why's that, lovey?'

'He runs hot and cold.'

'There's lots of people like that. You've just got to live your life despite them.' She edged herself into her chair. I took my position opposite, unfolding the paper and finding the right page.

'So, what have you brought me today?'

'January 1912.' I looked up. 'It's got the second part of that serial we started last week.' Nan loved a good serial. 'I could teach you,' I said. 'Then you could read all you want.'

'Hmmph. I would, if my eyes were good enough. But then I'd miss this.' She patted my hand. 'It's the best part of the day.'

For all Max did or thought he did during those early years, it's Nan who deserves credit for me being a good draftsman. Nan, with her uncanny ability to recreate any image she ever saw.

'There's nothing in it,' she'd say. 'It's just copying.'

It was a game for us, even then, when I was ten nearly eleven. She'd draw a face, or a horse, or a tram using a stick in the soot that settled around the stove, or if she had a stub of pencil and the empty back page of a Bookstall novel she'd draw something as big as the jam factory.

'There.' She'd hand me the stub of pencil or the stick or whatever she was using. 'Your turn.'

I'd put a wobble in the face, wings on the horse or draw a fire burning the factory. The game was to change the picture as much as I could from Nan's chocolate box image to my own concoction.

'That's the real trick,' Nan encouraged. 'To change what you see.'

Max Jenner did not agree. It was months before he gave me a sketchpad and set me half an apple to draw. I decided to show him just how good I was and sketched the beginnings of a tree emerging from the apple's seed. I improved on a bottle he set me too, sitting it in a billycart as if it were steering it down a hill. I filled pages, unasked, with sketches of safety pins and ads for beauty creams, covering the faces of the models with rashes and boils. I drew automobiles and aeroplanes, pictures of men fighting, women combing nits out of their hair, kids playing in the street and when I'd filled the sketchpad, I asked for another one. Max leafed through its pages, wearing that beady look of his.

'You'll get another when you show me you can take direction.'

'To where?' I asked, not understanding what he wanted from me.

'When I set you a task you are to replicate what you see. Not add these fanciful imaginings.'

'You think they're no good?'

'The skill is to draw what's in front of you.'

I'd been with Max for nearly a year before he trusted me with another sketchbook. The apple came out again – a full one this time. I copied it as best I could and Max showed me how to adjust the lines so that it looked more like the apple in front of me, than the one in my head.

The drawing tasks were repetitive, boring. What kept me going was the hidden sketchpad. I didn't pinch the thing. It was old and yellow and at the very bottom of one of Max's piles. I kept it behind the apothecary cabinet so that if he ever asked I could truthfully say that it had been there the whole time. I would draw my apple for Max then draw another in my hidden book, withered, inedible. I stayed back after Max had gone, came in on days that I wasn't meant to be there, found another sketchpad, not so old or yellowed and drew whatever I chose. In the meantime, I aimed to please Max by doing what he asked. I wanted to stay at the studio by then, with all those supplies.

By the time 1917 crept up I'd been part of Max's studio for three years but was still at school. 'And learning nothing,' I told Nan, complaining about the shared desks, lack of books and fact that I now had to teach the younger kids instead of learning anything new, but Nan didn't want the truant officer on her back.

'You'll stay till you're fourteen.' There were no buts once Nan decided something.

My father, who might have approved of me leaving to earn an income was nowhere to be seen. He didn't visit for months at a time. Even if he was dossing somewhere nearby we rarely saw him. Nan, ever optimistic, thought it a good sign that he didn't come around looking for handouts. 'He must be doing well, for himself,' she said. 'Maybe he's joined up.' I couldn't picture my father in uniform abiding by rules, but there were worse than him keen to join up.

Talk of the war made Max Jenner irascible. He was fervent about its politics. It became his favourite topic with the well-to-do men in uniform who commissioned portraits from him. And there was his friend Cyril Sandford, a landscape painter who was all for the war and loved to orate on the immigration debate and Australia's obligation to back the empire. I made tea on the gas ring while Cyril and Max talked, and cut up the hard, little rock cakes that Cyril's wife sent along with him, trying not to listen to their tedious banter.

On a day when the news wasn't good and they couldn't stomach the floury little slabs, I picked them up a bottle or two from the sly groggers. They turned out to be cranky drunks, both of them. Their voices pitched up and down and their conversation veered from war to art, somehow linking the two together.

'And what do you think Miss . . .' Cyril asked as if he'd only that moment noticed my presence.

'Muriel.'

'Miss Muriel. How do you think art,' he swept the room with his hand encompassing Max's canvasses, 'contributes to our understanding of the war?'

'Leave her out of this, Cyril.'

'The horse's mouth? You can't say you're not curious.'

I'd listened to Cyril's tripe, thinking smug thoughts. Max noticed.

'You have something you'd like to add to the discussion Miss Kemp?' Both sets of eyes were on me.

I should have said no, but instead looked at Cyril and said, 'As all good artists can only paint what they see, you, me and Mr Jenner have no chance of understanding the war.'

Cyril raised an eyebrow but it was Max who replied, his voice low, controlled. 'This little scrap thinks her talent for drawing and interpretation far exceeds yours and mine, Cyril.'

'What do you *dror* Miss Muriel?' Cyril exaggerated the vernacular then sneered. 'Pretty little flowers and bows?'

'Miss Kemp's work is best seen I think.'

I had enough wits to know that you can't reason with drunks and decided it was time to leave. What stopped me was the noise of the easel crashing to the floor as Max stood up, and the command in his voice. 'Fetch your sketchbook Miss Kemp.'

Despite Max's orders, I had no intentions of fetching anything. I folded my arms across my chest and didn't move. Max stumbled across the room to find the book for himself but tripped over the fallen easel, breaking his fall with his elbow. 'You will get your sketches.' He didn't raise his voice but he may as well have.

I stomped over to the table. 'No,' he pointed to the apothecary cabinet, 'those ones.'

So he knew. A buzz went through me.

'Get them,' Max repeated.

There was nothing for it. I pulled out one of the sketchbooks from behind the cabinet and let it fall open onto a crude sketch of a cavalry horse standing upright on its hind legs like a human. The horse, sword in its hoof, was not only lunging forward but had found its mark. The blade having being thrust through the khaki middle of a commissioned officer's torso. I held the sketch up as if I were the teacher's pet.

'As you can see, Cyril,' Max pointed a wobbly hand. 'Miss Kemp is undeniably one of the greats.'

Cyril laughed, choking, hiccuping and spluttering. So sodden he couldn't stop. Ripping the page from the sketchpad, I tore it in half then ran all the way from Darlinghurst to Surry Hills, back to Nan. The door rattled as I pushed through it into the square room with its dim unpaintable light and its damp mouldy smell. It seemed different.

'What is it, lovey?' Nan asked as I stood and looked around the room.

'Nothing,' I said, because I couldn't explain.

•

I expected Max to toss me out after that, but instead he made me work harder, extending my duties to include stretching and priming the canvasses, buying art supplies and helping him prepare for his portraits. He began to set me more complicated sketching tasks — hands which I found difficult to master and ears, for which I received little praise. He sent me home with a book he'd ordered from abroad on shading and I returned with lists of words and techniques I didn't understand and pestered Max about what they meant and how to say them until he allocated me a few minutes of his time.

I was apprenticed, that's how I saw it. I dared anyone to say I wasn't, but no one denied it to my face. Other artists, I mean. Established ones like Max and Cyril who had studios and tried to make a living from their work. Not that they bothered with me. They had their own apprentices to worry about. Boys too young to enlist, taken on to learn the trade. I knew them all by sight. Some too serious about their careers to acknowledge me and others willing to talk as long as I did the listening.

'But you're as good as them?' Alice Cooney was fascinated by the whole idea of painting.

'Of course I am.' We walked beside the Sunday closed shops with Alice pointing out everything she'd buy if she had the money.

'Then does it matter if they don't talk to you?'

'It's not *that* I care about.'

'Well then?'

'Their work gets looked at. Mine doesn't.'

'But yours will?'

'Being good isn't as important as being noticed.'

'You'll have to be both then.' Alice nodded, pointing to an upright piano that she liked the look of.

•

I drew the way Max wanted me to and learned everything he was able to teach until I was better than any of the other apprentices and young artists that lived around Sydney, but I was still ignored. Karl James, a protégé of the portrait artist Doug Adams, pretty much admitted it the day he came to the studio rubbing his hands and bemoaning the fact he was about to get his backside kicked because he couldn't paint anything worth his salt. This was after the war, in 1919. I'd left school by then and was now at the studio full-time. More than full-time.

'This game's not for me, not for me at all,' Karl said. He was right, he couldn't paint for tuppence and I was sick of him going on about it. I'd just finished working on a small canvas and was wiping the excess paint from my brushes and keen to get rid of him.

'You're wasting your time you know.' He looked at my work and shook his head. 'I mean it's good enough. But that's not the point is it? You'll be gone in a couple of years.'

'What do you mean, gone?'

'Married with kids and all that palaver. In the meantime here you are taking up a spot that could be filled by somebody who's serious about the whole thing.'

'Like you?'

'Yes, like me.'

'A moment ago you said this game wasn't for you.'

'It's not. I'm giving it up to become a writer. But I am serious. That's the point.'

I went to the other side of the room on the pretext of looking for my sketchbook. I figured if Karl didn't have an audience, he'd just go away. I got caught up though watching a slant of light as it fell across the floor. I kicked at the dust, watching the floating motes, then picked up a pencil and tried to capture what I saw. By the time I thought of Karl again, he'd gone and so had my painting.

I had to tell Max. He insisted on knowing what happened to the task he'd set and I was not a good liar back then. He was angry with me, not Karl.

'For not protecting your work. If you don't value it nobody else will.'

'Karl valued it.'

'That little rogue's appreciation is not a recommendation.'

'No, but it's not as if I'm without possibilities. Karl won't be the only one.'

The tight, watchful look was back. Max and his rat's face. 'There is no guarantee in this life, Miss Kemp, of anything.'

2.

Crowning the head

Autumn 1921

It's Max Jenner's hands I see when I think of him. The spots and folds that marked his thin, bluish skin. 'Old,' he'd say, fluttering his fingers against the light like butterflies. I should have painted them, with their knocks and scrapes and the permanent smear of paint on the palm. Or done a portrait of him, standing straight-backed and contemplative in front of my canvas, his hands together as if in prayer.

'Was your subject thrown from a horse?'

'No. He wasn't.'

'Then I pity the poor mother who brought him into the world.'

'Why? What's wrong with him?'

'All humans have the same bones, Miss Kemp, the same basic structure. But you've chosen to forgo the skull in favour of a cabbage. And not a very attractive cabbage at that.'

'You don't like it?'

'I would like the nose if it was half an inch to the left.'

I made the mistake of shifting my gaze toward his own canvasses. Portraits of women with pink sugary lips and unshed tears. There was something grander about the light and shadows in the men.

'I see. So, it's *my* work that's on trial here? Yes? No? Speak up Miss Kemp. What is it you object to?'

'You flatter.'

'Go on.'

'It's dishonest.'

'But it fills the belly. How are you going to fill *your* belly, Miss Kemp?'

Max, forever a traditionalist, maintained his belief in capturing a likeness. If I strayed from his teaching he declared the work not to his liking and me stubborn, too bloody-minded to be taught. Yet when he died he left me his easel, some of his books and all of his paints. He'd also paid the rent on the studio in advance, and I stayed there for the remaining three months of the lease. In the meantime, I got a job, working mornings in a cafe in Woolloomooloo. Corbett's. I did the breakfast shift.

At its peak, Corbett's was full of workmen moving eggs and bacon around their plates with slabs of toast, and sculling thickly brewed tea from enamel cups. It was a comfortable place, full of movement and noise, the type of scene I wanted to paint – *Wharfies at Breakfast* – not that I ever did.

I helped serve the meals and clear the tables, and took orders at the front desk. That's how I met Adam. He wasn't a labourer but part of the bohemian set Max had warned me against. He just wanted a cup of tea and I said all right because the breakfast crowd had gone. The table he sat at was smattered with bacon grease and slopped-over tea and granules of sugar and he looked gaunt and lean compared to the wharfies.

I wangled him a meal and let him know that books of breakfast tickets were available at a discount price. I thought no more of him until the end of the shift when he caught up to me on the pavement, altering his stride to match mine. I didn't want his gratitude on account of a cheap breakfast and increased my pace to try and get rid of him

'You were old man Jenner's assistant.'

'I was.'

'His heart, I heard.'

'Last month.'

'There's been a lot of speculation.'

I turned mid stride to face him. 'About what?'

'Who you'll sop up to now.'

I considered him – the raised brow, the fluttering hand – and realised I could take him. Tackle him to the road and rub his pretty face in the muck.

'Which way did you bet?'

'Me?' He pointed to his chest, lead player in a pantomime. 'Oh, I didn't bet anything.'

Stepping closer, I shoved him in the chest with an open palm. He sprawled to the ground, weaker than I thought or just surprised. It didn't matter to me. I left him where he was and that was that.

•

Adam disappeared from my thoughts, only reappearing a week or two later when an envelope bearing my name was left at Corbett's front desk. The envelope contained an ink drawing, a cartoon of me with my hands thrust toward Adam's chest and Adam flying backwards, limbs askew. Beneath the drawing was a caption.

The titian princess singles me out for attention.

Later that morning Adam stepped in beside me as I left Corbett's.

'You're a painter,' he said.

I was thinking of tea, wondering if Nan might like sausages with a bit of onion gravy, which left no room for Adam and his banter. I went into the butcher's, then into the Greek's to pick up some potatoes, carrying my packages back out onto the street where I saw Adam waiting.

'What do you want?' I said. His presence irritated me.

He attempted to help me with the groceries but I pushed him away. 'We're not friends, Adam.'

'No,' he said. 'But we should be.'

Let me stop and explain here. Regardless of what was said and what he wrote, there was never anything between Adam Black and me. This is not a love story. He was a man who did as he pleased and in those early days he thought I was the same. His stories about me were exaggerated; some of them were straight-out lies.

•

There were a lot of art schools scattered around Sydney at that time. The main one, Julian Ashton's, was held in a sombre building in George Street, near the town hall. It attracted a lot of students, but the school that stood out for me was run by Dattilo-Rubbo, a small Italian fellow with a large mound of hair who encouraged a liberal approach to art. Grace Cossington Smith went to him and painted exactly as she liked. That was the type of work I could admire.

As good as Dattilo-Rubbo was, I'd had my fill of instruction and stayed away from the schools and the cliques and the movements. After my shift at the cafe I'd go back to Surry Hills and Nan, returning to the studio to paint all night or until I fell asleep. Then I'd be off again to the cafe, mad from lack of sleep and resenting time spent away from my easel.

After I got to know Adam, he told me he'd tried Ashton's and fought with the man himself over his inability to take art seriously. 'Ashton's right. It's not that I can't cultivate the skill. I *can* paint after all, it's more that I don't want to. Everything that comes from my hand turns into a caricature, even the life drawings. So I dropped the classes, sold a sketch to *The Bulletin* and – *voila!* – I'm a political satirist.'

A half-lie. Adam could draw, but he couldn't paint. I thought he'd make a good sculptor. His drawings had that sort of look about them, but when I suggested he build what he drew, he dismissed the idea.

Imagine then, me, three years younger than Adam, who at twenty had a cutting wit and was rude to everyone. It wasn't my ability as an artist that attracted him but my perverseness, that and the dislike my work generated. Unlike everyone else, he claimed he saw its potential.

'I'm the only friend you've got,' he joked. But he wasn't – much of a friend, that is.

•

The First Man, or the idea of painting it, came after a visit from Max Jenner's widow, Flora, before the studio's lease expired. Max had kept her portrait on the wall above the gramophone for years.

I should have realised, though, that the sweet dewy face painted by Max was, in real life, more likely to attract blowflies than bees.

Flora, a once favoured artist's model, was a lot younger than Max. At the funeral, her black veiled figure was surrounded by supporters or admirers, I didn't know which – I didn't talk to her. A week later she pushed her way through the door undetected, navigating a path through the clutter until she stood by my side at the easel. The right thing would've been to acknowledge her husband's death and offer my sympathies, but I was startled by her unexpected appearance and only managed to lift my brush and shrug.

'So, you're Max's headache.' Flora, used to artists, stood as if posing. Arms by her side, shoulder diagonal, hat forward, head tilted down but eyes looking up. How to describe those eyes? I would paint them with the light glinting from their upper edge, luminous blue irises circled with black. She closed her lids, breaking the stare – one, two, three – then opened them again.

'Max went on and on about you. Well, not you so much as your palette.'

She leaned towards the easel, her tight, dark clothes a contrast to the tones in my painting. I searched among the tubes of oil, looking for the makings of a shadowy hue, not black but a murky olive green to paint her silhouette exactly as it fell on the canvas.

She cleared her throat. '*Her vile colours*: he said it all the time.' She stepped away. 'I can't see it myself.' I put my hand on her arm to detain her, still stuck on the idea of painting her silhouette. In response, she reached out, loosening a lock of my hair from its bind, tugging on it like a bell's rope. 'I've come to sort out the studio.'

I put my brush and palette aside, the idea of painting her shadow gone. 'Can I offer you a cup of tea?'

The air moved as she lifted her arm. 'It's not really your place to offer anything, is it?' She said. 'I'll look at the commissioned works first.'

Max's canvasses were stacked against the wall. She considered each one, then strolled around the room marking items with small red cards; the apothecary cabinet, the gramophone, anything of value or interest.

'I'll send someone to collect these. Do what you want with the rest.'

Belatedly, I realised I was wearing Max's smock.

'He had a weakness for girls of your colouring.' Flora moved towards me as if to kiss me goodbye. Clasping me to her chest she rose on her toes, sinking her teeth into my neck like Bram Stoker's Count Dracula. I slapped the back of her head and pushed her away, she smiled, a dribble of blood on her lip. Not cracked by grief, as I first thought, but jealous and nasty with it.

Later that same day Adam dropped by and I complained about her visit.

'How could she think something like that about Max and me?'

'How do you know that's what she thought?'

'"He had a weakness for girls of your colouring" – that's what she said.'

'She's grieving.'

'And I'm not?'

Adam spiralled his hand as he bent on one knee and though he meant to mock me, the image of his genuflection stuck.

'What's this?' He approached the easel to survey a portrait of Nan, dressed fussily with a peach in blossom behind her.

'A present.'

He scowled. 'It's pitiful.'

'Of course it is, but it's what she likes.'

'What happened to the other piece you were working on?'

Moving to the corner of the room, I rifled through a mess of discarded sketches until I found it. I replaced Nan with a small square canvas that showed a Surry Hills street flecked with children playing chasings, their bodies thin and sharp, their backs straight, topped by heads curved like lampposts. Adam peered at it, his nose almost on the paint, knowing as I did that no exhibition committee would accept it.

'You should submit it anyway. Stop complaining; prod the devil.'

He lit a cigarette and drew on it, filling his lungs. I squinted through the fug, listening to a litany of accusations. I was timid, I was a coward, I needed to take risks. His face shimmered then disappeared, replaced by smoky colours that arranged and rearranged themselves in a moving kaleidoscope. Adam's voice seeped through, spoiling the effect.

He unbuttoned his shirt. Shrugging it from his shoulders he declared that if I were serious, if I were as good as I said I was (and I was that good), then I would paint whatever I chose to paint.

He dropped his trousers and stood before me, naked. I was inclined to tell him to get dressed, that I would choose my own subject, not have it chosen for me, but then the light fell on him in a certain way, as if he were David himself. I circled him, assessing his slim frame and vibrant eyes, then drew near, sliding my palms up and down his limbs, dragging my nails across his hairless chest, smelling his sweat, dipping my tongue on his skin.

'There's no hurry.' He wound a hand through my hair. 'Take your time.'

I submerged my face in his groin, snuffling the inside of his thighs, following the curve of his scrotum with my nose and my lips, ignoring his half-closed eyes, the rise of his cock, the weight of his moan.

Then I stood and picked up my paintbrush. 'I want you on your knees and begging.'

3.

Near misses

There were three women. A triangle of crying women, standing in the corridor right on teatime when the trolley arrived, pushed by workers delivering food to the ward.

A phone rang on a desk. A nurse in a blue uniform stopped to answer as she passed. As soon as she hung up it rang again. Feet scurried in lace-up shoes. Green lights glowed outside of rooms as buzzers rang. There was a clatter as staff checked S8 medications from a locked cupboard in a recessed room and the sound of water spraying from further down the corridor in the pan room. An odour, disinfectant mixed with body fluids, wafted through the ward like a mist.

The three crying women stood in front of a door, blocking a sign that said NIL BY MOUTH. Inside the room, behind the door, Stella and I straightened the bed and tidied the clutter. Stella borrowed

30

a vase of flowers from another room and placed it on the bedside locker while I combed the patient's hair.

'How does he look?'

'Peaceful,' Stella said.

We walked from the dim room into the corridor. Stella turned right while I joined the three women, leading them through the door to their father's side.

Afterwards, back in the corridor, Dave, our wardsman, wheeled an empty chair towards the storeroom. One eyebrow lifted as he stopped to talk, low-voiced, through the side of his mouth.

'I bet you a block of chocolate you don't make it to the end of the shift without crying.' It was an old joke between us. He wanted to see me smile.

'I'm all right,' I replied and I was. Work was fine. It was only after I got home that the problems started. Most nights I'd get two or three hours sleep before it hit. Late-night nausea. Nothing helped. Once it began, there'd be no more sleep. At first light I'd pull on my stretchiest bike shorts and an old T-shirt and pace Shellharbour's streets until I was exhausted. It was the only thing that worked.

This is how I met Muriel Kemp.

Muriel lived on Boollwarroo Parade, the road that goes out to Bass Point with its single line of houses that back onto the Pacific. Hers was the last place before the reserve. The first couple of times I passed her house there was no one around. Not that I ever saw anyone much at that time of the morning. On that day, though, she was there at sunrise, watering her brown singe of a lawn. I raised my hand to say hello as I passed on the verge. She turned the hose on me.

'Holy fuck!' I stepped sideways but the stream followed my legs until I was out of reach. I walked on the other side of the road after that. By *after that* I mean until the end of the week, when I heard someone exclaim, 'Hell!' and saw the old woman, blood pouring down her arm as she fished a newspaper from the plumbago.

I turned back: duty more than inclination. By the time I reached her, she was seated on the front step, positioned at the side of the house rather than its front, cradling a cat. The cat yowled and writhed until it managed to break free, then clambered up and over the paling fence. I watched from the edge of the yard before I called out, 'Are you all right?'

'Bloody newspaper boy. I've rung the paper shop I don't know how many times to complain, but he still can't throw the damn thing straight.'

I approached. Her injury didn't look too bad. A concertinaed flap of skin that bled freely. The newspaper lay nearby, smeared with blood. I glanced at its headline.

'Puss, puss, puss,' Muriel called, but the cat wouldn't come. She lowered her head to her knees.

'Dizzy?'

She pushed herself up and onto her feet, steady, balanced. A magpie swooped from a tree onto the steps, undeterred by our proximity. Perhaps she fed it.

'I can fix that.' I pointed to her arm.

'Why would you want to?'

Why *did* I want to? I've asked myself that many times since. Whatever it was that drew me to Muriel, it wasn't her charm.

'I'm a nurse.' I shrugged. 'That's what I do.'

I washed her wound in a green-and-pink-tiled bathroom. 'Tranquil,' I said to make conversation. 'The colours I mean.'

'Not my choice.'

'Do you have tweezers? See how the skin's bunched up? If I pull it down over the tear, it'll heal better.'

The bathroom was claustrophobic. Muriel took up all the space; not physically, but she filled a room and there was the odour. It was either on her or in the bathroom – turps and linseed oil. I'd smelled it when we'd entered the house, passing a door that stood ajar. I'd craned my neck to look through the gap and saw crowds of colour. Someone likes to paint, is what I thought.

I kneeled on the tiles next to the bath, overcome by queasiness.

'You're a strange cut of nurse if you can't stand the sight of blood.'

I explained about the nausea. 'You're the first person I've told.'

She made me a cup of tea, her manner terse, despite the fact I'd tended her wound. I couldn't drink the tea but held the mug between my palms and told her I'd drop by the next day to take a look at her arm. I left when she started to protest.

There's more to that story; a layer I've omitted. I'll have to backtrack.

When I said I'd heard someone yell, 'Hell!' and looked up, Muriel had already fished the newspaper from the plumbago and stood reading the front page. Her reaction wasn't to the injury but to what she'd read. After I got home I was still unable to sleep, so I grabbed a couple of coins from the jar beside the bed and went back to the newsagents to buy the paper.

Claudine Worthington, much-loved patron of the arts, renowned advocate for the emerging, new and experimental, has died at the age of 84.

I finished reading the article, turned on the radio and got into bed. I needed a couple of good hours, at least, before that day's afternoon shift. Chrissy Amphlett crooned, her husky voice as good as any bedtime story. The nausea eased. Everything turned green and pink below my eyelids, like Muriel's bathroom. I slept.

•

Dawn, the next day. I was on Muriel's doorstep with a brown paper bag full of dressings. The cat, an orange tabby, appeared through tatters of the garden. It squeezed itself between my leg and a pot plant, purring as it rubbed its face against my shoe. Muriel's foot-steps approached the door. The cat shot off as if pelted by a stone.

Muriel led me down the bare L-shaped hallway into the kitchen. The door that had leaked the oily odour of turps was firmly shut. The rest of the house was devoid of paintings, photos, knick-knacks, knitted throws, doilies, flowers in vases, fruit in bowls. There was not a single artistic or decorative item on show, unless you counted the clock on the kitchen wall, which was nothing special; a black-and-white face in a round silver frame.

Blood had oozed through the bandage. I removed the cloth slowly, using water to loosen it. There was a splatter of paint on Muriel's inner arm and that same smell of turps on her clothes. At the kitchen sink I washed my hands then leaned against it, waiting for my stomach to settle. On the other side of the window the tabby sat on top of the paling fence, staring at me through the glass.

'Looks good. It hasn't retracted much.' I returned to the job. 'We'll leave the bandage off. The steri-strips will keep the skin in place. You can shower in them. Make sure you dry the wound with a clean towel afterwards, and if there's any signs of infection, like redness, swelling, heat, discharge–'

'I know what infection is.'

'–go and see your GP. I'm on dayshift tomorrow then I have days off. I'll come and see you then.'

'It's not necessary.'

'It's no bother.'

'It is a bother.'

'No. Not at all.'

.

Somewhere in one of those early visits, Muriel called me drug-gaunt, as if she were describing a physical trait, like big ears or white teeth. 'I'm not that thin,' I protested, but by then she'd moved on to my hair, which, she decided, was only marginally better than my undernourished state. 'Rust-streaked,' she called it. 'Part red.' Unlike hers, which had been the real deal apparently, before the grey.

'Brick red?'

'Titian.'

I was not drug-gaunt. I was haggard from not enough sleep and too much vomiting. I'd stand in front of the full-length mirror in my uniform: junior blue with a mauve, green and white leaf trim that banded the sleeves, neck and the placket, which buttoned to the waist. I'd removed the velcro shoulder pads and there were single pleats at the front and back of the skirt and between the shoulder blades. The uniform was roomy, a sack. Even so, as I raised my arms to pin on my fob watch and tie back my hair, I'd inspect the fall of the cloth for any tautness around my abdomen or across my swollen breasts.

•

Three months before meeting Muriel, prior to the nausea and the expanding waistline, two of my patients died on a dayshift. Every time Dave saw me I had my arms around someone, or someone had their arms around me, weeping. That was the first time Dave bet me a block of chocolate that I'd be in tears before the end of the day.

I headed to the pub that night, tired but unable to sleep, and downed three black Russians in a hurry even though I'm not much of a drinker. Pup Dumont was there. He tapped my shoulder and nodded hello over the noise of a local band. Then came the crash of glass behind him. A finger poked a sternum and shoulders jostled. I saw a mouth close over an ear. Teeth clamped, pulling at the lobe until a gush of the victim's beer rose in the air, did a U-turn and sprayed across my arm and neck.

I grabbed Pup's arm. 'I have to get out of here.'

Somebody threw a punch. I pulled Pup out of the trajectory. He drilled through the crowd, with me in his slipstream, and we emerged like two popping corks into the car park. Pup asked where I wanted to go.

'Away from here.'

'Are you going to be sick?'

'No.'

We were in his car by then, a white station wagon with roof racks for his boards, and he leaned across to wind the window down. 'In case.'

I guess he would have taken me home if I'd asked; it was only around the corner. But I didn't ask, so he took me to his home instead, a house on stilts right across from Warilla Beach.

'Groper's paradise,' he announced as he pushed through the rain-swollen door.

I'd secured my bra straps to my top with safety pins, so the sleeves wouldn't fall from my shoulders. Pup couldn't work out how to detach me. He fumbled and swore as he pricked a finger. There was a knock at the front door. He got up and turned out the light. I undressed myself in the dark, and when he returned I undressed him.

'Lie on your back,' I said.

'This is service.'

We were a mash of sweat, salt and semen, stuck together like glue, wordless until the morning, when I picked his T-shirt off the floor and put it on to go to the toilet.

'Take that off.'

I pulled it over my head and threw it at him.

'You're no better than all those chicks up at the housing commission. Single mothers after a skinny bit of arse for a change. Do you know how many T-shirts I've lost to them?'

This is my child's father I'm talking about – Pup. A one-night stand.

'Mindless sex.' I rubbed the T-shirt in his face. 'It's not the skinny arse they're after, Pup – it's the mindless.'

He laughed. I don't know why he thought it was funny.

•

'Should I tell him?' I asked Muriel, many months later.

'What for? He isn't any good to you.'

'But what about Olivia or Oliver?'

She looked at my belly. 'Adopt them out.'

37

'I mean what do I tell them?'

'I can't help you there.'

•

I'd told Muriel I'd take a look at her dressing on my days off. I worked dayshift then slept from 5 p.m. until 2 a.m. The most I'd slept in a while. My stomach woke me, clenching as if I had eaten roadkill for dinner. In between cramps I listened to the scrape of the ocean on the nearby shore and the vibration of a bass and drum as a band played encores at the pub. My stomach lurched. I tried to free myself from the bedsheets but they'd twisted around my legs and I fell from the mattress, reaching the toilet just in the nick.

Walking didn't quell the nausea, but the rhythm, if I got it right, was a distraction. What I needed was a four/four signature like a rock beat or the blues. It transformed me from Jane Cooper, responsible registered nurse to Jane Cooper, owner of decadent and nomadic thoughts.

My thoughts that night drifted to my ex-boyfriend who'd hung around long enough to witness my compulsive scribbling. Stamped and self-addressed envelopes posted to editors of obscure journals. How-to-write books stacked against the wall in piles and, on a day I forgot he was still in my bed, a single sentence recited over and over as I tried to get the words right. I told him I was moving to the city to pursue my writing. I'm a coward when it comes to a break-up.

Before I'd even had a chance to change the sheets, one of his mates, Steppo (not his real name), approached me at the pub. Coins rattling in his palm, he asked for five cents to buy a beer. Thinking he was broke, I offered to buy the beer for him. It turned out he just didn't want to break a five-dollar note. I gave him twenty cents and told him to keep the change. Instead of going to the bar, he sat beside me and extolled the assets of the pub, the beer and the town we lived in.

'Why can't you just write here?' he asked.

I cringed. What else had he been told? 'Imagine –' I leaned in so Steppo could hear me above the thump, thump, thump of the music '– living in a place where no one plays footy, they don't watch it, they don't talk about it and they definitely don't want to hear about it.'

'Yeah, all right.' He strode off to buy his beer.

That's the story that came to mind as I walked past Shelly Pub with a backache and a belly full of nausea. When I'd told my boyfriend I wanted to split up, he cried. This was unexpected. He hadn't seemed that interested. 'I'll try harder,' he said. Perhaps he would have.

A few weeks later I was approached by another mate of my ex-boyfriend's. He said he'd borrowed a couple of books from my ex and my name was inside their covers. By way of conversation, he told me he worked freelance as a mercenary. He had a flat, dead-eyed look about him so I thought it possible.

'There's stories I can tell that'd make your clitoris stand on end.'

I was almost interested. 'But what about the ex?' I said.

'Dog eat dog.'

I let him keep the books.

•

The air around the pub was sticky with salt and frangipani, beer dregs and cigarette smoke. A band packed their gear into the back of a reversed van while a couple, wrapped around each other's bodies, slithered on a patch of grass, dry humping like a pair of stray dogs.

I rocked through the streets, not meaning to drop in on Muriel, not that late. But the tabby flung herself at me as I walked by on the verge. 'Puss.' She rubbed her face against my ankle.

I picked the cat up, it purred against my chest, content. Then I noticed a light scanning the yard behind us. Before I could call out and let Muriel know I was there she appeared with a torch, warning me to: 'Putthecatdown.'

'It's all right Muriel – it's me, Jane.'

A set of headlights shone down Boollwarroo Parade beside us. The lovers from the pub, I thought, off to Bass Point to find a little privacy. The car quivered to the sound of Doc Neeson and The Angels played at full volume.

The car, an old EH, overflowed with a maggoty swarm of limbs and heads, one waggling bare arse and an empty can of beer cocked at a window, ready to be thrown. Not by any lovers.

But it was Muriel drawing near, not the ruckus from the EH, that upset the tabby. It clawed and scratched, then launched itself like a flying fox towards the oncoming headlights. There was the noise of a splintered muffler, a few *fuck you*'s sung in time to Doc Neeson's whoomph, whoomph, and the beer can landing on the blue metal that edged the tar. Above all that was the resounding thump of the cat being hit.

I ran out onto the bitumen, into the flare of the red tail-lights, but the tabby was nowhere to be seen. Neither was Muriel when I turned back to the verge to say, 'She must have been carried forward by the momentum.'

The streetlights came to a halt after Muriel's place but the moon was full and the sky clear. I searched the road and the sports-ground opposite, calling 'Puss, puss, puss.' Half an hour of useless looking and then I saw her, swaggering down the road towards me, untouched, a field mouse in her jaw.

She dropped the mouse at my feet, purring, not one ginger hair askew. Rolling her into my T-shirt I ran down the side of Muriel's house, tapped on her kitchen window then knocked at the door.

'I've found her, Muriel. She's okay.'

Muriel can't have been asleep because she was there, on the other side of the screen door, surrounded by her aura of turps, watching as the cat fought in my arms. I was worried it had copped a blow to the head and thought Muriel should keep an eye on it.

'You take it.' Muriel waved us away.

Instead of saying no, or just taking the tabby and going, I prattled on. Something I do when I'm over tired.

'The smell doesn't worry you?' I asked.

'What?' she replied, not understanding. 'The cat?'

'No, no. The turps. You paint, don't you?'

A mood crossed her face – anger, irritation? I'd said something I shouldn't have.

'I'm a writer,' I stumbled on, wanting to show we had something in common. I was no such thing. I'd had one short story published in the 'emerging writers' section of a journal. That was it.

Muriel stepped from behind the screen door onto the concrete landing and the cat panicked, sticking its claws through my T-shirt. 'If you were serious about being a writer,' she said, eyeing my pregnant belly, 'you'd get rid of that baby.'

'It'll be difficult. I know that.'

'Difficult? It will be impossible.' She slammed the screen door behind her. And there I was, alone with her cat.

4.

Promises, promises

(The short end of the stick)

Winter 1921

We, as in Adam and I, walked along William Street in the direction
of Hyde Park, our noses running from the sour horse dung that
permeated the Woolloomooloo night air. Adam was dressed in a
Prince of Wales suit and walked with his hands tucked under his
armpits and his shoulders bunched high. It annoyed me just to look
at him. By the time we reached Palmer Street I'd changed my mind
about the whole excursion and decided to turn back.

'I'm not going.'

'But we're here.' Adam's breath puffed like tobacco smoke,
drifting between us.

I moved the canvas, wrapped in a dust cloth, from my right
arm into the crook of my left. It was *my* painting. I'd decide its

fate. Pulling my coat tight I strode off, leaving Adam alone in the milky cold.

He followed, grabbing hold of the painting as if it was his.

'Don't, Adam. You won't win.'

He tried to pull my fingers from the canvas, but as he stepped in front of me, I grabbed his ear and twisted.

'You bloody goose, Muriel.'

I twisted harder. He dropped like a bag of chaff but mewed like a kitten. Two minutes down the road I could still hear him carrying on. Then came his footsteps skittering behind me.

'Wait. Muriel, wait.' He drew alongside, pale and sweaty, that short run as hard as he'd ever worked. 'Listen.'

'Unless you've got something different to say, I don't want to hear it.'

'Let them see what a real painting is.' That's what he said.

'Huh,' I scoffed. Adam, for all his education, had no real understanding of people.

'So what if they're shocked? Isn't that the point?'

'Once they know it's mine they won't even look at it.'

'Of course they will.'

'And if they do look, they won't see anything.' I raised my arm to push him out of the way.

'Listen, what if we say I painted it? A self-portrait.' He stood in front of me, an obstacle.

'You don't paint.'

'You don't want to admit it's yours and you don't want me to say it's mine. What *do* you want?' The cold had glazed his eyes and reddened his nose.

I paused, making him wait.

'All right. We say it's yours, then later, after everyone's commented, we admit it's mine.'

I handed him the canvas and we retraced our steps to Palmer Street, turning into a laneway that ran behind a line of shops. Dilapidated and obscured by crates, lengths of lumber, tin drums, wheels, the rusted body of a fuel stove, bottles, a fairly decent-looking ladder and a bucket of rotting oranges. A din came from inside but we couldn't find the way in until the carcass of a rat drew our eyes to the outline of the door.

'Like a cairn.'

I went in ahead of Adam, crossing the foyer to the staircase. The remains of a candle fluttered from the lowest stair, illuminating the cracked wooden panels of the risers and treads. Easy firewood. I licked my fingers and snuffed the candle out.

'Bloody hell,' Adam said.

'What?' I couldn't see a thing.

'On the railing, like thick dust.'

We followed the noise upwards. At a bend in the staircase a kerosene lamp beamed a path from the top-floor landing. In its glow, we saw a white chalky substance covering Adam's hand and the sleeve of his coat.

'Plaster.' He wiped it off on some hessian bags strung across the landing like washing.

We knew, without looking, what was on the other side of the rough curtain: an open space partitioned in two. The ground-floor shop used the larger side as their storeroom and the rest of the space was leased as living quarters to the three Alans – Alan, Alwyn and Allan: a poet, a journalist and a sculptor.

'What a rort,' the Alans fumed. 'We were had.' Not because the building had been scheduled for demolition but because they hadn't realised, until too late, that the tenants on the floor below were sly grog dealers.

Once they'd received notice to quit, the Alans had organised a send-off for the old doss, calling it the 'Last Hurrah' and warning there'd be eternal damnation for anyone who didn't turn up to pay their respects.

Adam and I pushed our way through the hessian screen into a fug of winter sweat, tobacco and noise. A cheer went up, conducted by a satyr waving a baton from a soapbox, a black tail sewn to the seat of his trousers. Adam bowed to the conductor then turned to the crowd and bowed again. Smoke rose from a shallow metal box positioned beside a blue line painted on the floor directly in front of us. It smelled of burning dung.

'You can't cross the river until you've paid the ferryman.' The conductor waved his baton at the blue line.

Adam grabbed a handful of my coat and skirt, raising the hem to expose my thigh and my lack of underwear. The sound of my palm hitting his face circled the room. We had everyone's attention.

'Welcome to Hades.' The conductor howled, chin tilted at the decaying roof. There was another cheer before the party resumed its shape.

'Why so hard?' Adam rubbed his jaw with his spare hand.

'Why so high?'

A man with protruding eyes, dressed in robes and carrying two pieces of a broken staff, greeted us from the other side of the Styx. He looked familiar.

'Aren't you with *The Bulletin*?' I asked.

'I'm with the ferry.' He handed me a mug that contained a sloshing inch of turgid liquid. 'Here, have a drink.' His lips were on my ear. 'There are tarts. We're eating them in the storeroom.'

'She's with me.' Adam raised his voice above the noise.

'Who do you think I'm talking to?' The ferryman tilted forward until his nose glanced off my cheek. Righting himself, he took his mug back, then staggered across the room with his two bits of staff. We followed him across the river.

'They're shickered, the lot of them,' Adam said.

'What did you expect?'

The corners of the room were dark and full of bodies writhing like blind grubs. A hand fondled my breast, another touched my thigh and a third used my sleeve as a hanky. We shifted from the edges, looking for somewhere to unveil the canvas.

'Everyone's here.'

By everyone Adam meant editors of *The Bulletin*, *Smith's Weekly*, *The Lone Hand*, newspapers, independent journals, reporters, freelancers, critics, committee members, art school directors and teachers. Then there were the artists and writers and actors themselves. Then everyone else.

We paused beside two men, leaning against one another like tent poles.

'So, your wife's a poet,' one said to the other.

Their foreheads and shoulders merged, their mouths almost touched.

'She writes free verse.'

'Ah.' The first pole kissed the second on the lips then licked his own. 'My apologies.'

The poles straightened their heads, extending a mutual arm to Adam.

'You're too far ahead of me,' Adam said.

Alan the poet waved us over, pointing to a verse he'd written in chalk on the wall. Stepping back to recite the lines, he trod on an upturned glass positioned on a ouija board, scattering the glass and the surrounding letters. The disrupted players slapped Alan's calves then his torso and scalp as they pulled him downwards, enclosing him in their circle.

Games scrummed back and forth across the room. A blindfolded Elsie Cunningham captained the kissing game. Opposition player Ronald Felton approached, tossed his jacket on the floor and tilted her back in his arms, covering her lips in a silver screen kiss before righting her.

'When I was a girl in Dubbo, I had an old cattle dog called Bully who kissed me the very same way.'

There was a roar of approval from a jumble of women sprawled across a thick layer of sacking as Ronald skulked off towards the storeroom.

'I was very fond of that dog, Ronald,' Elsie, blindfold still in place, called after him.

A drinking game that involved a bag of marbles and the recitation of a complicated rhyme got under everyone's feet. Discussions exploded like gunshot. Flappers danced a vigorous onestep to an Irish ballad played on an out-of-tune piano while an artiste with an audience of two performed a veil dance, removing a single diaphanous cloth then reinstating it, to rapturous applause.

'Over there,' Adam said, indicating a possible spot.

A figure pushed past, carrying a water jug filled from the tap on the landing. He poured its contents into a cast-iron tub by the window then turned to a blue-dressed girl slumped against the wall. He lifted her into the tub, pushing her dress over her shoulder to expose a breast. The girl opened her eyes with a gasp and tried to clamber out of the tub but was held in place by the man.

Adam dragged a card table to the short edge of the room. He balanced the canvas so it leaned against the wall. Removing the cloth with a flourish, he bowed low from the waist. Nobody noticed. Not until the blue-dressed girl pointed to it and called out, 'I could use a knife like that.'

The man with the water jug followed her finger. 'Don't show her that.' He said as she stepped out of the tub, breast still exposed. Unsteady, she rested a hand on his shoulder, stripped off her wet dress then got back into the tub. The piano stopped playing. A scruffy group of dark coats gathered around the painting. There was a collective shudder, a gravelly silence as they backed away from the canvas, avoiding its outstretched hand.

'Whose is it?'

I waited for Adam to say it was his. Instead he nodded in my direction.

'Well that explains the face – what there is of it. Faces are always difficult.'

There was a smattering of laughter. The coats dispersed. The nearest critic placed an arm around my shoulders and explained that Adam was nothing but a boy compared to him. Grabbing my wrist, he dragged my hand towards his bulge to show me. I obliged, slipping my hand down the front of his trousers.

'You're pinching,' he shrieked, prising my digging fingers from his flesh.

Adam watched over the head of James Dennison, a once-fashionable portrait artist turned reviewer who, hand on chin, was frowning at the painting. The water jug man, not put off by my run-in with the critic, approached. He stroked my arm and pleaded with me to get into the tub beside the girl who was now asleep. I elbowed him in the jaw and pushed him out of the way.

'James Dennison, this is Muriel Kemp.' Adam used his drawing-room voice and spoke as if everything was going to plan.

Dennison turned his back on me, excluding me from the conversation. I reached past him for the canvas.

'I beg your pardon,' he said.

'You do know James Dennison, don't you, Muriel?' Adam tried again.

I covered my canvas with its dust sheet, too angry to look at Adam or the old man.

'I was talking to James about some of your other work. I thought he might be interested in writing an article.'

'Ha.' I picked up my canvas.

'I'm sorry, it's the noise.' Dennison curved a hand around his ear and looked up at me.

I shoved my face close to his so there'd be no misunderstanding. 'I don't paint pretty pictures, Mr Dennison. Nothing for you to write about.'

Adam laughed as I crossed the room, my progress slowed by the shifting crowd. I was halted by a hand that latched onto my sleeve like a spider. James Dennison, face contorted, words drying like spittle on his lips. He was as angry as I was.

'I want to talk to you.'

Shaking him off, I veered past an entwined couple blocking the exit then descended the stairs, pushing through the door and along the laneway, breaking into the crisp, coal-tinted air.

William Street was still, except for the shuffle and limp of a ragged form on the other side of the road. He stopped and, facing the nearest building, fumbled with the front of his trousers before leaning one-handed against the bricks to relieve himself.

'Wait,' I called, crossing the road at a run.

He took off, a rabbit swerving a bullet.

'Wait – your hand. I just want to see your hand.'

But he was gone, merging into the shadows.

I propped the canvas against the street light and held my hand aloft. Shifting my feet, I tried different angles, wanting to recapture the ragged man's stance and the streetlight shining through his hand like the sun. Finding a stub of pencil in my jacket, I jotted notes on the calico dust cloth.

— *hand lit up, separate but joined*

— *corrugate dark and light, forehead, nose, chin edge of clothes*

— *chiaroscuro – stretch out thin*

— *warrior, on the hump*

Then I drew a quick study. The cold burned my fingers and there was the irritating hum of distant yelling and running as I worked. The sounds grew nearer, clarifying into a recognisable clatter of heels and a breathless voice that called my name.

I turned. 'Alice?'

'Am I glad to see a friendly face.' She linked an arm through mine.

'You didn't pass anyone did you? A man?' I said, my mind still on the ragged man.

She leaned into my arm, blotting up its warmth, then pushed me into a half-trot down the road. 'The only men I saw were the coppers.'

'Wait.' I ran back for my canvas.

'We need to step lively.' She looked over her shoulder then pushed me around the corner into Palmer Street. 'Maggie sent me up to warn the girls about a raid and I ran right into the bally middle of it all.'

'But you got away.'

She'd come out without a coat and was shivering in her thin blouse. 'Rose tripped one of them up.' She laughed. 'She was caught, so was Doreen.'

'Here.' I handed her the painting, took off my coat and swapped it for the canvas. Alice pushed her bare arms into the sleeves then linked her arm through mine once more. The studio was in Darlinghurst, not far from where we were.

'Let's go to Max's,' I said. 'They won't look for you there.'

Alice squeezed my arm in response.

'You look tired, Lissy,' I said.

'So do you.'

I drew her close, mentally sketching her as we turned into Liverpool Street. There'd be a time in the future when, for two or three good years, all I'd be able to paint was Alice. A dead Alice with skin more alive than any model's. I'd paint her sitting on a kitchen chair in front of a table set for breakfast or in the garden under a soft apricot sun. Always naked, her body a wash of blues, greys and violets.

And then would come a final composition – Alice and me standing in front of a window: her looking through its glass; me, one hand on its surrounding frame, watching her. Once it was done, I never painted Alice again, producing instead the best work of my career, paintings that no one else has ever seen.

But for now the sketch was of Alice Cooney walking along Liverpool Street in the winter of 1921.

A fire-fire-fire-brand.

Black and blue and greys and yellows, her skin the colour of quartz in between. 'Here she comes, little Miss Fit and Temper, won't she make someone a good wife.' I'd write those words in bubbles around the frame, or perhaps in a trough of spillage.

In this sketch her hand reaches through a swill: men, jammed shoulder to shoulder, bursting out of their shirts, sliding under arms and into gaps, up and over the bar to claim their orders before six o'clock closing. Mr Cooney's head squeezed between hips and rumps at the back of the scrum and a young Alice's fingers clutching his collar like a rein.

Alice interrupted my mental sketch to tug the wrapped canvas from beneath my arm. 'What's this?'

'Have a look when we get to the studio.'

She whistled a few bars and sang some words from a nonsensical rhyme she'd made up, then flapped her arms and teetered on her toes – her usual routine when she was dead on her feet and trying to stay awake.

We smelled the studio before we got to it. Turps and oil, mouldy dust and disinfectant.

'Can you smell the Lysol?'

'I can always smell Lysol,' Alice said in the dark, going up the stairs. 'The girls use it afterwards . . . you know, to stop a baby.'

'Max used to put it in saucers with horsemeat to kill off the rats.'

'They wouldn't go near it, would they?'

'He reckoned they'd eat anything if they were hungry enough.'

I lit the lamp then the gas stove and put a pan of water on the ring. In the burnished light, Alice looked like the cadaver I would one day paint. Her skin was tight over her cheeks, her jaw swollen and discoloured. She surveyed the near-empty room. Max's wife had taken most of the furniture by then.

'I wish you'd seen it before, when Max was still here.'

Alice shook her head. 'Wishing'll get you nowhere.' She placed the canvas on the easel, pulling off the dust sheet. 'Adam.' She moved a critical eye along his thighs and over his open chest.

I stirred a generous dollop of condensed milk into her tea before I passed her the cup. 'He couldn't wait to drop his trousers.'

'I bet,' she crooned, leaning in as I picked up the lamp and stood beside her. 'He'd do anything for you.'

'When it suits.'

'The blurring . . .' She pointed to Adam's head. 'What if you took it right across his face to here? And the colour, at this point where everything meets.' Bones skimmed like stones towards the nape of her neck as she bent towards the canvas.

'I can get you a job at Corbett's, Alice. They're looking for someone.'

'I'm not just running messages for Maggie; I'm running her books.'

'Corbett's would be easier.'

53

'It wouldn't be enough. And besides, I have a plan.' I waited for her to tell me the plan but she didn't.

'What about one of the girls?' I suggested. 'Marie's old enough.'

'I want to keep them in school for as long as I can. Does this have a name?'

'*The First Man.*'

She laughed. 'Our good priest won't think too much of that. The filthy old bastard.'

The priest wasn't the only problem. Antipathy towards my work increased after I painted *The First Man*. What was said about the painting is clearer than the work itself. That I'd mixed clotted blood into the paint, that I'd slain a pig and watched as its heart came to a halt, that I'd straddled the unconsecrated grave of a whore and channelled the image from her. I wasn't after notoriety, though; not that kind. I'd always been fascinated by the anatomy pages in Max's books and yes, I knew a butcher and went with him sometimes when he slaughtered his beasts.

That image was no more than common sense. Any girl could have explained its meaning as she steamed over her copper on a Monday morning. Adam naked and on his knees, reaching forward, begging, his eyes raw, his face blurred, slightly distorted, his chest open, exposing his heart. A bloodied knife, dropped by his side. I admit the blade was a little dramatic, but I was seventeen.

After the murder a big fuss was made over it. Adam dragged the canvas out for a reporter who'd remembered it and came knocking on his door. The painting was considered proof that I'd gutted a man's body of his heart then left him to die. My husband, the papers called him. WIFE SLAUGHTERS HUSBAND was the headline, above a quote from Adam: 'You never know, anything's possible with Muriel.' Years later I received a letter from him, delayed by my unknown whereabouts. In it he claimed he'd been misquoted, that what he'd actually said was, 'You never know, anything's possible with a genius like Muriel.' I guess he thought that bit of butter rubbing would please me.

And the title: *The First Man*. Blasphemy on top of all my other sins. The painting was no more than a young girl's manual on battling desire. Adam loved it. But then he believed in rebellion and was all for a war to get me noticed.

'Or killed. There are always casualties in war.'

Alice though, was never one of my detractors. 'I have to lie down,' she said.

We made a bed from a potato sack and a blanket then rolled my smock into a pillow, but she rested her head on my shoulder.

'All that eternal punishment.' Her nose was cold on my neck.

'What?'

'Eve.'

'Oh.' I stroked the hair from her forehead, feeling the flutter of her eyes as she began to run again from the coppers. Moving her head onto the smock, I went in search of my sketchbook and drew her bundled in my coat under the hessian blanket, eyes slightly open.

Alice slept for an hour, maybe longer, enough time anyway to do a preliminary drawing. When she woke, she was instantly alert. Eyelids lifting like shutters, hands clenched on the ready. She looked around, saw me, then relaxed.

'I have to go.'

'Stay. At least until morning.'

'I need to be home for the girls.' Ridding herself of my coat, she looked to see what I'd drawn, laughed, then kissed the back of my neck.

•

Time deflates when I paint, like a Dali clock. It was night when Alice left then it was morning. I'd highlighted her slumbering body in violet and blood-red lines no thicker than a single hair, then surrounded her in a glut of apples, chalked but not painted yet, in various stages of decay.

I was prised from my work by a slurry of noise. The front door opening, loud conversation and the thump of feet on the stairs. Adam and James Dennison entered, carrying the cool winter mist on their jackets and smelling of cheap claret.

'We've interrupted.' James Dennison was three sheets to the wind.

I took in their flaccid faces. Then contemplated drawing a baby, wriggling from the fruit like a grub – would that be too much?

Adam rabbited on about Old Masters. I heard Rembrandt mentioned and Renoir, although as far as I was concerned Renoir was no master, then they moved on to students who painted under their tutor's signature.

'Dennison would like to see your work.' Adam's voice sliced the baby from the apple.

I waved a hand at him. What Dennison wanted was someone to ridicule. They lifted my paintings one by one from where they were propped against the wall. Adam singled out a particular canvas and held it up, back turned to me.

'There . . . You see?'

Dennison moved his hand over his eyes, closing them fractionally before opening them again.

'Yes, it's exactly as you said.'

After that they followed the gush of cold through the open door and down the stairs and were gone.

I shivered, repulsed now by the thought of a baby crawling from the apples. I needed breakfast or lunch but there was nothing in the studio other than a last mouthful of condensed milk. I sucked on the can, wondering which of the canvasses Dennison had been shown, then saw it out of kilter, leaning against the wall. The portrait I'd painted for Nan's birthday with the flowering peach. The bile rose. Adam was such a bastard.

NO ~~DOGS OR WO~~MEN ALLOWED I had altered the sign that had been pinned to the edge of my easel as a joke. Looking at it now I decided Adam was right. I should prod the devil. From now on I'd only paint women. I thought of Vida Lahey's 1912 canvas, *Monday Morning*. Women at their work. It wasn't something you saw; waitresses, teachers, housewives, nuns, barwomen, shop assistants, nurses, women catching trams, walking, on the back of horses and sitting in traps – hanging out clothes, sweeping. There was an abundance of subjects. Women who ran brothels and sly grog shops. I'd paint them all.

But where? I'd been given notice to quit Max Jenner's studio and owned not much more than his old easel. I didn't have the money to rent something of my own.

Adam returned bearing a loaf of bread and a baked rabbit from the Ham and Bone. I could smell the food as he walked up the stairs. We sat on the floor and picked over the carcass, my unwashed hands leaving smears of paint on the bread as I tore bits off. Adam got up from the floor to make the tea, unhappy with the state of the leaves.

'How many times have you used these?' He looked at the slosh in the pot then left it there to brew.

I may have fallen asleep. When I opened my eyes, I was on the floor, my coat folded beneath my head with a still-warm mug at my side. I watched Adam through the steam, perched on the sitter's stool, eyes on my face.

'You could work from Dennison's studio.'

I sat up and lifted the tea to my lips.

'He needs an assistant.'

'He needs more than an assistant.' I thought of Dennison's trembling hands.

Adam shifted his bony backside to the left then to the right then decided to stand. 'He's working on a commission. A portrait.'

'Good luck to him.'

Adam moved to the painting of Alice. 'He's looking for an amanuensis.'

'He's looking for someone to do the work.'

'He's done a mile of preliminary sketches and mapped it out on canvas. He knows exactly what he wants.'

'Why are you telling me this?'

'You could move into his studio, use his supplies for your own work as well as his, and he could introduce you to some buyers.'

'Buyers? Interested in my work?'

•

'Dennison's last bloom,' Adam called it in his biography. Explaining how my steady hands, under the old man's tutelage, revived the painter's popularity for a few years. There was no tutelage – Adam didn't reveal that, although he did mention my trick of painting a maggot beneath Dennison's signature in retribution for having to sign on his behalf. I didn't want my name linked with the old souse. Which is exactly why Adam wrote about it in his book.

The Last Man. It was published decades after the announcement of my death, leaving Adam free to describe the great love that had existed between us, and the narcissism (mine) which had destroyed it. Our love was described in terms of a series of explicit sexual acts carried out in locations that didn't exist in the twenties. I wondered who'd checked the facts. Adam professed a passion not only for me but for my art, claiming to have recognised my genius long before anyone else had.

My response to Adam – typed on plain unidentifiable A4 paper and sent from a distant letterbox:

It reads like porn . . . And you could have picked a better title.

Dennison's paintings were your idea, not mine.

The day you came up with the scam we ate rabbit on the floor and you complained about the twice-used tea leaves. If you'd really loved me, you wouldn't have offered me up to that violent old drunk.

When Claudine held a retrospective of my work in the early eighties, Adam was there, scanning the crowd for my supposedly dead face in among the bloodsuckers. Anyway, enough of that.

•

Adam argued that assisting Dennison with the commission was
just that: *assisting.*

'He'll tell you what and how to paint. A lot of the greats taught
their students that way.'

'Greats?'

'I'll drink to that.' Adam raised his mug, slurping the tea through
his front teeth.

And so it was decided, without any explicit sex scenes, that I'd
play amanuensis to the great James Dennison in return for a studio
and free art supplies and time to spend on my own work.

5.

Something sweet

February 1992

Muriel invited me in for a cup of tea. She'd bought a cake. 'Something plain, because of the nausea.' I took the proffered chair, wary of her attention. The teapot wore a knitted cosy with stitched-on woollen flowers. Perhaps she'd bought it specially; there'd been a fundraiser in the car park near the harbour last Friday. She turned the pot three times anticlockwise then placed a warm hand on my arm and said, 'Tell me about your mother.'

I laughed. It had to be a joke.

Her lips pursed.

'My mother?'

'All right, forget about your mother. I'll tell you about mine.'

I would never have asked about her mother. I wasn't sure I wanted to know.

'It's the story that counts anyway. Not the writer.'

'The writer?'

'You.' She was terse, snappy. 'The writer. What do you think I'm talking about?'

'But *I'm* not telling your mother's story.'

'My mother's only a small part of it.' The table boxed me in. Was she looking for someone to write her life story?

'I could find you a writer. If that's what you want.'

'You'll do.'

'I don't think I will.'

'Think of the money.' Muriel leaned in. 'I'll pay you more than you're worth.'

'To write your story? Is that what you're saying, Muriel? You want to pay someone to write about your life?'

•

I *would* start with my mother, if I were to write my own story. I'd begin it in the summer of 1972, on a day my younger sister and I stood in front of the school, swatting flies as we waited for the bus. Mandy and I ignored each other until a pointy little Morris Minor cruised down the street and stopped just beyond the school gate.

'Get in,' Mum called through the front window. David, our four-year-old brother, leaned over the back seat and yelled, 'Run!' through the same window.

We did run. I made Mandy get in the back with David because I was ten and the eldest. *Amanda*, I can hear her correction. And while I should have asked where the car came from, I was distracted by David, bouncing up and down on the back seat bragging, 'We're going on holidays.' But our family didn't own a car and, as far as I knew, Mum couldn't drive.

'Sit down, David, please.' Mum negotiated the school traffic with surprising ease.

'What about school?' Mandy called from the back.

'Wouldn't you rather a holiday?'

'The play's tomorrow, and I'm the princess. I've been practising for weeks.'

'It's not as if you get to say anything,' I pointed out.

'The shoes don't fit anyone else. Nobody will know what to do.'

'I've already rung. Mrs Parsons said Beth could take the part.'

'Be-eth!' Mandy wailed, then slumped into a sulk.

'Dad's coming after work,' David told us.

Something wasn't right about this. How was Dad going to get there? And where *was* there? I looked at Mum, whose eyes were on the road, and decided not to ask questions. Not then. I'd wait.

We headed north past Wollongong. Mandy, who liked to put on a bit of a show, kicked the back of my seat and wailed, 'Be-eth.' David copied with a kick to the back of Mum's seat. Mum snapped her head around, wild-eyed, and this is the bit I remember most vividly. We skidded across the road on an oil patch – we found that out later. Mum tried to right the Morris but steered straight towards the coal truck.

Mandy and I remember things differently. She lamented (often) to my father, she knew something was wrong and had begged Mum to take us home. By then there was only Dad, me and the princess left. Mum and David were on the same side of the car. So, both killed. There was nobody to arbitrate our different stories.

On the day of the accident, Dad was delivered to us from the back of a police car. He asked me, 'Where the bloody hell did you think you were going?'

63

The princess: 'I told her, Dad – I said I wanted to go home.'

Dad to me: 'Why didn't you stop her?'

The princess: 'She didn't even try.'

Not that I blame Mandy; she was just a kid. And Dad, I guess he was in shock. I remember a policeman saying to him, 'Hey, hey – she's just a little girl.' Dad's eyes widened, as if he didn't quite know what he'd said.

There'd be no point in telling Muriel that story – her glance would wander out the window in search of the cat or any other distraction.

·

Muriel's cake was a large iced bun, more bread than cake. I scraped the icing off my slice and managed to eat it.

'See?' Muriel said. Not about the bun but about the two canvasses she'd propped against the wall to show me. The first two paintings from a series of three. A triptych, she called it.

'What?'

She pointed to the first canvas. 'My mother.' Two women stood on either side of a door that opened onto a street. Her mother, with her back to us, was on the street side.

Once I agreed to write the book, I suggested we tape her story. Priming, I called it. I thought I'd have to convince her but Muriel agreed readily enough, likening the experience to 'digging ticks out of your skin'. A relief – I guess that's what she meant.

But even though I hadn't agreed – yet – she insisted on telling me about her mother.

Her mother's hair was fairytale gold. It looked alive in the painting. Mobile and floating like seaweed on the tide.

64

'What was your mother's name?' I asked.

'I don't know.'

There was a lot she didn't seem to know.

On that particular day in 1904, Muriel's mother (painted an anaemic lead white with broad shoulders and Medusa hair that circled her head in a halo) walked along Campbell Street, then turned left into Samuel with a bundle that looked like washing. She knocked on a mottled green door part way along the street.

Painting number one: Muriel's mother hands her bundle to the woman who answers the door, Muriel's grandmother.

Painting number two: Muriel's mother walks empty-handed along the street, her back to the first painting.

Painting number three (a sketch drawn on a piece of paper by Muriel to represent the missing canvas): Two unknown women stand in front of a biplane – a Gipsy Moth, according to Muriel. The swaddling from the first painting had reappeared between the two women, held up by their four hands.

Muriel pointed out a tuft of 'red' at the apex of the bundle. 'My daughter.'

Muriel had a daughter? 'And?' I said, wanting to hear more.

She shook her head. 'I gave her to Claudine.'

'You're not much of a storyteller,' I said.

This was of no relevance to Muriel. *I* was to tell the story.

'I'm not interested in writing a biography, between my job and the baby and my own writing.'

'Did I say biography?' Muriel's eyes were clear and green. Marbles with heavy black centres, ready to shoot in my direction.

'Well, that's what it would be.'

'You can write it as fiction for all I care.'

What I didn't care for was her assumption that I'd do her bidding.

'As long you name me as the source,' she added. 'My surname is Kemp. That's enough information for today.'

But I stayed to argue the point. I couldn't write a story, I told her; not somebody else's.

'Why not? You're a writer. You told me so yourself.'

'Not much of one,' I confessed. 'Not yet. What if I stuff it up?'

'What if you don't?'

'I don't want to waste your time. Or mine.' I sliced another sliver from the bun and scraped the icing onto the plate.

Muriel picked up the plate and the cosied teapot. She deposited them on the draining board of the sink then gave me that killer look of hers. 'What I don't have time for is your simpering. Go away. Write something. If I don't like it, we're done.'

•

I drove to Warilla Library. Not because I thought I'd pursue the book, but because I was curious. Muriel Kemp. She'd said it like it mattered, but I'd never heard of her.

I started with a general book on the history of Australian Art, not expecting to find anything. But examples of Muriel Kemp's paintings were in among the modernists. She really was an artist. I scanned the black-and-white reproductions with no real interest, then came across a print in full colour: *Children Playing in Surry Hills* (1921). I was drawn to the colour, then to the children's thin bodies and their rounded heads that looked like beaks. How can I explain this? I don't know a thing about art, but I could have been in that picture, running with a cricket bat or bent over, hands on my thighs, ready to take a catch. I might have been the girl near the paling fence, whispering into the ear of her friend, my too-thin body wrapped in an oversized jumper, legs blistered by the cold. That was me at ten.

I came across another colour reproduction: *Girl on Riley Street* (1925), originally purchased by Claudine Worthington in that same year. I felt sure that I recognised it, then realised there was the same liveliness in the face of the Riley Street girl that I'd seen that morning in the woman with the red Medusa hair.

I flipped back and forth through the book, looking for details or some sort of biography, and found half a paragraph of writing under the heading; *MURIEL KEMP 1904–1936.*

I didn't know what to make of it. According to that reference Muriel Kemp was long dead but that couldn't be right. I searched the shelves and found two more books on Australian Art that mentioned Muriel's name. One said she'd died in 1935 the other in 1939. They both described her death as being controversial.

Intrigued, I went in search of the newspaper archives. Older copies of the *Illawarra Mercury* and some of the Sydney papers were on microfilm, but not a full collection and not searchable by subject. I'd have to read each paper individually. Back at the main catalogue, I looked for references on Claudine Worthington, the original buyer of *Girl on Riley Street*. I remembered the report of her death in the newspaper that first day I'd talked to Muriel. The library had a copy of an unauthorised biography.

•

There we were on my unmade bed: the cat, me, the biography and a bottle of flat ginger ale. The book was more than a decade old but revealing. Claudine Worthington, independently wealthy and a patron of the arts, had indeed known Muriel Kemp. A whole chapter was devoted to their relationship. Muriel was the first artist Claudine ever sponsored – to the detriment of her reputation, according to the biographer. Claudine continued to champion Kemp's talent long after Muriel's death, despite harsh criticism of the artist's work, narcissism and sexual misconduct. The critic argued that legend, rather than skill, had secured Muriel Kemp's position in history and cited other experts who shared this view.

The chapter resembled a Machiavellian drama with its talk of sex romps, beatings and scams gone wrong. It was trashy, but I couldn't put it down.

In summary, Muriel had grown up in the slums of Surry Hills but honed her artistic skills in Sydney's bohemian art world. She was discovered in her twenties by Claudine Worthington, who provided her with paint, money and a space of her own. The arrangement didn't benefit Claudine in the final wash-up. Muriel died in an aviation accident alongside Claudine's husband, Tommy Hasluck, with whom Muriel had been having an affair.

But that wasn't the only controversy. Before her death, Muriel had painted a series of canvasses meant to be part of a solo exhibition scheduled for 1936. However, the paintings vanished – stolen, the biographer implied.

And there was one more thing: Muriel Kemp was accused of murder in 1928. But that Muriel had died less than ten years later. And if that Muriel Kemp was dead, then who was the Muriel Kemp that lived in Boollwarroo Parade, also claiming to be a painter born in Surry Hills in 1904?

I re-read the chapter in case I'd missed something, but there were no answers in the printed pages. As late as it was, I was too wound up to sleep. The cat raised her head as I got off the bed to search for pen and paper. I wrote down some dot points from the biography, then a list of questions I wanted to ask Muriel. Muriel Kemp? – or the woman claiming to be Muriel Kemp? That was the question that absorbed me. Whoever she was, I was in. Because regardless of the truth, it was her story I wanted to tell.

The next morning I rang her. 'Give me three weeks to write you something. If you're happy with what I produce, I'll take on the biography.'

'We've already discussed this.'

'I just wanted to make sure . . .'

'You can have a fortnight.'

'Muriel . . .' What I really wanted to know was why she'd been reported dead in 1936.

'What?'

But maybe I should ask her that question in person. 'I've been reading some articles in the library.' I looked at the quotes written on my notepad. 'Claudine Worthington described you as being better than any artist past or present. Does that surprise you?'

'Why? It's a fair comment.'

I looked down at my notes again and thought about it.

She knew her worth. I'd give her that.

6.

A lifetime of gerunds

Early March 1992

Five thirty a.m. Bleary from reading Claudine Worthington's unauthorised biography, something I'd done repeatedly over the last two weeks, I picked up a thick black marker and wrote:

Do not believe everything Muriel says.

I stuck the note on the fridge then stood in front of the mirror to dress. Pulling my uniform over my hips, I told myself I wasn't showing – not really – then headed off to work.

It all broke loose, though, at the end of the shift, in handover to Sister Paxton; not Margaret, but 'Sister'. Sister Paxton frowned her way through my verbal report, tapping pen on paper. 'It helps no one, Sister Cooper –' she leaned in, confidential '– to run around after the patients the way you do.'

Up yours, I thought, but she left the room before I even had time to change the expression on my face. Sally, the enrolled nurse, mouthed, 'Ignore her,' then pushed her way through the meeting room door. I followed, into the gathering of afternoon staff.

The charge sister barrelled towards us from the other end of the ward, raising her finger to catch my attention. Oh God. She must have heard about my vomiting in the pan room.

'Jane,' she called. I should have told everyone by now that I was pregnant but hadn't wanted to deal with the gossip. Now I'd have to cope with the charge sister's probing questions instead. 'I'm pregnant, all right,' I projected in her direction. My face set in a fuck-off glare, the one meant for Sister Paxton.

'Jane?' Her steps faltered.

The other staff came to a halt, eyes turning towards the scene.

Alarmed by my obnoxious behaviour I escaped through the nearest exit, down the stairs and into daylight. I'd have to apologise but I was too on edge to do it now. Not because of the pregnancy but because I was supposed to show Muriel a sample of my writing the next day and I hadn't written a thing.

•

My car was three streets away and shimmered in the heat like a mirage. I slithered onto the arse-frying seat and gunned the engine. The radio kicked in, blaring prime ministerial rhetoric. Paul 'the recession Australia had to have' Keating. A potty-mouthed, arrogant bastard who called his colleagues scumbags, useless, flat out counting past ten. It's not as if *he* apologised. Why the fuck did I always feel so sorry about everything I did? I could design my own T-shirt. An anthem for all us mollifiers.

If that's all right with you . . .
If you don't mind . . .

If it's not too much trouble . . .

I floored the accelerator for a hundred metres, pulling back as I neared the T-intersection. Turning right onto Crown Street, I hit the horn as a pedestrian crossed the road in front of me. A face flashed sideways. It was the young intern from the ward. He slapped his left hand onto his right bicep and bent his elbow. When he saw it was me, his mouth dropped open. I blew the horn a second time and raised my middle finger.

I veered left onto the ramp road and merged with the F6. Ten minutes later I exited onto Springhill Road, going in the direction of Port Kembla, speeding past the steelworks, weaving through the traffic like a rally car driver.

I made it to the other side of Warrawong, right to the last set of traffic lights, pushing down on the accelerator to beat the orange light. But the driver in front was too slow and I got caught halfway across the intersection, just as the lights changed to red. There was a siren, the flash of an indicator, an arm waved me towards the kerb. I stepped out of the Laser at the same time as the cop stepped from his car. 'Aahh. No!' he said when he saw my uniform. The unofficial police–nurse code meant he wouldn't book me.

On the verge, I flapped my hand, warning him to back away – a gesture he ignored to his detriment as I hurled the contents of my stomach onto the grass.

'Big day?' He wiped his shoe against a straggle of weeds.

'I'm pregnant.' I moved to a clean patch of grass and kneeled, head over my knees.

'Wollongong Hospital or Port?'

'Wollongong.'

The uniform squatted beside me as I lurched forward again. He held my hair out of the way as I retched, then vomited. A small act of kindness. I could have cried.

'Were you on dayshift or did they send you home?'

'Days. I'm off tomorrow.'

He looked at the vomit. There was a lot of it. 'My partner can drive you.' He pointed to his partner, who watched from behind the safety of a closed window. 'I'll follow with your car.'

'Thanks, but it'll stop now.'

'Two vomits? A pattern?'

I laughed. 'I'm sorry.'

'No damage done.'

Back in the car, anger replaced the nausea. I didn't want this baby. I sat for a few moments, lower than worm's breath, an expression used to describe the morning after a big night out on cheap grog – not that I drank anymore. But that's how I felt: lower than worm's breath. I didn't want the baby. Whatever possessed me to think I did? I waved to my friend the cop, got back in my car and sauntered down the road, my lack of speed a facade for my frustration.

Too revved up to go home for a quiet lie-down, I drove to Warilla and the scene of the crime instead. Pup's was not far from the hospital where I'd end up giving birth. The ideal location, with its dope plants in a foil-lined cupboard, surfboards stacked in racks in the garage, porn mags in the loo, award-winning photos framed and aligned on the walls, crocheted doilies everywhere. 'A joke,' he said. Pup was no dummy. Just a wanker.

His car was parked in the gravel driveway beside the stilted house. I imagined him inside, tied to his bed by his four limbs while a contingent of housing commission chicks raided his draws for T-shirts and flogged him within an inch of comprehension. This: the father of my child.

A line from a poem by Philip Larkin came to mind: *They fuck you up, your mum and dad.* I cased the house for movement and contemplated how many babies Pup had fucked up in that little doilied room of his. A chainsaw through his stilts would have calmed me. I enjoyed the thought then came up with an alternative that wouldn't see me jailed.

At the servo down the road I bought a couple of cartons of full cream milk then parked around the corner from Pup's, out of sight. With the milk cartons tucked into a bag I walked, a nurse just finished her shift, up the road to the house and the white station wagon with the passenger door that didn't lock. I poured the milk along the back seat and as far as I could reach under it, then did the same in the front. It would ferment nicely in the heat. I took the empty cartons away with me. To dispose of responsibly.

Feeling a little better, I got in the car and headed for home. I was happy until I reached Shellharbour, and then it all seemed unfair again. Pouring a couple of litres of milk in the back of a car does not equal a child.

I thought of Mum's escape in the Morris Minor twenty years ago. Perhaps her leaving wasn't about revenge for Dad's failings, but merely a bid to be happy?

Dad never speculated; he said he didn't know why Mum had up and run. It was Lyn, Dad's new wife, who found the letters years later, in the still-packed suitcase salvaged from the Morris Minor. Lyn gave them to me, rather than my sister. No envelopes, no addresses written in the upper right-hand corner, just pages signed by someone called Harry who described his life on the New South Wales–Queensland border and asked which of the children would prefer to sleep in a room and which on the verandah. Who would've told Harry about Mum?

I pulled into my parking space behind the flats and the tabby ran the length of the backyard to greet me. She rubbed her whiskers against my pantyhosed legs and the laces in my shoes and we walked inside together, two partial redheads, one tabby and one streaked. It wasn't possible to be angry when the cat curled itself on my lap and purred.

I slept for a few hours then woke with the cat moulded to my lower back and an idea in my head that I couldn't quite work out. I got out the typewriter.

At dawn, I ripped the note off the fridge – *Do not believe everything Muriel says* – and left the flat with sheafs of typewritten words in my hand.

•

As Muriel ushered me into the house I wondered if the cat had worked out something about her that I hadn't. Don't be ridiculous, I chided myself. It's probably the smell of the turps that the cat can't stand.

In the kitchen, I cleared my throat.

'Don't fidget, just read it. Or give it to me. I'll read it myself.'

The increasing sounds slowed Joseph's rhythm. He groped for the next person in the queue, then the next. Head injury, stroke, cancer, blood pressure, seizures, delusions. He moved hand over hand down the line, a bounce at each stop.

He touched the shaky hands of a man with Parkinson's who leaned in to whisper the name of his disease as if he thought it was necessary that Joseph know.

'I live in the body of an old man too,' Joseph explained in return. 'Even older than yours and I don't know the name of my own disease.'

But the man had gone, replaced by a woman who patted his hand. 'It'll come,' she told him. 'Not that a name really matters.'

Joseph nodded, not to the woman but to a teenager, skinny, short hair. It could have been a boy or girl. He felt himself swell, feed on the healings. There was a throb in him like a second heartbeat.

'Yes, that's how it feels,' answered someone in the queue. 'Like a throb. I didn't realise anything was wrong at first.'

Joseph didn't think there was anything wrong at all. It was going well. He touched a man's sternum and felt the stabbing rhythm beneath it.

'I've had it for thirty-odd years, haven't been able to get out of the house much in all that time.'

Joseph touched the spot lightly to even out the pace, then plucked himself from the sky. It was important to keep his feet on the ground, to try to remember that he couldn't fly.

'I did pluck it out.' Whose voice was that? Joseph was millimetres away from the purulent pores of a screwed-up face. 'And it grew right back like an elephant's arse, right here on my chin.'

Bodies pressed forward, necks craned. Messages surfed the crowd. 'Joseph Clymont is curing the dead.'

The PA system announced that the healings would stop if the crowd did not submit to direction. 'Those already healed must proceed promptly to the exit.'

'That's not about me,' Muriel interrupted.

'Of course it's not.'

Muriel snorted and looked away.

'I said you mightn't like it.'

'I didn't say I didn't like it.'

'So, you want to hear the rest then?'

'No, that'll do. You're hired.'

I smiled, gratified. Afterwards, Muriel shuffled me out of the house refusing to answer any of my questions about her reported death in 1936 or where she'd been since then.

'Everything you need to know will be on the tapes.'

'I understand but I have some questions, before we start . . .'

'Everything.'

7.

The hot iron

Spring 1921

I've never met such a stubborn bitch nor anyone, male or female, as convinced of their genius as Muriel. She was a leech. I moved on before she sucked every last drop out of me.

Adam Black, The Last Man (1958)

I didn't see anybody after I moved into James Dennison's. I'd gotten used to the comings and goings of the old studio. Max had attracted visitors and it was the group he referred to as the disciples that I missed most – with their outdated prints and their ideas on the avant-garde – especially William Green who'd draw me into his discussions. Bill fell in love with Cézanne from an art book posted to him from France and every time I saw him after that he tried to convert me. 'Don't bother with light and shade.' He took my brush to demonstrate, building a shape based on the subtleties of colour.

'What is it?'

'A pear.'

'It doesn't look like one.' It didn't look like anything much.

'Give it a burl. It takes some getting used to.'

By then Cézanne's techniques were already unfashionable. That was the way of it. Any ideas or news on art movements were a decade or more out of date by the time they reached us.

'We're not Europe, Bill, or England. We should have our own art.'

'*We?* What *we*? Who are you referring to as *we*?'

'Australia – Australians. There's no reason we can't start our own movement.'

'I can see it now – us, captivating the world with our art.' He laughed, then slapped me on the back, laughing again.

Bill chose his masters carefully, slaving over their lessons until there was nothing left of his own inclinations. As irritating as this was, I dropped his ideas into the conversations I had with Max. An indiscretion – much like admitting to a dose of VD.

'All that hocus pocus. It won't last. People want to understand what they see.'

'You mean like God or the Great War or–'

'Have I forced you to stay?'

'What an old . . .'

'Speak up, Miss Kemp. Don't keep me in suspense.'

My appreciation of the old goat escalated after I moved into James Dennison's studio. Dennison and I fought from the very beginning. About painting and everything else.

His studio was not far from Max's, in an alleyway that ran off Liverpool Street. The day Adam and I arrived, lugging my bits and pieces, I said I was disappointed the rooms weren't in Rushcutters Bay or Potts Point. 'It'd be nice to see a glimpse of water.'

James Dennison's face set like tar and he disappeared. I didn't see him for a couple of days after that.

'He can't take a joke,' I observed.

'You can't tell them.'

On my own, I organised the studio the way I wanted it. I assessed the supplies and wrote a list of what was needed, then began my series of women. Not began really; the beginning was the painting of Alice. I started on the second one, working from memory on a sketch of big meaty Ava Wilson, beating the dust out of a carpet as the fowls scouted around in the dirt near her ankles, searching for a feed.

Dennison came back sour-faced but calm. He found the preliminary drawings and the colour study he'd done for the portrait commission and told me what he wanted done.

'When's the next sitting?'

'The sittings are finished.' He waved a hand toward his preparatory work as if the answers were all there.

'Absolute rubbish.' I showed them to Adam. 'There was a canvas too. But it was so bad he wouldn't show it to me. It looks like a woman. But I'm not even certain of that.'

'It's not finished yet,' Adam defended him, though he agreed there was a paucity of material for me to work from. 'But I don't see what I can do about it.'

'This whole thing was your idea. Ask him who the sitter is.'

'I know who it is. I can even introduce you.'

It turned out Adam had recommended James Dennison to the

sitter then, having realised his mistake, coerced Dennison to employ me. So now I knew.

'I'll tell her you're my cousin.'

•

The morning we set out to meet the sitter was cool. The street was foggy with the breath of horses. Not our horses; we were on shanks' pony. Adam carried a walking stick over his arm – carved, he said, from yellow boxwood. It was an ugly thing with a silver snake coiled around the shaft.

'Where'd you get it?'

'Present from an admirer.' He swaggered, best suit on, hair full of pomade, the broken sole of his shoe tied and the string camouflaged with ink. We crossed the lawn of the botanic gardens towards the path that circled the wishing tree. Adam doffed his hat as two women approached from the opposite direction.

'The Misses Trudeau,' he declared.

There was no flick of parasols or flutter of fans. The Misses Trudeau, Virginia and Adele, were thoroughly modern in their short dresses and dropped waists. This didn't stop Adam from fawning as if they were landed gentry.

'My sister and I come here quite a lot.' The taller Miss Trudeau, Adele, was the subject of Dennison's portrait and, as a consequence, drew my attention. 'Even during the Spanish flu.' She pushed blunt-cut tresses behind an ear. 'My mother was all for fresh air, although everyone told her she was wrong to let us out.'

I'd managed to coax Adele away from her sister towards a flowerbed. She had a soft face with bright blue Nordic eyes and a twitch that pulled the left side of her mouth towards her jaw.

'Are you really Adam's cousin?' she asked.

'No, it's his excuse for being seen with me.'

Adam was stuck with the twittering Virginia, who insisted they make a wish on the large Norfolk pine designated as the wishing tree. The process included circling the tree three times forwards then another three backwards before making a wish. Adam cast looks in my direction.

'Surely not. You could hardly embarrass him.'

'Take a good look. I'm no fashion plate.' I threw my arms above my head and twirled, noting the way her head tilted and one eyelid drooped lower than the other.

'What about *him?*' She snorted as she lifted a small embroidered handkerchief to her nose. 'With that awful cane.'

I turned my head and gazed at Adam, taking my time so he could see me assessing him head to foot. 'You're right. I've got nothing to worry about.'

The handkerchief flapped in front of her lips. I linked my arm through hers and led her guffawing frame away.

'Don't get me wrong,' she said. 'I'm very fond of Adam.'

'But?'

'There are no buts. I laugh too much, that's all.' The sunlight bleached her skin and filled her eyes with phosphorus.

'He's worried that I'll ask to sketch you.'

'You draw?'

I nodded.

'You don't need to seduce me. I'm more than willing.'

I pulled my sketchbook from the waist of my skirt and found the pencil in my pocket.

'Oh, you mean now.' She laughed again but sat on the nearby bench to pose, arms by her side, gaze direct. 'You know, I've just finished sitting for a portrait.'

'For James Dennison?'

'Adam told you?'

'You were wearing that dress.'

'Have you seen it?'

'It's a beautiful dress, that's all. And the beading around the neck is flattering.' She blushed as I ran a finger around the neckline. 'I can imagine that's what you'd wear.' I did a number of quick studies then looked up and smiled. 'Would you mind removing your hat?' I asked.

She pulled out the pin and flattened her hair. 'Lovely,' I said.

I wrote some notes about tones and colours then sat beside her on the bench to sketch the intricacies of the dress's neckline. Putting the sketchbook away, I ran a finger over the beadwork once more, not stopping this time until I reached her breasts. She laughed nervously then looking around, covered my hand with her own.

'You don't bind them, do you?'

'There's no need.'

I cupped my hands around the loose mounds, feeling their weight.

'You're as good as my doctor.' She checked once again to see that we were alone then leaned back against the bench.

'If I was doing your portrait, I'd pose you in the natural.' I reclined on the bench beside her. Adam, no longer attentive to Virginia, stood at a distance, hands on his hips, eyes in our direction.

'You paint portraits?'

'Much better than James Dennison ever will.'

'In that case, you should contact me.' She twisted sideways, skimming her mouth gently over mine. There was nothing in it, a friendly touch of the lips, but her arm snaked between the fold of our bodies, her hand grasping my breast curiously. Then she resettled herself beside me.

Adam walked towards us, eyebrows meeting over his nose, Virginia trailing him like a fish on a line.

'Why didn't you say your cousin was an artist?' Adele cooed.

●

I never saw Adam again, after that day.

'You were trying to provoke me.' He raised his arms, furious with me.

'You're easy to rile.'

'I'm serious about her, Muriel.'

'She's too pretty and she won't be enough. Not after me.'

He lowered his arms and his voice. 'You never promised me a thing.'

I shook my head. 'It's not you I'm worried about. I liked her.'

'So you've said.'

'We flirted a little, it was nothing. Women do that sometimes.'

'Not women. You, Muriel. You do that sometimes.'

This argument took place at the studio, or maybe it was on our way back from the park. Adam was a like a harsh dose of salts when he was angry.

You should include a picture of him in the book, Jane. Not the portrait I told you about – *The First Man*. Adam kept that. No one else wanted it at the time. [Laughter.] Claudine borrowed it for the eighties retrospective. It was worth something by then, but he wouldn't sell. He liked to stand beside it and spout his half-arsed lies about our love-life. I saw him once on *Midday* with Ray Martin, looking like the peacock he was. But enough of that. I'll do a sketch of him, so you can get a sense of his character. Include that in the book, if you like.

•

Biographer's note: Once Muriel mastered the recorder she began to tape on her own. In this particular session, the recorder picked up the sound of what could have been her sketching. I couldn't find a drawing among those she left me which corresponded to her description of Adam. It's quite possible she wasn't happy with what she drew or changed her mind about the whole thing and destroyed it.

•

After the fight with Adam, I went to Surry Hills to see Alice. It was going on dark and the weather had changed. One of the Murphy boys – Joe, I think – lumbered past in tatty grey shorts and what could have been his father's jacket, pushing a sack of flour and a younger brother in a pram. I heard him before I saw him, mimicking the horn from a motorcar for his brother, who clapped his hands and laughed each time Joe made the sound.

'Are you still drawing those pictures?' Joe said as they came alongside.

'Why?'

'I was after something for me mum.'

'You still working Reservoir Street?' Joe was a sometime cockatoo for the local two-up school and that was where he'd be later, if he was on the job.

'Yep. What about the morning?'

'Come first thing.' I turned into Riley Street. The sound of Joe's Klaxon and his baby brother's laugh continued along Campbell.

The Cooneys were at their tea. It must have been after six because Mr Cooney was at the table, red-eyed and in braces and undershirt. Mrs Cooney stood beside him, ready to put his plate down, but waited until Marie settled the large teapot. Edna, the youngest, followed a cat beneath the table and copped the boot that was meant for the animal. She emerged howling with a blood nose.

Mr Cooney reached past the teapot, grabbing for her dark curls. 'Stop that racket or I'll really give you something to cry about. By hell, a man works hard and all he asks for is a little peace.'

Marie raised a sullen eyebrow as she pinched the bridge of her sister's nose with her fingers.

'You can count on a turn of the strap too, Marie, if you don't shut that sister of yours up.'

I followed Marie and the sobbing Edna out of the kitchen to ask where Alice was.

'She hasn't been here all week.' Marie shushed her sister. 'If you see her, tell her Mum needs the money for the housekeeping.'

There was a clatter behind us, dropped crockery followed by the sound of lungs deflating as somebody was thumped. Whoomp, whoomp, whoomp. No wail, no cry. Then came the crackle of crockery being picked up.

'Mumma.' Marie wiped a hand over her eyes, tired. 'I'd get a job myself but I promised Alice I wouldn't, not yet. But maybe I'll have to. Tell her that if you see her.'

Alice had taken over the responsibility of her sisters ever since — I'm not sure if I've mentioned Hugh, the eldest of the Cooney siblings. He'd run off as a fifteen-year-old to enlist in the Great War and got himself run over instead by the electrified tram on George Street, right in front of Peapes & Co, the menswear store.

'But he's so sure-footed,' Mrs Cooney said when the police turned up with the news.

They couldn't tell her anything other than what they'd been told: he'd stumbled and fallen in front of the tram.

'But what was he doing there?'

'Buying a new suit.' The coppers were laughing as they left Riley Street. No one liked them around there.

•

Peace and quiet behind Nan's old green door. 'Is that you, Muriel?' She was a lump moulded into the rocking chair, her leg raised like a busted snag on a fruit box.

'What happened?'

'Fell, didn't I, right on my behind in front of the apple display at Addison's, where everyone could see me. No, no, don't fuss. It's all right other than me pride, and I can't do much about that besides watch where I'm going the next time.'

I pulled the sketchbook from my waistband and bent to kiss her forehead. 'I'll put the kettle on.'

'There's a loaf in the box and a new tin of jam.'

'No apples?'

'You're a funny bugger.'

The gas jet guttered and light flickered upwards, illuminating a finger of the wall behind Nan. It fell on the painting of her and the peach tree, newly framed and hung.

'I was wondering when you'd notice. It took him a good couple of hours to get it up there and he wouldn't take so much as a cuppa in return.'

'Took who?' Even in the half-dark the painting looked stiff and out of kilter.

'Adam.'

'Adam was here?'

'A couple of days ago. Didn't he say?'

'No, he didn't.'

'You haven't signed it yet. Bring a bit of paint with you next time.'

'I will.'

•

Joe Murphy arrived the next morning as the sun came up. 'Going to church, are you?' I asked as he wandered in barefoot, dressed in the same clothes I'd seen him in the day before.

'I'll go if you go,' he said as he looked around. 'Where's your nan?'

'Having a lie-in.' I put the water on the gas ring to boil and cut two slices of bread. 'Dripping or jam?'

'Can you spare the jam?'

We took our breakfast out onto the street where the light was better. After we'd eaten I asked Joe what he had in mind then sketched it: the Murphy's front door framed by a climbing rose, half-a-dozen butterflies (one for each kid) and two fluttering birds.

Joe grinned as I tore the page from the book. Shifting from foot to foot, he took the sketch as if it were a pound note and tucked it beneath his shirt. Back in the flat I slid into the bed next to Nan, my ear between her shoulders, listening to the wheeze as her lungs forced their way to her ribs.

'That was Joe Murphy.'

'I thought so, lovey.' She scratched her upper arm and flakes sprung into the air. We lay in the warmth.

'Those Murphys are good kids,' she murmured drowsily. 'Busy, always doing something.'

'Your heart jumped,' I told her.

'It does that sometimes. Doesn't mean anything.'

Nan was my great-grandmother. When she was young she'd had a daughter called Mary, who gave birth to my father, Lionel, at sixteen then ran off to find her son's dad, who was away picking fruit in Victoria, or it might have been Queensland, and had been gone so long he didn't know about a baby. Mary never came back.

'It would have done her no good writing. Not to me. I expect she's made a life for herself somewhere.'

Lionel, Nan always said, was no trouble at all. He brought himself up. And down, as far as I could see, but there was no convincing Nan of any deficit. Even when the girl turned up on her doorstep.

'She had to be from around here but I couldn't place her.'

From Frogs Hollow, I'd decided, with its shacks built one on top of the other, dripping vermin and damp and hidden people. Lionel didn't have far to go to find her. The girl had remarkable hair. Nan used the word 'remarkable'. Picture story hair. I imagined fairytale gold. 'Much like your own,' said Nan, 'with that same curl.'

'And her face?' I'd ask.

'You'd never forget her face. That's how I knew I hadn't seen her before or since. Because of her face. It looked as if someone had pulled it apart then put it back together again in a hurry. Something was missing. I couldn't tell you what, only that there was something not quite right about it.'

'She wasn't pretty?'

'No, she wasn't. And better off for that.'

I imagined her face and agreed she was better off. 'You need more than a face.'

'That's true, you do.'

'But you didn't know her name.'

'I never knew her name. She came to the door, the whitest skin and pale blue lips, carrying what looked like a bundle of rags. She was as thin as a bit of paling, straight up and down, couldn't have been more than fourteen. Probably younger. She shoved the parcel at me. I thought she was selling something. She looked that desperate. Then I saw the blood on her neck. "This belongs to your son," she said.

'I should've asked her in, given her something to eat, made her a cuppa. I might have been able to help. But then I looked down and saw you in my arms. It was a bit of a shock – more than a bit. And when I looked up she was gone.'

'But there's something you remember about her most,' I prompted.

'What I remember about her most was the calmness.'

'She knew what she was doing.'

'She knew exactly what she was doing. She spoke as if she was handing me a gift.'

'I was the gift.'

'Too right you were.'

•

Back at the studio nothing was a gift.

Day one: James Dennison struggled to keep his body upright, smacking dry lips over a dry tongue. I showed him my sketch of Adele gazing from the paper on the cusp of a snort. He thought he'd drawn it. Impressed with himself, he headed off to celebrate.

Day three: Dennison wandered into the studio – from the back of a stable, by the look of him: flies undone, filthy shirt pulled about, braces drifting down his shoulders. He rolled himself into a blanket and began to snore. He woke some hours later, red-eyed; puzzled, I think, to find himself in the studio. He closed his eyes for another half-hour then got up.

'You're on the job early, Miss Kemp.'

It was two o'clock in the afternoon. I was glad when he left.

Day six: Dennison marched up the stairs and across the studio as if he'd never touched a drop of the stuff and came to a halt behind the easel to watch me work. He was silent for a long time. Then he snatched the brush from my hand.

'Too heavy, much too heavy, and these are not the colours we agreed on.'

I tried pulling the wool. 'You painted that bit yourself only yesterday.'

But Dennison wanted me to know he was on the wagon. 'I wasn't here yesterday, Miss Kemp.' He picked up a jar of turps and threw it at the canvas. 'We'll start again.'

Dennison sober was a torture. He raged and stomped around the room, insisted I prime the canvas, thin and mix the paints, clean the brushes and, worse, paint the portrait to his exact specification.

He arrived at nine each morning to ruminate. 'You could paint well enough, Miss Kemp, if you were willing to learn.'

His only good attribute was that he left by three each afternoon. I might have gone too, if it weren't for his supplies and the hours I had to myself. Each time I saw his tremor or looked into his black-gouged eyes I reminded myself that I had the better side of the deal.

•

I don't remember doing anything other than painting for the next year or two or even three. I was going to say that was all I did, but the magpies just started up outside the window, reminding me of a man I knew during that time who went by the name of Paterson Curse. He had plenty of other pseudonyms, but that was the one I liked best.

Paterson worked for *Smith's Weekly*. Besides that, he published freelance articles and poetry in *The Bulletin, The Triad, The Lone Hand* and even *Truth*. This is the memory the birds have dug up; me coming across Paterson in Hyde Park one morning. He was seated on the dewy grass near the trees as if he hadn't noticed the damp, watching as a couple of magpies sang in the early light. I took it all in. Paterson humped over his knees, chin on his hand, the intent look, fingers of light, sharp beaks, black wings. I would sketch it when I got home.

'Ugly birds have the best voices.' He held out an arm to be pulled up.

'I wouldn't call them ugly.'

'Not the birds – me. Have I ever sung for you?'

He had, many times, but I said, 'No,' and, 'I'd like to hear that,' as I reefed him up from the ground.

'What do you say then, Mure? Let's go find a drink.'

We did find a drink, although there was nowhere to buy one at that hour. Paterson was good at finding drinks and was a fair singer, but he was a much better writer than he was anything else. When he wasn't writing, he'd wrap a piece of purple cloth – *silk*, he said – around his head like a turban and sit in wine bars or pubs looking into his glass as if it were a crystal ball. Paterson was the first man to take me seriously. We'd talk about jazz, Nietzsche, Arcadia and how we'd start the world from scratch if we were God. I was attracted to him and he knew it.

'What bloody rot.'

We stood in the street in Woolloomooloo overlooking the docks and tried to talk above the clanging trams and the clop and puff of horses and a group of boys who yelled and laughed as they ran behind a motorcar.

'I'd ruin you.'

I wanted to be ruined at the time but couldn't convince Paterson of my sincerity.

'If I were you, I'd get out of a place like this and away from old codgers like me.'

He died soon after, not of the consumption he'd long claimed would take him, but blind drunk falling through the window of a third-floor front room in Victoria Street, Kings Cross, his pockets full of bottles. That could have been as late as 1924.

•

Back to 1921. I would paint the me of that time in sombre greys. Adam was gone, Dennison was sober and I was being fended off by

Paterson. Trivialities, gristle between the teeth, but that's because
I haven't explained the worst of it.

The grey tones I'd choose would be sombre rather than luminous
because I'd lost the thread – of the paintings that is; the paintings.
My work. Then: in came Alice, looking around the studio as if
she might take to it with a broom. 'Marie said you'd been. What's
wrong? You look as if you've been smacked by a horse's tail.'

I showed her the day's efforts on the Dennison portrait. The
painting brought on a smile, which didn't help. 'It's a shocker all
right. Is she alive or is it meant to be a memorial?' She lifted the
canvas and took a closer look before putting it back on the easel.
'Where's *your* stuff?'

But I was glum and didn't want to show her *my* stuff. 'Dennison's
commission is like gas gangrene. It infects everything I touch.'

She sighed long, loud and hard. I felt guilty but wasn't sure
why – yet. 'You agreed to it, didn't you? You're up to your belly
in paint, have the use of a studio and the time to do your own
work. Go home and get a better job, if you think you can. Plenty
of drunks with dirty mouths in the Hills who'll give you nothing
in return for listening to their shite.'

Alice found her way to the gas ring and managed to light it
without looking at me. She seemed done in, but it was too late to
point that out. 'Fruitcake.' She prodded the lump in the tin.

I went over and cut off a chunk. 'You're right.' I handed her
the cake.

'Of course I'm right.' She sunk her teeth into the wedge. 'You're
nobody's pet, Muriel, you never were. Besides, I've come to talk to
you about earning a bit of pin money.'

'After you've had your tea.' Generous for me. 'Sit down, I'll make it.'

•

Whore painter. That's what I was called for a long time. I was called a whore too, often. It never seemed an insult to me. Those women earned their money. But forget about that. It's the work I want to talk about.

Alice took me to Maggie's house on Campbell Street after the fruitcake and the tea. Two storeys high with lace-iron edges, busy lizzies growing down the side and geraniums across the front. There was a painted blue door with a brass knob that opened onto an entrance hall, a sitting room to the right with a piano, a scullery out the back and at least half-a-dozen bedrooms upstairs. The house was an oasis. Maggie's money house. The moneyed rolled up in motorcars and tailored suits to see the girls, coiffed and manicured, dressed in the latest evening wear by the live-in seamstress. Business was good.

'Maggie's bought a Model T. She can't drive it yet but I've had a few goes. I can teach you if you like.'

Alice led me up the stairs, finger on her lips because the girls were resting. We followed a hall runner to its end. 'Take a look at this.' She pushed open a door. The room was a horror, decorated with small glass prisms that hung from the window, the lampshade and the ends of a brass bed that was plump with white linen. Alice raised the blinds and the facets caught the light, filling the room with twirling colours.

'I sleep here sometimes when the room isn't needed.'

We headed downstairs in search of Maggie, who had what was called a study, a room not far from the kitchen with a desk and chair, a divan, mirror, hatstand in the corner and a deep blue and white patterned rug.

Maggie came into the room behind us, buxom and beautiful in a navy-blue dress with simple straight lines and a stole draped over her shoulders. I knew in one glance exactly how I'd paint her.

'Not me,' Maggie said. 'But one of each. An Adonis and a Venus. There's plenty of men who enjoy their lavender.'

We talked through the costs. She wasn't stingy.

'Do you mind?' she asked, looping a strand of my hair through her fingers. 'If you're ever short of a bob, you might come and see me.'

•

The next day, Dennison stood too close behind me as I worked. Annoyed, I lifted the brush from the canvas.

'Is there a problem, Miss Kemp?'

'No, I'm just thinking.'

He moved into my vision. 'Perhaps you need a rest.'

'I'm fine. It's nearly finished.'

He stood for a full minute, hands behind his back. 'I've been approached about another commission. Something a little more challenging.'

I didn't hesitate. 'You'll have to find someone else.'

'The same conditions would apply. You'd have the use of the studio. It would be the last for me – commission, that is.'

I shook my head.

'You would have to accompany me to the sittings, of course, take responsibility for some of the preliminary sketches yourself. It's a group, did I mention that?'

I collected my brushes to clean them, wiping the excess paint on a rag.

'I doubt you'd need the same level of supervision, now that you know how I work.'

Only his mouth moved. His hands remained behind his back. He stood rigid, thighs and lower back aligned like a rod, shoulders pulled taut, head an unmoving husk. Did he mean what I thought?

'How much say would I have in the composition?'

'It would be my signature on the painting, Miss Kemp.' The skin around his nose and on his forehead glistened.

I said nothing.

'I would be interested in your ideas,' he said after a long silence.

•

Still sober, and mean with it, Dennison managed the sitters. They were officials, that's all I'll say. Too many of them and objectionable, the lot of them. Dennison cajoled them into their required positions with handsome words and flattery. They believed they were to be part of a masterpiece.

If you asked any of those officials about Dennison's assistant, they would tell you he had none. I sketched furtively, took notes, and painted in a style that Dennison could call his own. Dennison and I got on for a while. If you can call being in a routine getting on.

'We're rubbing along, Miss Kemp.' He remained formal, a stiff bugger, but we didn't fight. I almost liked him. I did like him on one particular day, when I was full of a fever and the aches and shakes that came with it. He brought me soup and made fresh pots of tea, using the leaves only once, running out to buy fresh milk, then condensed milk because I preferred it.

Dennison knew he was cooked if I didn't help him with the painting. He could paint a broad stroke if he needed to but the tremor in his hands made finer work impossible. We carried on, as Dennison put it, for a good couple of years, working on his commission during the day while I did my own work during the evenings. Sometimes I slept at Nan's. Other times I got a couple of hours on the studio floor, where I'd catch sight of the pig-rooting horse I'd drawn on the underside of Dennison's work table. I needed all the luck I could get and touched it each day before I began my work.

I stayed in the studio for six months or so after the final commission. Dennison put it about that he'd retired but would still work on his reviews. In those last months he'd arrive after I'd begun my day's work, fill his pen with ink and put nib to paper. Then he'd put it down again to have a cigarette. Occasionally he'd scratch out a few words, but I don't think he ever finished anything.

Paterson had died by then and I went through a dreary stage, streaky muddy paintings that I scraped off and repainted then started anew, not settling on anything definite until Dennison threw an ink-filled pen at one of my canvasses and said, 'We're the same you and I.'

That moved me on. The work began to flow – my work that is, I never painted for Dennison again.

8.

Chasing mirages

Late March 1992

It had been at least a year – I counted the months in my head – since I'd seen the odd prickly eyes of the mercenary and heard him whisper, *Dog eat dog*.

Less than a month after I'd read my story to Muriel, I saw him again. It was a hot Sunday and I was out on the square piece of grass I shared with the other renters. I'd positioned a chair by the fence under the mottled shade of the neighbour's pepper tree, the best spot in the backyard. When I looked up, there he was.

I raised my hand against the glare but it was him all right, walking down the driveway, a plastic bag swinging from his hand.

'Hello,' I said as he came to a halt right in front of me, blocking the sun. Foregoing any preliminaries, he replied, 'I can find him if you like.'

I looked down at my T-shirt, which had rucked up baring a slice of my belly, but I wasn't showing, not yet. Someone must have told him. 'It's all right. I know where he is.'

The mercenary righted the square slatted table from its upended position near the fence and found himself a chair. He placed the plastic bag on the table in front of me. It contained my books, I presumed. The ones I'd given my ex-boyfriend.

My ex-boyfriend was not the type of person who read fiction. 'I bet you'll read this,' I'd said to him about the first book I lent him: *The World According to Garp*. He'd taken it to please me and returned it months later, black with grease and curled at the corners. That was when he worked at the steelworks as a fitter. He laughed so much in the crib room, he said, that there'd been a queue to borrow the book.

The mercenary's stare was a burn. 'Have you heard from him? Since . . .' He nodded at my midriff.

The ex had disappeared; well, not disappeared, really, but walked away from me and the town a few months ago. The mercenary must have thought the pregnancy was a result of a last unfortunate fling. 'This isn't his.' I nodded to my belly. Flat, I told myself, still flat as a tack.

The mercenary pushed the plastic bag towards me. Up close it was warm and not book-like. The tabby arrived tinkling the bell I'd placed around her neck, drawn to the mercenary's legs. He picked her up and let her knead the folds in his T-shirt.

Inside the bag I found pieces of crumbed fish wrapped in the local newspaper. He obviously hadn't heard about the vomiting. I ripped off two pieces of paper, placed a piece of fish on each of them and pushed one towards him. Licking the salty oil from my thumb I realised I felt all right and told myself the morning sickness must be near its end.

The mercenary tore through the crumbed coating. Taking a piece of white flesh, he waved it in the air to cool, then fed it to the cat.

'You don't remember me, do you?' The cat ate the fish from his palm in small gulping bites. At first I thought he meant from a year ago and was about to say of course I did. But something about the way he said it made me stop and take another look.

'1972,' he said.

I didn't get it.

'I had tea at your place once.'

There was only one boy who'd eaten at our place around that time. But no. It couldn't be. It wasn't possible. His gaze shifted from the cat to me, softening, and that's when I saw it.

'Matt?'

His stiff lips tried for a smile. Matt, Matty, Matthew Vittore. It couldn't be, but it was.

'My name – it was written in those books you borrowed from my ex. You must have known who I was when you saw me at the pub. Why didn't you say something?'

He stared into the pepper tree. A wattlebird squawked. I looked instinctively at the cat but it didn't move, waiting like me for Matt to answer.

'You were reading that book by Nina Bawden.' His eyes flicked towards me then back to the pepper tree. 'In the library.'

'*Squib.*'

'Yes, that's it.'

Matthew Vittore arrived at our school in 1972 wearing a blue jumper instead of the school's regulation bottle green, permitted because he wasn't staying long. I didn't want anything to do with Matthew Vittore; I didn't want anything to do with anyone. It was not long after the accident. Mandy, desperate to return to school, insisted on wearing the princess costume and pimped our mother and brother's death to her friends in the playground. I, on the other hand, spent the recess and lunch breaks reading in the library. Alone usually, until the day Matt came speeding in, running his hand along the books in the shelves and coming to a stop in front of me, his shadow teetering over my open book.

'Any good?'

I nodded without lifting my gaze from the page.

'I'm giving some of my books away.' He bent to scratch his ankle then stood again. 'If you come to my place you can pick out a few.'

I looked up at him. His eyes were a strange hue. I couldn't think of a colour that described their mix of purple and grey.

'I'll meet you at the gate this arvo if you like. I've got me bike. I can double you.'

He careered past the shelves and back along the corridor. I crossed to the window and watched him hurtle down the stairs, howling like a dog as he joined one pack then another, throwing, running, catching, and then he was a different boy, head tilted to the side as he talked to the teacher on playground duty.

I had no intention of going back to Matt's, but he was waiting at the gate and wheeled his blue Malvern Star to a halt in front of me. 'Get on,' he said, holding the bike steady. At ten, I was too embarrassed to say no. He doubled me up the hill, past the saleyards and told me everything I needed to know without me asking.

'We've come from Victoria. Dad's got a job at the steelworks. We're going to buy a house by the beach. We've had to bring all our stuff here and then we'll have to move it again.'

His house was full of boxes.

'Mum?' he called as he led me through the door, skidding his bag across the floor. 'Mum!' There was the smell of food and the sound of a radio, and a woman with the same strange eyes as Matt walked out of a room with a washing basket. She asked how things had gone at school.

'This is Jane, Mum. I told her she could have some of my books.'

'Hello, Jane. Matty, there's cordial in the fridge. Make yourselves a sandwich if you want.'

I don't remember eating a sandwich or drinking the cordial, but I remember the books, piles and piles of them. I was slow, tentative, shy. Matt got a box and filled it, making recommendations.

'Have you read this?' *The Hobbit* in a pristine hardcover.

'Are you sure?'

'I've got two of them.'

When the box was full, he strapped it to the seat of his bike and wheeled it to my place. He lowered the stand and lifted the box from the seat onto the lawn. 'I can help carry it in if you want.'

I shook my head. I didn't want him to come inside.

'Watch this.' He somersaulted back towards his bike, waggled his backside at me then jumped on the pedals and zigzagged away.

I cast a furtive look at him now over the fish and chips. Matt's eyes had darkened and his face had grown coarse with age, but still, I wondered how I hadn't recognised him before.

The cat leaped from his lap and stretched.

'Do you remember the garden down by the cemetery?' I asked.

Matt's face tightened. A twitch started below his left eye. I wanted to know what had happened to him after primary school but couldn't bring myself to ask. We sat a while longer, the tops of my feet reddening in the sun. Matt stood up to leave.

'It's good to see you looking so well, Jane,' he said formally.

As he walked down the driveway he passed my friend Annie, who'd come to visit. Annie bent to rub my belly and kiss my forehead. Her hair smelled of a recent perm. My stomach railed against its chemical scent.

'He reminds me of someone,' she said, looking over her shoulder as Matt retreated along the driveway.

'Bruce Reid?'

'Huh?'

'The cricketer. Six foot eight, skinny as. Fast bowler.'

'No, not him. The guy who does that mattress ad – you know, the one with the ukulele.'

I shrugged.

Annie took another look at Matt. 'He looks dangerous.'

My gaze joined Annie's. I found it difficult to reconcile this tall, lanky man with the Matt I'd known as a ten-year-old. Not that I'd known him long; four or five months at most. But for a short while he inserted himself *holus bolus* into my life.

•

'It's Matt,' Lyn called from the front door.

Dad had returned to his labouring job at the steelworks right after Mum and David's funeral, working three shifts, on a rotating roster. Mandy and I'd thought we'd look after ourselves while Dad was at work, but then Lyn turned up.

Lyn was married to Chevo Petrie, who had one of those coveted council jobs that involved leaning against a shovel by the side of the road. Although she was only in her mid-twenties, Lyn had been married to Chevo for years. According to Mrs Turner from over the road, it had been a shotgun wedding, but Lyn had lost the baby, and every baby she'd fallen with since. It was Chevo's idea that Lyn help Dad with us kids. He thought it would get her over the latest miscarriage and give her a bit of pocket money to boot. Chevo had failed to mention this new vocation to Lyn until the last minute and so she arrived that first day unkempt and bleary eyed, and denouncing Chevo for the *heartless bastard* he was. Mandy and I had been prepared to resent Lyn, but instead we found ourselves lighting the gas stove for the kettle and making her tea as she wept.

Years later she would finally have a baby that stuck, Sean. He turned out to be Dad's, not Chevo's. Lyn and Dad did a flit to Queensland and took Mandy with them. I was eighteen by that time, so I applied to do my nurse's training and moved into quarters at Wollongong Hospital.

On the phone to her not long after they'd done the bunk, I queried Lyn's choice.

'You think Dad's better than Chevo?'

'Not much, he's a surly bastard, but there were terms. I'm going to study accounting and when I get a job he has to stay at home and look after the bub.'

'And he agreed?'

'My oath he did. Your poor mum. I got the best of him.'

Lyn had only been with us a month or so the morning she answered the door and called out to me that Matt was there, as if it were perfectly natural that he should be on our front step. At first I was dismayed, thinking he wanted his books back but then he looked around Lyn and said, 'I thought I could double you.'

'What?'

'To school.' He looked at my bare feet. 'Aren't you ready yet?'

'Come in, Matt,' Lyn said before I could answer. 'She won't be a minute. Get your shoes on, Jane. I'll pack your bag.'

And that was that: our friendship decided between Matt and Lyn.

I sat on the seat of Matt's bike, while he stood and pumped the pedals, oblivious of my reluctance to engage, and full of questions about the town. Too many.

I cut him off, giving him the highlights as I saw them. 'Old Mr Preston lives there. He'll tell you his finger dropped off and the dog ate it, but he worked in a sawmill when he was a kid. That's how he really lost it.'

'They're Helga's goats. The lot of them. She seems all right to me but everyone says she's a nutter. They take her away every few months and she comes back washed and in clean clothes.'

'The tennis club uses that building every Tuesday and Friday night. Lyn says they throw their keys in a bowl and pick out another set that's not theirs, like a lucky dip. But you never see them driving each other's cars around.'

'I had piano lessons in that house. Mrs Winton holds a ruler over your knuckles and hits them if you make a mistake.'

Not long after, Matt discovered the cemetery down by the old road. The one that curved past the Electricity Commission. It all disappeared once the library and the swimming pool were built, but back then it was a derelict bit of bushland full of grey paperbarks, dumped rubbish and large concrete drain pipes that were littered with porno magazines and empty bottles. The cemetery itself was made up of a dozen graves, which were so old the writing on their headstones couldn't be read and most of the graves were split or eroded.

'We should tidy it up.' Matt stood beside a small rectangle of cement, no bigger than a fruit box.

'What for?'

'Would you be happy if this is what your grave looked like?'

'I'd be dead. How would I know?' I thought of Mum and David and wondered if it was wrong to say that.

A goat on a runner from Helga's scavenged through a small mound of refuse among the trees. Matt pulled up a clump of weeds and held it out to entice the goat towards the long grass but the goat, more interested in the taste of an old magazine, ignored him.

'Forget it,' I advised. 'It's not interested.'

'How old do you think this one is?' He kicked the edge of a small grave.

'At least a hundred years.'

'I mean the kid when it died, not the grave.' Matt stood beside it, hands behind his back. I found myself unwilling, but unable to look away from the decaying cement then reluctantly saying,

'Okay, I'll help.'

Matt had already started, in his head at least, and began to list what we'd need: 'Shovels, trowels, mower, watering can, seedlings.' He looked at his assistant and smiled.

Dad was on afternoon shift and Matt stayed for tea: fish fingers, mashed potatoes, peas and hot chocolate.

'I'd forgotten about that old cemetery,' Lyn said, and promptly offered the services of Chevo and the council crew to mow and do the edges.

'Do you think he would?'

'He will if he knows what's good for him.'

Mandy, who had no interest in the cemetery, walked her Barbie doll through Matt's potatoes. Matt took Barbie's hand and led her to the peas, one of which she kicked like a soccer ball.

'Goal,' he screamed, and raised Barbie's hands above her head.

'Thank you for dinner, Lyn,' Matt said as he left.

'He's such a nice boy,' Lyn said.

That weekend, after the cemetery had been cleared of debris and mowed and edged, some smart arse – Chevo, most likely – erected a sign, painted on an old bit of fibro:

The Living Dead Project

Entry Prohibited

Without Authorisation

From the coordinators of the Living Dead

In the meantime, boxes labelled 'Matt and Jane' were dropped off at school, seedlings from decrepit Mr Preston, an assortment of garden equipment from the members of the tennis club, a pair of gardening gloves from my old piano teacher and a bag of goat poo from Helga. Mrs Lomas announced the commencement of the project at the school assembly and rambled on about the history of the town.

'You've told everybody,' I accused Matt. 'I thought it was *our* project.'

Matt shrugged; he didn't see what I was so worked up about. 'Well, it is our project.'

'There'll be people everywhere. They'll trample over everything.'

'We could start really early and finish before they get there.'

He had no idea how it was with people in our town. 'You're a dope,' I told him.

I said to Lyn that Matt was a show-off and the whole thing had been a stupid idea right from the start.

'You're not going down there tomorrow then?'

'No way.'

'Oh, that's a bit of a problem.' Lyn picked up a plate from the sink and dried it.

'What do you mean?'

'I'm not supposed to say.' She pursed her lips. 'But you know Maureen?'

'Down at the bookshop?'

'Well, I might have mentioned the project to her. And you know Maureen, loves a bit of community spirit, chuffed at the thought of a couple of locals–'

'Matt's not a local.'

'–a couple of kids doing something for the town. She's made up encouragement awards which entitle you and Matt to pick a book each from the shop. A bit embarrassing. It's my fault; I shouldn't have bragged.' She put the plate in the cupboard and picked up another.

'I didn't know.'

'No. And she got that book in that you were talking about especially.'

'*The Green Ghost?*'

'That's the one.'

I was ready when Matt arrived early the next morning on his Malvern Star.

When we got to the cemetery, Matt reefed the tarp from the crate of donated equipment delivered the night before and pulled some folded pages from his jeans pocket.

'Mrs Lomas gave me some copies of old photos of the cemetery. See that bit of headstone over there? It belongs to this grave here. It's like a jigsaw.'

Matt was particularly interested in the child's grave. 'Same name as me, Matthew.' He looked at the pages Mrs Lomas had given him. 'Three months old. No wonder the grave's so small.'

Chevo and his mates had piled bits of stone and cement into a mound on the mowed lawn. We searched through it for pieces that might belong to the child's grave. Matt picked up a fist-sized lump and placed it in a hole in the middle of the grave.

'It fits,' I said.

He shook his head. 'It's not right.'

'Just jiggle it a bit.' I leaned towards it, but Matt slapped my hand out of the way.

'Ow. What was that for?'

He was looking past me: eyes wide, mouth open, breath a fast pant.

I turned my head, braced to see the green ghost itself or a snake or at least one of Helga's goats ready to charge. But there was nothing.

'Matt?'

His hands clenched the edge of the grave as if they were glued. He closed his mouth and swallowed then groaned, his mouth rigid, unable to form a word. I grabbed him from behind and tried to pull him back from the grave. When that didn't work, I yanked at his fingers and palms, scraping them along the cement until they let go of the crumbling lip. I pulled him from behind again, my arms around his chest until he was clear of the site.

He curled onto his side.

'I'll get help.'

He shook his head.

I held his hand and wiped his brow with the edge of my T-shirt because I didn't know what else to do. Minutes later he sat up.

'What happened?'

He shook his head again.

'Are you all right?'

'I've wet my pants.' He began to cry. 'Please, don't tell anyone.'

And I put my arms around him and stroked his hair, because what else could I do?

•

'He looks dangerous,' Annie said as we watched Matty step from the driveway onto the road. 'Tantalising but dangerous.'

'He does, doesn't he?' I replied.

After Annie left I went to see Muriel. I'd dropped a tape recorder and some blank tapes at her place a couple of weeks before and had promised to give her some space.

She opened the door as I walked up the steps. 'I've run out of tapes.'

'What?'

'I've run out of tapes and I don't have your phone number. I need you to get me some more and another one of these machines that does the recording.'

Muriel's kitchen table was covered in piles of papers. She moved a stack out of the way so I could sit down, then handed me a bunch to look at.

'Why do you need another tape recorder?' I unfolded a letter from the top of the stack. The year in the right-hand corner read 1935.

'How are you going to listen to the tapes while I'm using this one to record them?'

'They're not cheap. What's this?' I flattened the letter onto the table.

My dear Muriel, the letter began.

'It's from Claudine. But don't read it now. It won't make any sense until you've listened to the tapes. I'll keep this old machine. I'm used to it. You keep the one you buy. I ignored her and went through the rest of the pile. It was made up of letters, a deed for the house, a passport in Muriel Kemp's name and another under the name of Muriel Rose – both passports bore the same photo of her, both were unused.

'Put those down and listen to me.' Muriel whipped the documents away. 'I wanted you to know that I have them, but I don't want you to read them yet.' The papers scattered, a letter slid from the pile, catching my eye.

I read:

Write to me as soon as you can.
Claudine

'Here.' Muriel wafted an envelope under my nose. 'What's wrong with you, Jane? Take the money.'

'What's it for?'

'For the new machine and more tapes – but I want bigger tapes this time. The last ones didn't record enough.'

The envelope wasn't sealed. I flicked a finger through the notes. 'This is too much.'

'What do you want, a bodyguard?'

'It won't cost this much.'

She lowered her voice so I had to lean forwards to hear her. 'I'm not short of funds, Jane.'

'I'll bring you the receipt.'

'Just bring me the tapes. Stick them in the letterbox on your way back. Don't forget the new machine for yourself.'

'I don't know if I can go tonight.'

'Yes, you can. It's late-night shopping.' She rummaged in a kitchen drawer for a plastic bag, which she started filling with tapes. 'Take these to start with. Don't lose them.'

I was on the front step. Muriel had shut the door behind me with a bang then almost immediately opened it again. For some reason, I thought she was going to ask about her cat.

'I need your phone number.'

I walked inside and wrote it on the pad beside the phone. The door shut behind me with as much force as the first time.

•

I didn't like being ordered around by Muriel, but I *was* keen to listen to the tapes so headed over to Shellharbour Square to do the shopping. On the return, I popped half-a-dozen ninety-minute tapes in her letterbox then headed home. I opened the door to a ringing phone. The tabby came in, probably hungry.

'Did you get another recorder?'

'I've just walked in the door.'

'The recorder?'

'Yes. I got it.' I'd upgraded to a portable Walkman, an improvement on the old tape deck that Muriel was using but I'd still had to convince the salesman I wanted one that played tapes rather than CDs.

Muriel hung up.

I put the tapes she'd given me on the table, scraped a tin of sardines onto a plate that now belonged to the cat and checked her water. It wasn't until I put the kettle on that I realised I hadn't vomited all day. In celebration, I opened a packet of chocolate biscuits to dunk in the tea and found that I'd lost my taste for them.

I set up the tape recorder and inserted the tape marked #1 and fiddled with the volume button on the side. The first voice I heard was mine.

'You press the play and record buttons together. The red light means it's recording. Say something and we'll play it back.'

'What if I make a mistake and want to rub it out?'

'You can do that, although it might be easier just to say you made a mistake and correct the details verbally.'

'I'd rather rub it out.'

'Yes, but once you erase something you can't get it back.'

'Stop fussing. I know what I'm doing.'

9.

Luminous bathers

1925–1928

I'm going to tell you the true story of what happened in 1928. This was on a day when the sky was blue and the sun was warm and Alice and I took Maggie's latest Model T for a spin. A holiday we called it and sang like lorikeets.

Daisy, daisy,
Give me your answer do!

We headed to Brighton-le-Sands and the recently built shark-proof baths. Over two acres of water enclosed by a semicircular mesh fence, we'd read, topped by a timber-planked promenade and a wharf where the steamers docked.

We pulled into the picnic grounds and parked the Model T in a patch of shade. Alice went in search of some lunch while I strode towards the new baths. The place was crammed with bodies; in deckchairs on the sand, leaning over the promenade, diving from the tower, strolling, running, backflipping into the water. Everything was luminous, the green and blue of the water, the soapy edges, the crystalline sand, the hazy heat.

I tried to work out how I'd paint the moving bodies and the wet dog shaking itself dry. Advice, not the kind I wanted, came to me in Adam Black's voice. *No matter how vibrant your composition, it'll fade once you move it inside.*

I bent over the edge of the pool to watch the light on the water. A young man brushed past me at a run, knees lifted against his chest as he bombed, backside first, in between the swimmers. Salt water splashed. I kept my eyes open through the spray and watched as his body changed shape, short and squat as he sank through the depths then long and lean as he rose and stroked forward under the surface. His head broke through the glare, dark and disjointed from the rest of his body as he swam to the edge of the baths and looked up, eyes incandescent, skin a rubbed-raw red. He looked heroic as the sharp light speckled on the water behind him. I kneeled to take a closer look.

'I could go a trip to the cinemas with a girl like you.'

His teeth were not as white as you'd expect from the rude healthy look of him and some of them were missing.

'My treat.'

His mouth was a fascination though. Pink gums, tongue and uvula tunnelling back from crimson lips. I reached out and touched the shadow above his collarbone then stood and wiped my hands on my skirt.

'Moll,' the boy called as I walked away.

Faces looked up, slapped by the word. I reached for my sketchpad and pencil, captured his look, then tucked the pad into my waistband and out of sight; Alice had insisted I leave my work tools behind.

Back at the picnic grounds, Alice and I ate pies on folded bits of newspaper. The pastry was flaky and light and the gravy rich and thick and it dripped on my skirt. I wiped it off and licked my fingers, washing the food down with a bottle of lemonade. We recollected how as kids we'd chase Tam O'Brien's cart along the streets to the call of *hot pies, hot pies, hot pies and peas,* the smell of the gravy a torture.

'We were like a pack of swarming rats. The lot of us.'

Alice, with no concern for decorum, stretched out on the grass and closed her eyes while I watched a woman and her small boy coming from the direction of the baths. The boy bent and picked up a feather from the ground then passed it to the woman to hold. She glanced at Alice, asleep in the shade, staring as if I wasn't there. I wanted to sketch the bold disapproval of that look but rather than risk being caught by Alice, I memorised it instead. Immersed in the woman's expression, I waved a fly away with the newspaper. The movement broke her gaze and she ambled off after the child.

We motored home, smelling of salt and gravy.

'Why don't we move to the seaside?'

'Why don't we?'

There were less demands on Alice by then. Marie had started her nurse's training and had moved out of Riley Street into the hospital accommodation. Grace was still at home, though she'd begun as a typist at the furniture factory and would be off and married and moving out as soon as she could; then there'd only be Edna to worry about.

'We could take Edna to the seaside with us,' I suggested.

'And Mum. Dad can stay put. We don't want him along.'

'So your Mum and Edna, me and you in a house by the sea.'

'Why not?'

It was pitch when I got back to Surry Hills. I lit the lamp and looked at my handful of shells. Then I saw the empty bottle of rum on the table. Bloody Dennison. He'd turned up drunk the night before, which he did far too often, and I'd let him sleep it off on the floor. That's where he'd been when I left for Brighton-le-Sands. The empty bottle of rum wasn't a puzzle so much as the handbag that sat beside it, and the suitcase I found stowed beneath the table.

•

I'll have to take you back, Jane – otherwise you won't understand the importance of what happened in 1928. There are some details you need to know.

I'll start with James Dennison who, as far as I knew had a working man's flat and a wife in Bondi. This was back in 1925. I'd never seen either of them, the wife or the flat, but he'd retired there to write his art reviews once his lease expired on the studio. As for me, I went home. Two months later, Nan died. No fuss, no bother. She went in her sleep.

I stayed put in Surry Hills because the rent was cheap and I only got the odd shift or two at Corbett's. Other than that, I sold the occasional painting from the *Working Women* series to brothels or friends of Maggie's. Mostly, though, I gave the paintings away.

Somewhere near the end of 1925, James Dennison turned up at my door in Surry Hills bloated and filthy, with a cut over his eye as if he'd been fighting. When I saw the state he was in, I pushed him straight through the house and into the backyard.

To get rid of the lice, I added a good dose of metho to a bucket of water and poured it over his head. He opened his mouth wide to catch as much of the diluted mixture as he could, then picked up the bucket and drained the dregs. I gave his clothes the same treatment then hung them out to dry, shrouding his skinny shanks in a grey blanket that the moths had taken to. All the while he quivered and begged me to shoot him.

'I'm not going to be hung for doing *you* a favour.'

'Shoot me. I'm as good as dead anyway. Shoot me,' he repeated, until I clipped him around the ear and told him to cut it out.

He rolled himself in the blanket and slept until the vermin woke him. 'Green worms,' he said. They glowed like lightning, he told me, and crawled from under his skin, up over the walls and along the ceiling.

'What shade of green?'

He thought about it for a minute, then screamed blue murder until Ivy Lee, the tenant from upstairs, came down to see if I was being attacked. I invited her in and asked her for suggestions. She'd raised four boys.

'There's nothing you can do. Not if you don't want to give him a drink. It has to see itself out.' She shook her head. 'Come up if he gets too much. We can lock ourselves in.'

I went down to the sly groggers, bought a bottle and poured a bit down his throat. Tossing his damp clothes at him I told him not to come back.

Calmed by the effects of the medicine, he said, almost coherently, that he thought we could do it again, him and me; take on another commission and for a good price. He'd see that I was well paid.

I got him out the door. Had there ever been a key with which to lock it?

•

The problem with the tenement was the poor light. There was only the gas lamp to paint by and that wasn't much better than a candle or the embers of the fire.

Plein air, the streets were narrow and mottled. Objects – buildings, hats, shoes, horses and drays – were the colour of steeped tea. Flesh, whether it belonged to men, women or children, looked as if it were smeared in dripping. I wanted to strike a box of matches and light the place up.

On a miserable day, when the sky was as sombre as the street, I saw a girl in an ochre-coloured dress on Riley Street, singing as she walked. Pasty, stringy-haired with a runny nose and red-rimmed eyes, she held her chilblained hands to her lips to catch the warmth of her breath. When we passed one another, she looked up and I looked down.

I painted her from memory, scraping the grime from the road and the buildings, thinning the white until she was transparent. A spectre, everything visible through her body.

I finished the painting in the dunny with the door open to catch the light but angled to escape the slant of rain. I was on my way inside with the finished canvas when James Dennison stumbled in from the hall. This was a month or two after he'd asked me to shoot him. I hadn't seen him since. He was half shot and carried a live fowl in a sugar bag as if it was Christmas. He smelled of urine, sweat and tobacco, and as he handed over the bag he cursed me, my pictures, my dead eye and my barren cunt.

I sent him packing, wrung the chook's neck and baked it using the last of the coal.

He reappeared the following day in a presentable condition, not sure what had passed between us but remembering a painting he saw or thought he saw. I showed him *The Girl on Riley Street*, knowing he wouldn't like it.

'That's sellable,' he said.

'I've heard *that* before.' I let him take the picture in the end. There was nothing I could do with it and I knew I'd paint over it once I ran out of canvas.

The Girl on Riley Street triggered a change from the *Working Women* series. I began to scrub the suburbs with light, linking merged bodies in doorways with rainbows, painting drunks curled up beside buildings that glowed, the Chinese shopkeeper in his sunlit store, children at their games or on their sickbeds glistening with fever, men returning from work or the pub, young women in front of factories haloed like saints, nuns on welfare visits, men crouched in radiant circles tossing coins. Light and lean shadows filled my spaces.

James Dennison returned with a dead man's cough and skin the colour of muddy buttercups, hawking and yelling about being robbed, carrying on as if he'd had riches to steal.

'What happened to your place in Bondi?'

'Not mine anymore.'

He came and went smelling of metho and filth and his own vomit. God knows why he kept coming back. It wasn't for sympathy, because he got none of that from me. I got stuck with him for a few days when the stormwater drains flooded the streets, driving the rats inside.

'They're looking for me,' Dennison howled as the water sloshed around our feet and the red-eyed vermin scampered from the floor to the bed and over the rickety furniture. He squealed as a large rat, bold as brass, darted forward and nipped his toe. Then it was the rat's turn to squeal as Dennison smashed its skull with his empty bottle, showing a speed and flair I thought him incapable of. Once the water subsided, I booted him out and painted my two remaining canvasses back and front using charcoal, Reckitt's blue, ground leaves, dirt mixed into a paste. And then I went and saw Maggie.

•

The geraniums in front of the Campbell Street house were a tangle in two tones of pink. The busy lizzies planted along the shaded path to the side were a contrast in vibrant clusters of red and crimson, broken by a pearly white. Alice opened the door. Her face creased when she saw me. 'About time. I thought you'd changed your mind.' She led me to the study which contained Maggie, smooth in her voluptuous navy blue.

'Dearie me.'

'She'll be all right with a bit of a scrub,' Alice assured her.

'She'll want to be.' Maggie rose from her desk, crossed the blue-and-white rug and seated herself on the divan. 'Alice has explained what's involved?'

I nodded.

'I look after my girls, Muriel, and I'll look after you too if you decide to stay. But there'll be no running out in the middle of a job, no nervous giggles or changes of mind. I don't take kindly to that, neither do my men. You need to be certain.'

She approached me like a boy crossing the floor to demand a dance.

'What do you think, Alice?' She ran her hands over my arms and breasts and down the backs of my legs then wrinkled her nose. 'Should we feed her or stick her in the bath first?'

Alice took me to the tub room and told me to strip. She diluted the wash with metho to get rid of the lice then brought me a tray of sandwiches and a pot of tea while she filled the bath a second time and scented the water.

'Are you sure this is what you want?' She took two towels from a cupboard and hung them over a rack.

I nodded, mouth full of sandwich.

'Whatever Maggie says, remember: it's you doing her the favour.'

I took a sip of the tea and when I laughed the liquid frothed from my nose. 'Where do they get these ideas?'

'Oh, you have no idea, lovey.'

•

Are you keeping up with this, Jane? These men, the ones that frequented Maggie's, had too much money and spare time. Alice and I laughed at their *special requests*. They wanted a schoolgirl to pee on their face, to be whipped, dressed as a baby, humiliated, revered or, in one man's case, seduced by the artist he posed for. No penetration required and only a little baring of flesh. I was made for the job.

Alice stood behind me, untangling my hair in her first run through with a comb. Once the knots were gone, she brushed it. Her arm moved in long smooth strokes down my back as she spoke. 'I'll help you with your hair and get you settled. You should have a sleep. There'll be nothing to do until it's well and truly dark.'

Maggie consulted me about an outfit. 'I normally wear men's trousers,' I told her. Trousers amused her because they were unseemly and got you looked at in the street. She had Vera, the seamstress, adjust a men's pair for that night and later had her fashion me a pair that buttoned down the side and fit better than anything I'd worn before. I wore a plain cream blouse with the trousers and a blue calico smock over that. I usually pinned my hair up to keep it out of the way when I painted, but Maggie insisted I wear it loose and with no adornments. 'George will want to see it out.'

I waited for George in a room with whitewashed walls, a simple brass bed covered in a white quilt, plumped-up pillows and a bedside table with a lamp. A gilt-framed mirror hung on the opposite wall above a dresser topped by another two lamps. I stood sideways between their glow, a sketchpad across one arm and a piece of charcoal resting on the paper. My eyes were on the door as George entered.

George was younger than I expected; mid-thirties and in fair condition, wearing a good-quality three-piece suit – the kind Adam would have worn, if he'd had the money. Once inside the door, he paused.

'Over there.' I directed him to the bed.

He fingered the lapel of his jacket.

'You can put it on the rack.'

George undressed then sat naked on the edge of the bed like a patient waiting to be examined. I approached, placed my sketchpad and charcoal on the bedside table then lifted the lamp.

'Beautiful.' I ran the light over his body, imagining a fat plucked fowl or a thick slice of dripping beef. 'Lie back over the pillows, hands behind your head . . . that's it. Bring your legs up a little, feet together, now drop your knees. Perfect.'

I swapped the lamp for the charcoal and pad, and made a simple sketch of his shadowy body, concentrating on the torso, legs and groin, omitting the head.

Afterwards, I rolled the soft charcoal in my hands and asked George to stand. I ran my palms along his thighs and chest and back. Opening the sketchbook, I rubbed him with the paper, drawing side down, until he looked as if he'd been playing in the coal bucket.

I told George to stand in the corner as I opened the door of a small alcove in the wall and removed the jug of warm water that had been placed there. Pouring half its contents into a basin, I washed George slowly. Moving down his body from his face to his feet, I warned him that I'd tan his hide if I found so much as a single smudge on him when he arrived the following week.

'Do you understand, George? You don't play without me.' I bent his pink, warm body over the bed, pillow under his hips and slapped his rump twice. 'Next time it'll be the switch.'

Then, leaving him to dress, I took the back stairs to the scullery, where half-a-dozen jugs were lined up on the bench, ready for Maudie to run up the stairs and place in alcoves at the allotted time.

Alice was there talking to a woman in a low-backed evening gown. The woman looked up as I entered.

'Were you in room six?'

I nodded.

Maudie said, 'Give me a few minutes, Ailsa, and I'll tidy it for you.'

The woman straightened her dress and fluffed her hair. 'Do I look all right?'

'You'll do.'

'Good-oh.' The woman left the scullery, her heels clack, clack, clacking along the hall towards Maggie and the reception area in search of her beau.

'Come and eat.' Alice put a plate on the table. 'Beef stew and dumplings. If you're here when I'm not, help yourself to whatever's on the range. How'd it go?'

I shrugged.

'Maggie'll let you know soon enough if there are any problems.' She handed me an envelope. 'Here's your pay.'

George was a regular over the next couple of years. There were others too, not quite like George. Some I got to whip, one I dressed in a bonnet, another liked to be punished for not doing as he was told. *Muriel's specials*, Maggie called them. I enjoyed dishing out the whippings – you're not to put that in the book, Jane – it made up for the pandering, which there was much too much of. I earned enough to get by. Which meant paying the rent and buying art supplies, nothing more.

And then, Freddie Kitchener's cherubic face turned up at my rattly green door, cap in fist and a note from Claudine Worthington, whom I'd never met but whose pictures I'd seen in the society pages of the magazines at Maggie's.

These photos included: Claudine posing on the deck of a ship with her parents after travelling abroad; Claudine on a tennis court, dressed in a sleeveless white dress and holding her racquet aloft; and Claudine on the arm of her fiancé, aviator Tommy Hasluck, in evening wear, her outfit described in the article as an angel wrap in a deep rose over a paler blush of georgette. And then there was the favourite up at Maggie's: a grainy grey-and-white picture clipped from *The Sun* and pinned to the back of the pantry door, decorated with hearts and lipstick kisses: Tommy Hasluck diving into a pool, fingers tapping the water's surface, torso perfectly arced.

The note handed to me by Freddie said Claudine wanted to meet me at Sargent's Tea Rooms in George Street to discuss the commission of a painting. I looked at Freddie's earnest face. Was it a joke? Freddie looked much the same as any other cove from Surry Hills in his shirt and flannels, although he and the clothes showed less wear and tear than most. I found out later that Freddie, a driver for Claudine's father, grew up in Potts Point and knew all the tricks, which included leaving the motorcar behind and taking the tram. What convinced me, though, was Freddie himself, straight-backed, clear-eyed and well fed. A man with a job. He wouldn't have wasted his time on a joke.

When I got to Sargent's the next day, I found Freddie waiting outside. 'Change of plans.' He escorted me to a waiting car, a Bentley, narrow up front where the driver sat but roomy in the back for the passengers. 'We're going to Mascot.'

'The aerodrome?'

'The Aero Club, for lunch.'

He led me to the back of the motorcar, but instead I opened the front passenger door and got in next to him. The Bentley was a different vehicle to the Model T, less noise and rattle. I opened the window so I could smell the benzene and bitumen and the dry scratchy dirt. I wanted to feel that I was on the road.

Mascot was busy. As Freddie walked me across the grass to the club we passed a couple of businessmen standing in front of an ADASTRA AIRWAYS sign waiting for a flight and a group of students milling about, watching a training plane as it descended. The plane proceeded to perform, what Freddie called, a perfect three-point landing – right up until the wheels touched the ground and the machine toppled onto its nose.

Freddie pointed out an inverted Gipsy Moth among the traffic in the sky. It growled its way in from the south and over us. As the biplane righted itself, a pair of goggles leaned out of the open cockpit and raised a glove before ascending vertically.

'That's Tommy Hasluck, Miss Worthington's fiancé.'

The Moth reached its apex and cut its engine, dropping like a leaf, not pulling out of its fall until it seemed it would crash. Then it climbed again on the diagonal, flipping sideways into a barrel roll and looping the loop, completing a final circuit before coming in to land.

Freddie led me to the door of the Aero Club and pointed out Claudine Worthington. She crossed from the other side of the room to greet me. She wore her cloche hat tilted and her skirt much shorter than mine.

'Miss Kemp.' She clasped my hands in hers, smelling like a Pear's advertisement. First impression: I'd paint her but without the smile and the hat and sit her in a cooking pot to simmer like a green prawn. But, then, I was hungry when I met her.

'We'll eat over there.' She led the way, bypassing a large table – 'That's where the pilots, the engineers and the mechanics sit' – to take a smaller one near the back wall.

'It's beef usually, and something with apple for sweets and as much tea as you can fit in. Please, take a seat.'

There was the smell of roasting meat and a pudding on the bake; lemon, I thought, not apple. Claudine was saying something about James Dennison painting a family portrait when she was a child but the smell of the food distracted me.

'Can we order?' I asked.

'I'm sure they'll have something ready.' Claudine left the table to organise the meal then returned smoothing her skirt and straightening a tie at her hip.

Within minutes, the food arrived. Roast lamb with baked potatoes, pumpkin, peas and jugs of gravy and mint sauce. I ate and ate. It was only as I was mopping up the last of the gravy with a piece of bread that I remembered to look up.

'Tea?' Claudine offered.

I wiped a dribble of gravy from my blouse with a chunk of bread as she turned to order the tea.

Claudine poured. I spooned in a great heap of sugar, stirring it well.

'Where have you seen my work?' I asked.

'Mr Dennison showed it to me. He didn't mention it?'

The old bastard had *mentioned* nothing.

'I bought *The Girl on Riley Street* from him.'

I frowned. 'I painted that some time ago.'

'I bought it some time ago, along with another one.' She described a second painting that, as far as I knew, was on the wall of a brothel in Woolloomooloo.

'My fiancé tracked that one down. I've had hell's own finding you, Miss Kemp.'

She wore lipstick and face powder and looked perfect. I questioned her interest in my seamy pictures until I thought of Maggie and her house rules; *Any fraternising, duckie, and you're out. Even if it's them that start things. And they might. Some of them like a little roll in the dirt.*

'What have you got in mind?' I asked.

'Something small to start. Let's call it a sample.' Claudine pushed three five-pound notes across the table.

I picked up the money and tucked it in the pocket of my skirt alongside a slice of bread and a potato I'd already secreted there.

The sweets were brought out as a straggle of newcomers entered the room: men in overalls, stout trousers and flying jackets, jostling for places at the large table, laughing, sledging, chiacking. Claudine nodded at the last of them. Tommy Hasluck, the swimming pool diver from *The Sun*. He looked in his early thirties and wore a Ronald Colman moustache. Handsome but stupid was my best guess. There was a woman with the group. She glanced over at Claudine then trailed a finger down Tommy's arm. He bowed his head, whispered in her ear then moved across the room towards us.

Claudine did the introductions. 'Miss Muriel Kemp, Mr Tommy Hasluck.'

'We finally meet.' Tommy took my hand. 'I've seen your paintings.'

The charm was a bit thick. I retrieved my hand and wiped it against my skirt. He saw and laughed but took the hint along with his charm back to the large table. The woman looked our way, then touched her head to his, a conspirator. Claudine's eyes scanned the room, taking in the woman and her fiancé as if she were glancing at nothing more interesting than a chair.

I ate my lemon pudding then ate Claudine's. She insisted. What else can I tell you about that meeting? I got fifteen pounds and a good feed out of it, and then walked across the aerodrome with Claudine to the waiting Bentley. Claudine pointed to the Cook's River and told me she'd nearly ditched the plane in it when she was learning to fly.

I talked to Alice about it later. 'She was all smiles and politeness. I couldn't work her out.'

Alice, flushed from the pot she was stirring, looked up and said, 'That was the money talking, not her.'

Even in the city people stopped to watch the Bentley pull over on George Street. I stepped out, the collar of my blouse frayed, my hat out of shape. At the art supplies shop I purchased a small piece of hardboard, a sketchbook and paints and considered taking the tram to Surry Hills but decided to save my pennies instead. Close to home, I bought a tin of kero, tea, a bag of tangerines, a loaf of bread and thruppence worth of corned beef.

Joe Murphy's younger brother, Danny, was on the road ahead of me, pushing the perambulator. I called out and he crammed my supplies in next to his, taking the proffered tangerine.

Danny was full of news about a big raid on the two-up school at Albion Street and the demolition of certain tenements – the council were calling it the Brisbane Street resumption. It was to be cleared of its undesirables and the land set aside for factories. The council (more likely the councillors) stood to make huge profits.

Danny wheeled the pram through the door and unloaded my parcels. I cut him a slice of bread and put a bit of corned beef on it. 'Ta.' He took it with him. 'Mum's expecting me.'

•

I worked on Claudine's sample using a piece of hardboard the size of a family Bible. The painting wasn't of Claudine, although I used her cloche hat with its dark-banded edge to frame the subject's face. I called it *The Broken Gaze*. Sunlight fell over a woman's upper body from an unseen window. The woman scowled at the viewer from eyes that wicked into the surrounding flesh of her face. A strip of skin between her shoulder and sternum was peeled away, exposing the muscle and bone beneath the left breast. I was pleased with it.

It rained heavily the day Fred was due to collect it. He didn't turn up. The next day, not long after sunrise, I heard a ruckus in the street and went out the door like everyone else to see what was going on.

'Whoa there . . . whoa.' Les Frances reined in his mare, cursing the filthy bastard – 'excuse me, ladies,' touching his cap – on the filthy bleeding contraption at the far end of the street.

The filthy contraption was an Indian motorcycle with a red petrol tank and panniers slung over its rear rack. The driver turned off the engine, pushed his goggles onto his leather helmet and parlayed with the milling group. Les got off his horse, coaxed it around and led it back out onto Campbell Street and away.

Someone called, 'Oi, Muriel, he's here to see you.'

It wasn't Freddie come for the painting. The rider was tall, too large overall, and the crowd too respectful, as if Herbie Collins – the Australian cricket captain – had dropped by for a visit. There were no derogatory remarks or sly noises, no ribald comments. The women at my end of the street sensed the anomaly and watched.

'God Almighty, isn't he the one from the papers?' Alma hitched up the shoulder of her dress and flattened her hair.

'How can you tell with all the clobber he's got on? Oi, Dosey, put that down. It's for your tea.'

'The flyer, I mean – you know the one.'

'Ask Muriel. She oughta know.' Bea took off after her mother, the dim-witted Dosey who'd tucked half a loaf under her arm and was headed off up the street.

The remaining women looked over their shoulders at me. I shrugged.

'It's you he's come to see.'

I shrugged again.

'He wants his drawing.' A kid ran ahead with the news.

'Well, well.' Maureen Percival thrust out a hip. 'I wish I could draw.'

Tommy wheeled his motorcycle up the road, escorted by men and boys.

'Move along, Addie, you'll get yourself run over.'

Delivered, he acknowledged me with a nod, took a cigarette – tailor-made – from a pack then offered them my way.

'I'll have one.' Maureen stepped forward to pluck one from the packet.

'Since when have *you* smoked, Maureen?'

'Who says I'm going to smoke it?' Maureen laughed at her prank and someone said, 'We'll look after your bike, mister.'

Tommy followed me into the tenement. Pulling a bottle of rum from his jacket he placed it on the table and said, 'For Dennison.'

'He doesn't live here. He just turns up when he's had a skinful and needs somewhere to doss for the night.'

Unconcerned, Tommy sat himself on the only chair as if he were staying for dinner. 'I don't suppose there's any chance of a cuppa?'

'Out of tea, sorry.'

He eyed the bottle of rum while I wrapped and tied the painting in string. I handed it to him then led him to the door. The crowd was standing vigil around the bike. Hands touched Tommy's leather jacket as he moved from the doorway to the road.

Tommy straddled the bike, started it, then gave me a nod. 'If you need anything, the aerodrome can always get a message to me.' He hit the throttle and lifted his foot speeding down the street and away.

•

Alice loved machines. She had her head in the engine of Maggie's Model T when I told her about Tommy's visit.

'We should go.' She looked up.

'What do you mean?'

'To the aerodrome.'

'Tommy said they could get a message to him. It wasn't an invitation to visit.'

'But that's what he meant – come and visit.'

'You won't like him, Alice.'

Alice wiped her hands with a rag then closed the hood of the Model T. 'It's the planes I'm interested in.'

It wasn't Alice's fascination that got me there three days after Tommy's visit, but curiosity about what the view from a plane would look like and how I would paint it. Tommy was nowhere in sight when we crossed the grass towards the hangar. What we found instead were two men working on an engine.

'We're friends of Tommy Hasluck's.' Alice was brazen. 'He invited us to take a look around.'

The men assessed Tommy's friends and one remarked, 'There's not much to see. We're only on routine maintenance.'

'Well, I'd like to see that.' Alice removed her coat.

The talk was of checking tappets and greasing rockers when I left the hangar, attracted to the chaotic sky that was filled with planes taking off and landing, some barely avoiding collision. A figure made its way towards me in a leather helmet and goggles. Tommy. I could tell by the shape of him and the way he moved. He pushed up his goggles, his eyes stark in the clean circle of flesh that surrounded them.

'You here to see me?'

'No. My friend, Alice, wanted a closer look at the planes.' I nodded in the direction of the hangar.

Tommy laughed. 'I'd offer to take her up but I've torn a wing.'

In his flying gear, with his thoughts on his plane, Tommy was grave rather than smarmy and I felt civil towards him. 'Come and take a look at her,' he said.

We walked back the way he'd come, around the side of the hangar towards the biplane. 'Claudine was pleased with your painting.' He eyed the wing, calculating the repair.

'Was she?' I hadn't thought too much about whether she'd like it or not.

Tommy moved his scrutiny from the wing to me. 'You should take her interest seriously.' He kept his eyes on my face. 'Her backing wouldn't do you any harm.'

'Is that what she is to you? Backing?'

'My oath.' He tapped the fuselage of the plane, unruffled.

On the return journey to Surry Hills, Alice went on, not so much about Gerrard and John, the mechanic and the engineer, but the plane itself and in particular its engine. She had grease across her chin and talked of flying as if she were already an expert.

'Tommy said he would have taken you up,' I told her. 'But he'd torn a wing.'

•

Three weeks later Tommy turned up at the tenement on foot. The bottle of rum he'd brought for Dennison was still on the table. He raised an eyebrow.

'He'll turn up sooner or later,' I said, lighting the gas under the kettle for tea. There was no sign of the easy behaviour he'd shown when we'd first met. He stood, hands behind his back as if at attention, his eyes on the blue jet of the gas flame. I made the pot and poured the tea and still, he'd said nothing.

'Are you here for a reason?' I prompted.

He brought his hands from behind his back to take the cup and I saw the tremor. 'Claudine is interested in commissioning another work.' He pulled his eyes from their distant stare and settled them on the tea. We were standing either side of the one chair I owned. The other, Nan's rocking chair, had disappeared after she'd died.

'What did she have in mind?'

The answer was slow to come. 'It's up to you.'

I could have blamed Tommy's absent manner on a heavy night or the grog, but I could see it wasn't that. Tommy had the same look about him I'd noticed on other returned soldiers. Shell-shock they called it back then. There were men who were crippled by it. For others, it seemed to come and go.

'What I'd like, is to paint the view from up there some time.' I pointed to the sky.

'You'd trust me to fly you?' Tommy lifted his eyes from the cup.

'Why? Shouldn't I?'

'You'd be all right.' He said and gave a half smile. And I imagined that I would be – all right, that is.

Tommy drank his tea without saying anything else then placed five pounds next to the rum for supplies. Not long after I went out for a canvas and some paint and on my return spent the afternoon working.

Dennison turned up late that night, sodden, and when he saw the drying canvas started ranting about painting another commission. I took it up to Ivy Lee's for safe keeping and let Dennison sleep on the floor.

•

I've already told you about the excursion to Brighton-le-Sands with Alice, that was the next morning, with Maggie's latest Model T and the meat pie and the luminous bathers. I'd left Dennison sleeping it off, not thinking about the rum. It was when I got home from the beach and lit the lamp, that I saw the empty bottle and the handbag and suitcase.

The suitcase, I noticed, was embossed with the initials C.M. but I recognised the handbag, anyway, as belonging to Constance Mawson. She'd worked as an artist's model for Max Jenner and had also been a favourite of James Dennison's. She came by occasionally looking for Dennison, though God knows why; she didn't seem to think too much of him.

'How do you put up with him?' she'd ask me. 'He's putrid. Scratching himself raw and gushing from both ends. Who cleans that up? Not him I bet.'

Dennison had once suggested Constance and I model together. 'You could be sisters,' he'd said. We shared the same colouring, the same wavy red hair. I was taller and younger and she had more curves, but there was a definite resemblance. I had no interest in modelling for Dennison or anyone else.

Staring at the handbag and suitcase, I could only think that Constance must have come here looking for Dennison and then gone out with him somewhere. When they hadn't returned by 11 p.m., I searched the handbag and found a letter from a guesthouse confirming a reservation, a ticket for a train leaving from Central in the morning, and a drawstring calico purse containing money.

There were two murders that night, but I'm only guilty of one of them. It was Dennison that killed Constance Mawson. He turned up a few hours later, drunk from the rum and whatever else he'd had, blood and grass staining his shirt. I could see straight away what he'd done.

'Why?' I asked.

'She was leaving. Did you know? She was leaving me.'

He'd dumped her body in the marshes and said the feral dogs had already made a start on her by the time he'd left. Slumping onto the chair, he took a swig from the empty bottle.

'How do you think I'll look on the end of a rope?'

'What marshes?' I didn't believe him about the dogs and thought she might be lying hurt somewhere.

'You can't undo what's done.'

I slapped the table to get his attention then pulled the bottle away from him. He leaned towards me, his breath saturated in methylated spirits, and said he could see exactly where the devil was in me then offered to cut it out. He was quite gentle about it, only using force once I resisted.

•

In the early hours of that morning, I left Samuel Street with Constance Mawson's suitcase and handbag. It was a stroke of luck that I found Alice still at Maggie's.

'No such thing. Maggie's teaching me the business. These are the hours I work.'

We stowed the suitcase and handbag in the Model T. Alice drove. There was only one place I could think of to go.

It was dawn when we got there. The planes were already on the move, growling along the runway into the wind and stuttering across the sky.

'I'll see if I can find him.' Alice walked in the direction of the hangars.

It was luck that Tommy Hasluck happened to be there that morning.

'No such thing,' Alice said. 'It's the best time of day if you're a flyer.'

Tommy looked at the suitcase and gave me a canvas bag in lieu of it. 'Fit what you can in here.'

I grabbed a handful of Constance's belongings and shoved them into the corners. Then I hesitated.

Alice shook her head. 'You don't have a choice.'

Tommy handed me a pair of goggles, leather helmet and jacket, and I walked incognito towards the biplane. 'Be careful,' he said. 'If you put your foot through the wing we'll be going nowhere.'

I climbed into the plane and positioned myself in the front cockpit while Alice helped Tommy untie the machine. Then he was in the cockpit behind me, yelling, 'Contact.'

'Contact,' Alice responded, before swinging the propeller and removing the chocks from the wheels. How did she know what do?

We trundled across the bumpy paddock. Alice watched, one hand slightly raised ready to wave. At the end of the track we turned, bumbling over the ground we'd already covered, picking up speed. The wheels whirred over the tussocks. The nose tilted upwards. Alice's hand lifted then everything stilled. Banking to the right, we passed the Cook's River. The air plucked at the struts and fanned the fumes from the fuel over me. I felt nauseous until we were above the Pacific. Then the sky merged with the ocean, enveloping us in blues, greens and greys. I twisted in my seat. Tommy raised his thumb and I returned the signal, feeling all right.

•

SURRY HILLS MURDER

Prominent artist killed. Wife suspected.

Prominent artist James Dennison was stabbed yesterday in his Surry Hills home.

Neighbours told detectives they heard yelling and banging coming from the house early that morning. Shortly afterwards, Mrs Maureen Percival, who resides in the flat opposite, called in to see the deceased man's wife and found Mr Dennison lying beneath the kitchen table in a pool of blood with a knife protruding from his chest.

Neighbours have supplied detectives with a description of Mrs Dennison, whose whereabouts are unknown. They also stated that Mr Dennison had a temper and often set against his wife.

While Mrs Dennison is a suspect in her husband's murder, detectives have not ruled out the possibility that she may have been taken from her home by force.

10.

Ready or not

April 1992

Five months pregnant, and I'd lost my sense of time. Other women lose their sense of taste or smell, but for me it was time. I was on a fortnight's leave, booked before I knew I was pregnant. My plan had been to spend it in Queensland with Dad and Lyn and Sean, but I'd changed my mind. Sean would be at school, Lyn at work and that would leave me alone with Dad, who, when I'd rung to tell him I was pregnant, said, 'I'll put you on to Lyn.'

I was on the lounge in front of the TV watching the morning news when Annie walked in the door and said, 'The water's warm — warmer than it was in summer. Let's go for a swim.'

'Okay,' I said, but I must have dozed off, and Annie was gone when I woke.

Ray Martin's face flickered at me from *The Midday Show*. I made a cheese sandwich and took it back to the lounge to eat.

When I woke up, the cat was eating the sandwich and Annie was back.

'You haven't moved since I left,' she said.

I pointed to the remains of the sandwich, proof that I had. 'I don't know what's wrong with me.'

'Really? You puked for months, barely slept, worked days, afternoons and nights then ran around after that old woman of yours. If anyone needs a good sleep, it's you.'

It was dark when I said for the second time, 'Okay, let's go for that swim.'

Annie called from the kitchen, 'I've made spag bol. Sit at the table and eat it before you fall asleep again.'

We walked to the pub, towels over our shoulders. Annie ducked in to deliver a message while I stood outside because I couldn't stand the cigarette smoke. Luke Tremaine – or Thug, as we called him – saw me through the doorway and came out for a chat. We'd talked before, many times, but he didn't recognise me now. He smelled of bourbon and Coke and stood too close. I stepped back but he followed, hand on my arse, as I bumped into a low brick wall.

'Steady,' he said, but didn't move his hand. He sprouted his usual gibberish: 'Great-arse-great-tits-what's-ya-name?'

'Piss off, Thug.' I pushed him away.

Thug thrust his face into mine then turned and punched the glass in the door. It shattered. 'I'll fuckin' break your skinny little neck the same way.' He held his hands in front of him like Frankenstein's monster and lunged.

'Thug!' Annie walked carefully through the broken glass. 'I was behind that door and nearly lost an eye.'

'Oh, sorry, sorry.' Thug wiped a shard of glass from Annie's shoulder then turned back to me, intent on murder. He was interrupted by the angry publican, who wasn't happy about the damage done to his door.

'Let's get out of here.' Annie grabbed my arm.

We moved at speed into the warm autumn night. We laughed as we passed the rock pool and were delirious by the time we reached South Beach.

'He would have killed me.' We lay on the sand and looked up at the stars.

'You should have told him you were pregnant. That would have put him off.'

'You reckon?'

'Come and stroke my belly, Thug.' She wiggled her hips in the sand. 'The baby will love it.'

I started to laugh then started to choke and sat up, indicating Annie should whack me on the back.

'You'd laugh at anything.'

'It's been a while.'

The moon was a sliver. We undressed beneath its dim light, no swimmers, just flesh and wobbly arses as we ran to the waves.

'It's freezing,' I gasped.

'Beautiful once you're in.' Two more strides and Annie dived under.

I splashed water over my face and arms then briefly submerged my head. Moonlight hit the foamy edges of the waves and my pale rounded belly.

'Look at it.' I rubbed my hand over its curve.

'You're showing. At last.' Annie's hair sat in perfect ringlets on her scalp.

We waded through the shallows towards the beach. There was no breeze, not even a glimmer, as we lay on towels on the strip of sand that fronted Muriel's house.

'Do you regret keeping it?'

'Sometimes. Most of the time I don't think about it.'

Annie talked about her plan to start a community vegetable garden on a spare block of land outside of Wollongong.

'Who owns the spare block?'

'I don't know, but they're not using it.'

Annie's chatter was rhythmic, soothing. I drifted upwards, a dandelion seed floating above our bodies, mine pale and lumpy, Annie's darker and warm. The ocean was a dull sheen of low-moving waves and fluorescent edges that broke then spread like a net as they reached the shallows. I drifted in the opposite direction over the dunes, past Mr Henley, Muriel's neighbour, stomping down rubbish in his garbage tin.

Muriel's yard was a straggle, trees positioned along the side fences for privacy but open at its end so the ocean could be viewed from the large back window where she painted. The room oozed the usual odour of oil and turps as she stood backlit in front of an easel, her paintbrush raised against the canvas. It would be my job in the future to scrutinise each of the paintings stored in that room. One of them, *Madonna with Her Friend*, was not a portrayal of the musician but two women romping in the night surf, one with a rounded belly.

For now I returned to the dunes, transfixed by a small orange ember not far from our towels. I sat up.

'Put your clothes on.'

'What?'

'Somebody's watching.'

'Where?' Annie swivelled around as she dressed.

'To the right, in the dunes. I can see their cigarette.'

We shook the sand out of our towels as we walked north along the beach.

'Do you think it was Thug?'

'Nah, no way. He didn't see where we went.'

•

Back at home, Annie produced a video she'd rented – *Ghost*, starring Demi Moore and Patrick Swayze. We ate Caramello Koalas and scraped the grains of sand from our toes. After the movie, I walked her to the car. 'Just in case Thug's still on the stalk.'

'It's you he's after, not me.'

I was walking back up the driveway when I heard my phone ringing. I ran back inside to answer it.

It was Lyn, drunk, upset that I was in Shellharbour and not on the Gold Coast with her.

'On the Gold Coast with Dad, you mean. You'd be at work.'

'And your sister doesn't visit. She's never taken to me.'

'Mandy doesn't take to anyone.'

'Your dad's a good man –' Lyn slurped her wine '– but he's no communicator. He needs to resolve some issues, especially where your mum's concerned.'

'Issues? Resolve? What've you been reading?'

'Transformative learning. Don't ask. Well, do ask. It's a course I want your father to go to.'

146

'Not interested?'

'Not yet. But I've stopped all sex. That should bring him round.'

'Lyn, he's my dad!'

'Exactly.'

Lyn was more familiar to me by now than my mother, though I had occasional flashes of Mum. At Christmas time with tinsel in her hair as she handed me the cake bowl to lick. A cool hand on my face when I was ill. Fragments of a story read aloud from a book. And there was the accident, of course. My memories didn't match the photos shared between me and my sister, though. Mum in her wedding dress, tall and lithe like a *Vogue* model. A woman in a pair of old trousers and shirt standing beside a paling fence, with a scene from *Snow White* painted on it. The same woman with three children bunched on a skirt that parachuted over her knees, her smile so broad it crinkled her eyes.

'I was ten when she died, I should remember more.'

'Your dad says that they were happy, that she had no reason to leave,' said Lyn. 'But you know your father: everything's a secret.' She rang off.

I'll tell you a secret, Mum had said to me. Was it in the car? *But you can't tell your father.*

I picked up the receiver and dialled.

'Hello?'

'Hi, Mandy – Amanda.'

'What time is it?'

'It's not too late.' There was a scuffle, the click of a switch. 'It's nearly midnight.'

'I have to ask you something.'

She groaned. 'What about?'

'The day of the accident, in the car. Do you remember what Mum said to us? I mean anything out of the ordinary?'

'All of it was out of the ordinary. What are you on about?'

'A secret, one that we weren't supposed to tell Dad. Maybe the reason we had to leave town.'

Mandy sighed. Her movements rustled like static. 'Leave it alone, Jane.'

'Don't you want to know what happened?'

'What if she was no more than a common tart, or she really did want to kill us as well as herself, like everyone said?'

'Then I'd want to know.'

'No, you wouldn't.'

There was the accident. Then there was after the accident. Mandy and I were dropped off at Mrs Turner's over the road. She let us sit on her good lounge in front of *Kimba the White Lion* with a box of Cheezels while Dad went with the police to identify Mum and David.

I didn't like Cheezels but conscientiously dipped my hand into the box while Mrs Turner watched. When she moved from the doorjamb, I went to the bathroom to wash my hands. Mrs Turner caught me in the hallway. She looked in Mandy's direction, then back at me.

'Whatever your father says,' she murmured, 'this was not your fault. It was your mother's.' She smelled of Avon Roses, Roses, and her neck creaked when it bent.

'That's nothing compared to what I heard,' Mandy said with a snort.

I waited, but she wanted a drum roll. 'What did you hear?'

'That she ran away to be with another man—'

'We already know that.'

'—and that before she ran away, she offered herself to just about every man in town, whether they wanted her or not.'

Amanda's words triggered nothing, no recollection. 'Do you believe it?'

'No. Look at the photos. She was beautiful. How many men in that town would have turned her down if she'd thrown herself at them?'

'Mandy, I don't remember her.'

'It was a long time ago.'

'I was ten. I should remember a lot more than I do.'

'You try too hard, that's all.'

There was a pause. Mandy's earring clacked against the receiver, which made me think she wasn't in bed at all.

'There's one more thing,' she said. 'You won't like this though.'

'Go on.'

'Dad and Lyn started their affair before the accident.'

'Who said that?'

Mandy sucked in her breath. 'Me.'

'Why would you—'

'Because I saw them.'

'You saw them? Where?' Lyn was right: Mandy had never liked her.

'Down by the hockey fields. Remember the old sheds that were there? I was at Minta's place, playing hide-and-seek. Her house backed onto the fields. I was it and I had my face pressed against the palings to count when I saw Dad drive in on the gravel track. I was about to climb the fence and call out to him, and then I saw another car. Lyn's.'

'But did they . . . ?'

'They had their arms around each other. They kissed.' Mandy's voice was dry, neutral.

'This was before the accident?'

'Before.'

'Why didn't you say anything?'

'How could I?'

'I had as much right to know as you.' A prickle coursed through me.

'Do you remember what you were like back then, holed up in the library at school or digging holes down at the old cemetery with that loopy friend of yours? And I was eight. I didn't fully understand what I saw, what it all meant. Not till after.'

'Matt wasn't loopy. I thought you liked him.'

'He was as mad as you and me – that's why he liked us, why he hung around you and tolerated your little sister. He was the same as us.'

The tabby unfurled herself and shifted towards me, winding in and out of my legs.

'I didn't take a whole lot of notice of you back then. I'm sorry, Amanda.'

'Well, I always blamed you for wanting to go away with Mum in the Morris Minor and not telling her she should stay.'

'And you *don't* anymore?'

'What?'

'Blame me?'

'For Christ's sake.'

This is how it was between me and my sister. Generous one moment, hands around each other's throat the next.

'It's a simple question.'

'No. It's not. You blame me just as much as I blame you for what happened. Tell me that I'm wrong.'

But I couldn't and, for a change, kept my mouth shut.

PART II

PART II

11.

The collaborators

1928, 1929, 19??

The paintings are a catastrophe. There is nothing to see, other than well-lit and incomprehensible violence.

The ginger snap falls into the tea before I can catch it. I'm getting slow. More than slow. I've barely given James Dennison a thought since the murder and now I can't pin down the exact year I escaped Surry Hills. The shark-proof baths were built at Brighton-le-Sands in September 1928, so it had to be after that. Maybe October, but the more I think about it, I'm wondering if it was early '29 rather than the end of '28 that we flew out? I conjure Tommy, running his hand through the dark slick of his hair. 'You're no help,' I chide.

I press the record and play buttons. 'Jane, I'm not a hundred percent sure on the dates in that last tape. You'll have to check them against the newspaper stories on the murder.'

•

Biographer's note: Although it was implied in the previous tape that Muriel had stabbed James Dennison, she did not at any stage give specific details about the actual murder.

•

Flying was two shades of blue. The square blue of the ocean separated from the square blue of the sky by a sliver of gold, a hinge along the horizon. I'm not the first artist to see it like that. Some paint foregrounds and backgrounds as solid blocks of colour: *my five-year-old could do that*. Record prices have been paid for squares of orange, red and yellow, sunflowers and irises, cans of soup, reproduced comics.

'We have to concentrate on you,' Claudine had advised as I guzzled my lemon pudding at the Aero Club. 'You as a person, I mean. We have to sell you.'

But it wasn't Claudine that first got me noticed. It was James Dennison's murder. Actually, it was the inquiry into his murder that got me noticed. My painting of Adam Black, nude and slashed by a knife, drew a lot of attention, as did the *Working Women* series. The newspapers critiqued my dark and violent subjects in dribs and drabs over the two years it took Claudine, or Claudine's lawyers I should say, to sort things out.

And where was I during these two years?

•

'Where to?' Tommy eyed the horizon, licked his finger and held it up to check wind direction. We headed south, following roads, railway lines or Tommy's school atlas, landing in paddocks, hardpan plains or on packed sand, sleeping near the plane, under a tarp, in an abandoned shack, in the sand dunes or in the nearby scrub. We settled on South Australia. Concealing the plane under branches and leaves, beside a bungalow, far enough from the town to be left alone.

'More of a lean-to than a bungalow.'

It was a bungalow to me. The postie delivered bread and meat twice a week, and other groceries too if I left a list in the old tin letterbox. The creamery truck delivered ice on its way past, if I wanted it.

'It'll be a couple of weeks before I can get back to see you.' Tommy sat behind me on the sand, his legs on either side of mine, his arms around my waist, 'It could be longer.'

•

Jane, before you go turning this book into something it's not, you need to understand – what happened between Tommy and me was anything but a romance.

•

Tommy was two men. The first did as he pleased. The second was governed by a group of World War I pilots. Novices, perpetually caught up in dogfights they were incapable of winning. Entering each fray with volatile machines that were destined to fail.

'Stick to my tail.' He'd sit upright, eyes open though he was sound asleep, trying to guide his aviators through the flak. Most were lost by morning. Cinders in crashed planes. This was the worst outcome for Tommy, who couldn't stand the thought of being trapped in a fire.

'Don't send anymore.' His hands around my throat, almost throttling me.

There was a danger that Tommy would one day go too far. His dreams made him reckless. I'd watch him shave the trees with his undercarriage, rise in a barrel roll, loop in the air, land too fast.

His proximity to death sharpened our appetites. We'd lay in the lean-to, our legs tangled beneath a sheet, the gaps in the wall the only thing between us and the South Pole. There was the smell of salt and the texture of our skin and a richness to everything.

'You should paint me.' Tommy was jealous of Adam's portrait.

'I think I'd rather paint the sea.'

He stubbed out his cigarette and rolled me onto my stomach. 'The sea can't do this.' The hair from his chest scratched the back of my legs and the skin of my backside as he slid upwards then stopped.

'All right, all right.' I gave in.

The next time he flew in he had canvas and paint so I could start on a portrait of him.

I painted Tommy a lot in those two years of exile, leaning back with a cigarette in his mouth, guiding novices through a flak-filled sky, running out of the ocean, removing his leather helmet, always with that same insolent look on his face. Claudine would have it that Tommy wasn't a talker, but that's because she was too busy giving orders to listen. He talked, as he posed, about being demobbed in London back in 1919. Tommy was stuck there, along with a lot of other airmen waiting to go home, when Billy Hughes announced a ten-thousand-pound prize to be awarded to the first Australian to fly from London to Australia. He and his mates pooled their money and drew straws for the pilot and navigator spots, but they couldn't raise the hundred-pound entry fee and had to come home the long way instead.

'That's why you're still alive.'

'Maybe.' He sucked on his cigarette and blew the smoke upwards. 'But what a way to go.'

Those two years were full of movement; different states, different bungalows. We'd look at the school atlas and work out our next location. Tommy would set me down and see me settled, then fly back to visit when he could. The first thing I did in each new place was mark out the best landing strip, and when I heard him approach I'd wave a red piece of cloth over my head. When he'd landed Tommy would jump out of the cockpit like a charging bull and kneel in front of me, arms around my hips, head on my belly. And though it might sound like a romance to you, it was something else.

•

As time went on we became careless, less concerned about being recognised. No, I'll change that. *I* became careless. Tommy never lost his concern. Towards the end of the exile I travelled by train from the Blue Mountains to a coastal town north of Wollongong. I wore a veiled hat, an old woman's shawl and carried a walking stick. That was during the Depression. On the other side of the train's window I saw people swarming around makeshift camps or tramping along the road, making do. I thought it would be easy to disappear in all the chaos.

At Thirroul, plumes of smoke and steam rose from a distant colliery. From the station, I walked east, turning into a road that butted against low scrub, peppery dunes and the Pacific. FOR LEASE signs fronted the first two houses on the corner of the street. There was one more house after that, then an expanse of grassy vacant lots before I reached a cottage on its own at the road's end. It was a timber affair with a corrugated-iron roof, a deep verandah, a water tank at the side and an unassuming Model T parked on a rectangular verge out the front.

I stood on the grass verge, canvas bag in my hand, squinting at the verandah through the sunlight. There was nothing to see but an opaque block of shade. I stepped over the wrought-iron gate with its pink flaking paint and walked along the path then up three steps. A red ember appeared in the shadow. It moved upwards in a vertical line, expanded then somersaulted over my head as I stepped onto the wooden floor.

'Tommy?'

He leaned against me, smelling of tobacco, salt and soap. A low whistle sounded.

'The colliery.' His hand knocked the hat from my crown. Stooping to retrieve it, we bumped heads.

'I left my port at the station.'

'I'll motor up and get it if you like.'

'Later.'

We spoke in sleepy afternoon voices, gravitating into wicker chairs to watch a bird dive for fish in deep water beyond the breakers. I rested my head on Tommy's shoulder and he pulled the pins from my hair, stroking my hatless head.

Tommy said, 'We should go away, just you and me, and never come back.'

'We'd have to take Claudine.' I lifted my head from his shoulder to see those incandescent eyes of his.

Puzzled, he raised a shoulder in question.

'To keep you in planes and me in paint.' I lowered my head and listened as cigarette smoke entered his lungs with a whoosh. We stayed like that for hours, not talking or moving, but somehow I woke in a bed and it was the next morning.

The sun fell in a bar over Tommy's feet. Two years of patchy access to pencil and paints had left me greedy. I scrabbled for my sketchbook, drawing a few lines before Tommy opened his eyes and stretched his limbs through the light.

'*Nude Man, Early Morning*.' I tapped his shoulder with my pencil.

Tommy rolled onto his back and lay there, one hand behind his head, the other under the sheet. I pulled the sheet away and drew him in that pose, hand on his shaft, gazing at the ceiling.

•

Nude Man, Early Morning was not part of the exhibition Claudine planned for 1936. I gave her that painting as a gift and she kept it on the wall above her bed. As a result, it was the only painting I produced for Claudine between 1931 and 1936, other than the triptych, that wasn't stolen. Forty-five years later, the paintings were retrieved and in 1982 Claudine held a retrospective. It was the biggest news in art since the Ern Malley affair. I wasn't meant to be there. That was the exhibition's drawcard – I was dead. Claudine shuffled me through the crowd and out the back while Adam Black walked around inside, peering into the eyes of every woman over the age of fifty, unsure if I were still alive.

'It's too late,' Claudine said on a cement block behind the gallery. 'You're dead, Muriel. That's what you wanted, remember.'

She placed her hand on my shoulder. I noticed the rings, slightly too large on her fingers. She infuriated me. I shook her off. The death had been her idea not mine.

'And what happened to *Nude Man, Early Morning*?' I asked her. 'Why isn't that here?'

•

Tommy was a patient sitter and I was quick with my preparatory sketches. Once I'd finished he threw his legs over the side of the bed, reaching for his trousers. Buttoning his flies, he frowned then looked over his shoulder.

When I presented the painting to Claudine, she wanted all the details. How Tommy had put his trousers on as if he wasn't interested, then crawled back onto the bed, reaching beneath the sheets to stroke my flesh, rolling me in his arms until I was on top of him in the gauzy light. The curtains flicking over my back as I placed my hands around his upper arms, pinning him down.

'How did you get his trousers off?'

'He hadn't buttoned them all the way. They fell below his hips, which was enough.'

'And then?'

I had to think. Claudine liked specifics. It was far easier to let her watch. But if she watched, we had to make it worth her while.

'I lowered my breasts onto his chest.' The painting and the details were a gift for everything she'd done and everything she said she'd do.

•

'Come on.' Tommy banged on the verandah in front of where I sat, eyes closed in a patch of sun. He'd found a bike in the back shed, a rusted bit of metal on buckled wheels.

'Unwreckable.' He crossed the road to the embankment and tumbled over its edge down the slope, catapulting with some speed over the handlebars. 'Come on.' He picked the bike up and ran towards firmer sand.

We took it in turns to ride along the water's edge, skidding in and out of the shallows, heading south until we reached the rocky dais at the base of the headland. Waves broke over the edge of the platform, spraying us. Tommy stood shirtless, wet shorts folded around his legs, dripping onto the flat purple rocks. The next wave rolled past and he began to sprint, jumping as he reached the edge, knees against his chest, elbows in, falling into the rolling blue gutter, then he was gone – his dark hair resurfacing, his face breaking free of the water.

'Muriel.' He waved his arm back and forth. 'Muriel. Come on.'

I looked into the sun, then at the satin sheen on the water. Tommy yelled, 'Run,' and I did, over periwinkles, jumping as the wave flattened out, rising into the sky then dropping through white smoky bubbles, sliding upwards over Tommy's torso, tangling myself in his limbs. Tommy threw his head back and opened his mouth, catching the sun in his white teeth and iridescent eyes. 'Let's go again,' he shouted.

•

Late afternoon, the bungalow was in shadow. Modern conveniences included a separate washroom with a chip heater that trickled hot water into a bath.

'It's so slow. It'll be cold before it fills an inch.'

I heated a bucketful of water on the range and poured it into a tub that I positioned by the fireside. Tommy had grazes everywhere. He squatted while I swirled the washer between his knees, dabbing at the torn spots on his shoulders, kissing the back of his warmed neck. That's as far as we got. No details for Claudine.

We were interrupted by someone yelling and a knock on the door. It was a boy's voice.

'Go into the bedroom,' Tommy ordered as he pulled on his trousers. 'It could be a trick. The coppers might have come for you.'

I listened from the bedroom to the panicked conversation. The boy's older brother was in the ocean somewhere or drowned, washed off the rocks while they were fishing. I stepped out of the room in a shirt and trousers.

'You go with the boy, Tommy, I'll bring a lamp.'

They ran off and I grabbed the lamp and some matches and followed. It was the tail end of the day and there wasn't much light left by the time I found them standing on the platform near the southern headland considering the water.

'Cooee,' the boy yelled through cupped hands. 'Floyd!' But the wind had come up and it was hard to hear over the rush and roar of the breaking waves.

I held the lamp high, scanning the water, but it wasn't quite dark and I was throwing too many shadows. Then I saw something.

'Tommy!' I directed his attention to a scattering of rocks between the platform and the beach, to what I thought was a pale arm, slung across the top of a sharply angled facet. The arm and the rock vanished beneath a wave then reappeared.

Tommy sprinted to the edge of the platform and, without hesitating, he jumped.

'Will he get him?' asked the boy, who had told us his name was Billy.

Tommy re-emerged through the bucking waves.

'Yes. He'll get him all right.'

We lost sight of him in the backwash. Then we saw him again, caught on a jutting rock not far from the platform. He launched himself, using the oncoming wave to reach the adjacent rock and Floyd. The same wave pounded over Floyd's head. When it receded, the boy was gone.

'Floyd!' his brother screeched.

'There.' The water sucked back then surged again, battering the figure against the corroded rocks.

Tommy manoeuvred himself into position then stretched out, but the gap was too wide. Thrusting forward with the next rush, he propelled himself towards the boy. We didn't see what happened next; there was too much foam, and when it cleared they weren't there.

'They might have been pushed sideways by the current.'

Billy and I ran across the rocks towards the sand. We sprinted back and forth, shouting hopelessly into the wind. Then I noticed waves pounding against a sandbank a few yards from the shore. I left the lamp on the sand as a marker and waded through the shallows towards it.

Floyd's body skimmed the sandbank, lifeless. I clutched his leg before the retreating wave could claim him. He was skinny but heavy. I dragged, rather than carried him back to the beach. Billy reached me as I turned Floyd face down over my knees and hit him on the back. He vomited a raft of water then vomited a second time, fighting as he tried to draw breath.

Once he was sitting on his haunches, breathing steadily, his brother by his side, I ran back to the sandbank. I waded its width, despite the grip in the current, searching, but Tommy wasn't there. Desperate, I waded back to shore and ran north up the beach, almost tripping over him lying face down at the water's edge. I grabbed him by the shoulders but he rolled onto his elbow without my help.

'I've lost him,' he gasped. Blood was running from his limbs and his torso.

'He washed up on a sandbank further back. He's all right.'

We took the boys back to the bungalow, where I wrapped Floyd in a blanket. I wanted to make him a hot drink but Tommy was against it.

'I'll drive them home.' He got in the motorcar with the boys. 'You pack. We'll leave as soon as I get back.'

I sat our ports side by side on the bed and threw in our belongings, running to meet Tommy when I heard the motor.

'Left them at their house. Took off like a bunny when someone opened the door. They'll think me a queer sort of bugger.' He threw off his wet clothes and grabbed dry ones from the top of his bag.

'Let me take a look at those cuts.'

'Leave it. Let's get away.'

I said, 'I'll drive.'

He got into the passenger side without protest.

I stalled at the end of the road then stuttered around the corner.

'You'll want to improve on that,' Tommy said, and I laughed because of the haste, which seemed unnecessary, and because of the serious way he said it. I laughed so much I got a pain under my ribs and had to pull over.

'Where to?' I said once I'd settled down, but there wasn't much choice. We knew where we had to go. I drove smoothly after that in the direction of the highlands.

•

A flock of pink-and-grey galahs fed on the dew-covered grass. They rose as we drove by, merging into one coordinated screech. We'd been travelling for a day and a half with no lack of trouble. Tommy had a turn at the wheel a few hours into the trip and ran us into a ditch. Pushing the Ford out had reopened his wounds, and the blood had to be staunched. Then we'd had to wait outside a garage until it opened so we could buy fuel. We argued after that. Tommy wanted to drive again but I refused to get out of the driver's seat.

The galahs continued their screeching. I pulled over and Tommy got out of the car to vomit. He wiped his mouth with his shirt. 'I've been worse.' His left eye was bruised, there was a gash on his forehead, and his hair was matted with dry blood.

'I didn't ask.'

He squinted, drowsy and irritable. I'd let him sleep but I needed him to stay awake now to give me directions. Propping his head against the window, he closed his eyes then opened them again as I steered into a rut.

'Left, Muriel. Left.'

I drove along the tamped-down track, pulling up in front of a Victorian weatherboard with a front verandah and iron roof.

Tommy grimaced getting out of the car. 'Leave the bags,' he said, but I brought them in.

We moved along a hallway through squares of foggy light. 'Which room?' I asked

'Any you like,' Tommy said. 'Claudine chops and changes.'

He wanted to go straight to sleep but I insisted on checking his wounds and made him have something to drink. 'It's not too late,' he said, head on the pillow. I didn't know what he meant by that and didn't ask.

•

I woke in the middle of the day. Tommy lay on his back beside me. He wasn't feverish and his breathing was even. The room was full of sunlight that fell in rectangles over a tallboy and caught the edge of a cloth-covered chair with a shawl thrown over its back. I put the shawl around my shoulders and followed the dust motes along the hallway into a kitchen that was as big as the tenement I'd shared with Nan. There was a brass tap below a window, wood stacked beside the stove and a sizeable table. I turned on the tap and water ran into the sink as a rosella flew past the window in a flash of vibrant red and blue.

Outside I could see blossoming fruit trees, a post-and-rail fence and paddocks of rich grass. Inside I found a pantry filled with jars of jams, preserved fruit and pickled vegetables as well as canisters of flour, sugar and tea. I opened a jar of stewed apples and drank a glass of water then continued towards the back of the house and a semicircular room with oversized windows. One of its walls was lined with shelves of books, another stacked with art supplies and an easel. I picked up a tube of cadmium yellow, removed the cap and touched its colour to my tongue.

That's where Tommy found me. It must have been late afternoon because the light outside glanced off the leaves at a dull angle. Tommy stood in the doorway, his face puffy, coloured by bruises. My canvas had the same look; faded yellows and greens alongside a deep thick purple. I smiled at him then returned to my work. His footsteps receded along the hallway. The front door opened and the motorcar started. Wheels crunched as they rolled along the track towards the road.

I was still at the easel when he returned. I'd found kerosene lamps and set them up at intervals to minimise the shadows on the canvas.

I heard Tommy blunder through the door and stagger down the hallway, colliding with the walls. He appeared beside me, stippled by the lamps.

'All those little bits of paint wanting to get into Claudine's cunt.'

Tommy was a tall man and broad. With his face as it was, covered in cuts and bruises, he looked like a pirate. Years later, I'd think of Errol Flynn in *Captain Blood*. Even drunk, Tommy had the same sort of grace that Errol flaunted on the big screen.

He lurched forward, fists clenched, smashing the easel to the floor. Winding a handful of my hair around his fingers, he pulled me to the ground then sunk his teeth into my shoulder. I rolled out from under him, pulled back my arm and punched him in the face until he let go.

I ran through the house and out the door, crossing the verandah then the grass, my bare toes catching on rocks and stubble. The moon was full. To escape its light, I crouched in a dark cluster of scrubby bushes, knees against my chest. Tommy stumbled out of the house, howling like a wounded dog.

'Muriel,' he yelled from the verandah. Then he counted, one – two – three – four, right up to eleven, after which he yelled curses and insults, then slumped to the ground.

The leaves around me were laced with creatures that scrabbled and creaked. Overhead, two crossed branches rubbed against each other like cicada legs. I crawled through the scrub until my head butted against a wrought-iron fence. A rusted square marked the perimeter of a gravesite. I stepped over it to read the headstone.

IN LOVING MEMORY OF
VICTORIA ELLEN DALTON
Who died 6 May 1895 AGED 31
Also Her Beloved Husband
GEORGE HENRY DALTON
Who died 8 April 1906 AGED 54
'Reunited'

Weeds grew through cracks in the slab. What a wretched place to be buried, lost among the debris and rust. I cleared away lumps of dirt and gravel then lay on the smoothed surface and watched the moonlight fall on the leaves. Caught in the flux of light and shadows, I didn't move from the grave until the cold seeped in. Then I stepped over the fence, crept through the bushes and past the trees towards the house.

Tommy was still on the front verandah, but asleep now. His limbs twitched as I balanced on the step below and listened to his laboured breathing. He raised his hand, reached forward, then lowered his arm. I went inside to retrieve my sketchbook and a lamp, which I positioned so I could see his face. Nothing would wake him now.

'Follow me.' His voice was hoarse. 'They'll come out of the sun. Stay behind, stay behind.'

I would paint him as I saw him, I decided, putting pencil to paper.

•

I've been back to that house since. Claudine has left it pretty much as it was. Tommy liked to say it was ill-gotten, that old man Worthington won it on a bet and passed it on to his daughter because he had no use for it. The truth is, many properties were sold for a fraction of their value during the Depression and Claudine's father, who liked a bargain, gave this one to his daughter. She loved that house and chose it as a place for the three of us to meet after Tommy and I had had our week in Thirroul. She had some good news, she promised.

•

In years to come, Claudine would say she'd recognised my genius from the start and would have done anything to support me. I had no doubts, none, that I was indebted to her – and after 1929 I had even more reason to be grateful to her. Just like me with Tommy on the steps, she thought nothing would wake me.

•

Even if you don't know a lot about Claudine, Jane, you must have heard of the Worthington Museum in Surry Hills – where the Muriel Kemp Foundation is housed. Claudine started collecting art in the early thirties. Australian art could be bought for almost nothing during the Depression and its value didn't escalate much afterwards.

One of the most common accusations made against Claudine over the years was that she promoted mediocracy, the argument being that she promoted her lovers, most of whom were artists and writers but none of whom were particularly talented. According to Claudine herself, it was her promotion of local artists that got up the establishment's nose. Her response was to start a museum, collecting not just art but poetry and prose, music and Indigenous pieces – works nobody else thought were important. In the forties and fifties, she became known as the Frock Buyer after she bought up works by female artists and promoted them while she was at it. She liked to buy from unknowns; young or old, she didn't care. She had an eye did Claudine, and an ear. When her artists gained a reputation, she sold off their works to fund the museum.

The museum was considered radical. Paintings were slung between the ceilings and floors on universal joints. You could grab hold of a canvas and rotate it three hundred and sixty degrees. Readings were piped through the building, poems hung in frames. Sculptures were meant to be touched, music danced or listened to while lying in deckchairs in low-lit caves or in front of screens filled with oceans and forests.

Claudine was flamboyant but she was also well read and clever. Her irreverence was appreciated in Europe and America, and once the rest of the world had taken her up, so did Australia.

You've heard of Kerrie Chan, Simon Nyland, Patricia Walker? They wouldn't have been recognised in this country, let alone internationally, if it hadn't been for Claudine.

What else? Who else?

In the fifties Claudine mentored a group of artists that called themselves The Beasts. The most notorious among them was the androgynous Le Bon, who used his or her own blood to make frozen sculptures. At her peak, Le Bon painted a blood cage on a cement slab beside a six-metre-high building site, which she threw herself from. Her intention may have been to land in the cell on top of a mattress but, if it was, then she miscalculated because she landed outside its boundaries. This might also have been her intention. Le Bon didn't die but was left a vegetable. The Beasts disbanded after that.

I'm trying to think of other examples. There are plenty.

The artist in the seventies who filmed his own death.

The sculptor of the giant condom who canvassed the community for donations of sperm.

The diamond-crusted toilet seat.

The red tap shoes handed out to Sydney's homeless.

Look her up. She was always in the paper or on the television commenting about something.

As for me, I didn't like Claudine any the better because of her achievements or despite her insisting publicly and repeatedly that Muriel Kemp was the most talented artist she'd ever met or was likely to meet. Because as true as that was, it was she that ruined me.

•

Anyway, back to the Southern Highlands in 1931 with Tommy, a black sky, diamond stars, a full moon and a frog on the hunt for a mate. I stepped over Tommy and returned with a blanket, tossing it over him.

Then I went to bed.

It wasn't the sun edging its way between the curtains that woke me, but Tommy, smelling of rum and thawing himself against my back. 'I'm sorry,' he whispered. 'I'm sorry.' His hands moved over my scalp, finding the gap where he'd pulled out my hair. 'I'm sorry.' He kissed my throat and breasts. I pulled his head tight against me until he struggled, suffocating. Then I got out of bed. He knew not to follow.

I found some kindling in the woodpile and lit the stove, boiled the water, opened a can of beans as well as a jar of rhubarb, then made a pot of tea. The back room wasn't as badly destroyed as I thought and the painting I'd worked on was strange and compelling in the daylight. I cleaned up the damage and got back to it.

Mid-morning there was the sound of an engine then Claudine's voice ringing through the house. I'd seen Claudine several times since the day at the Aero Club when she'd filled me with food, praised my work and given me fifteen pounds to paint her a sample. Tommy had flown her to a number of my hiding places, something she bragged about later in her life. At the time, she would never have admitted to consorting with an alleged murderer.

'Hello!' She was in the hallway stirring up the sunlight as I walked out of the back room. 'Haven't you two been busy?' She held up a newspaper and pointed to the headline. WAR HERO SAVES DROWNING BOY.

She put her arms around my shoulders and held me briefly before wiping some paint from my cheek. 'Where is he?'

I nodded towards the bedroom.

She picked up a bag from the floor and I followed her into the kitchen.

'How did they find out it was him?'

'My guess is the real estate agent. I told Tommy to use a false name, but you know Tommy.'

She unpacked the bag, placing packages on the table. 'Fortunately they didn't mention the floozy he was with; out of courtesy to their hero, I suppose. They want to give Tommy a medal.' She leaned against the table and laughed. 'Can you imagine it?'

'And I have some even better news,' she went on, before I had time to answer her question. 'You're no longer wanted by the police.'

And there it was. I'd been exonerated, after it was discovered (by Claudine's lawyers) that the police had ignored the testimony of my upstairs neighbour Ivy Lee. She'd told them I'd visited her three days before James Dennison's murder, suitcase in hand, to say my goodbyes because I was leaving the tenement. In their turn the lawyers were able to produce a record of my stay at a guesthouse on the night in question

Witnesses were reinterviewed: Maureen Percival, the Greek fruiterer, the landlord, the coal and wood, and peg and clothes prop men. Not one person could say they recollected seeing me after Ivy Lee in the three days leading up to the murder. Of course, no one liked the cops around there.

'So that's it?' I asked.

'Yes, it's over. You have some loyal friends, Muriel.' Claudine nodded to the packages on the table, 'Oh, I stopped at the dairy,' then tilted her head as if listening to Tommy snore. 'Has he given you any trouble?'

•

The sky was a bleeding sore. That's how I painted it; a combustion of fuel and falling men. Those not destroyed when they hit the ground dragged their bodies in a multitude of directions. In the bottom left of the rectangle, I painted a tree and filled it with women, phantoms, sitting on the branches. I stood back from the easel. Something was wrong with the women. I wasn't sure what . . .

I woke up lying on the floor, my feet under the easel. It was cold and dark. The fire and lamps had gone out. I disentangled myself from brushes, bits of paper and an open book and took myself down the hall, crawling into a bed that smelled of Tommy. I was asleep, then I was awake. Thinking of the painting and the sun that I'd dented with dark falling bodies. The women, I realised, should be painted in green hues. Unripe fruit, falling from the tree to the ground below it. I reached over the slumbering body towards the side table for the matches to light the lamp but couldn't find the box.

Early light filtered into the room between the wavering curtains. Enough to see by. I got out of the bed. Claudine rolled into the warm dip I'd vacated beside Tommy. I was thinking of the women with their hard, green peel and thick bitter pith and didn't need a lamp anymore.

12.

The skin of it

April – August 1992

Much of my two weeks' leave in April was spent in Muriel's company.
I transcribed tapes during that time and she corrected the written
copies, querulous and impatient if I questioned her about details.

'It's on the tapes.'

'It's not, I've checked.'

'Go back and listen again.'

I'd arrive in the afternoons, transcript in a plastic sleeve. Muriel
would make a pot of tea, hunt up the ceremonial cosy, then we'd
argue. The problem for me were the gaps in her story.

'You stopped painting for twenty-five years. Are you saying you
just walked away from it?'

'By choice.'

'How was that a choice?'

I can still see her face through the steam as she poured water into the teapot, enraged by my ignorance. 'I was a woman and a painter. The two don't go together.' She pushed a plate of Iced VoVo's towards me. 'Damn well eat something, would you? You look like a drug addict.' That was in April; by July my face was a full moon.

'Claudine Worthington called you a genius.'

'Don't trust anyone who calls you a genius. They'll stab you in the back just the same as anyone else.'

Muriel painted instead of sleeping in those winter months. Mr Henley said the light was on in that back room at all hours. The last hurrah, she might have called it.

•

In the last two months of my pregnancy, I was concerned by our lack of progress on the biography. Muriel rehashed the same scenes over and over. Surry Hills, the painting she'd done for her grand-mother: the tree in the scrap of dirt out the back – was it a peach or a tangerine?

'It's not the years before 1936 people will question,' I reminded her. 'It's the years after it. You have to convince the critics you didn't die in that plane crash.'

'I know, and I'll get to it.'

But she didn't, not in any detail. She briefly mentioned seeing Adam Black in the sixties and made a vague reference to living on the money Tommy embezzled from Claudine.

'He kept some of it as cash but we didn't trust cash after the Depression. There were properties, investments and a lot of gold.'

'What about the grave?'

'What grave?'

'Yours. If Claudine and everyone else claims you died in 1936, then where's the grave? Unless you were cremated.'

'I told you about that,' she snapped, as if I were deliberately provoking her.

'I swear you didn't, Muriel.' I crossed my heart.

'It's outside Bowral, on Claudine's property. I went back to see it. I already told you that.' She glared at me. 'Away from the house and the other two graves that were already there. On its own, overgrown with lantana and bracken fern, surrounded by ant's nests. There was a full-grown black snake curled up on the cement the day I saw it.'

This was the first time I'd ever seen Muriel distressed and I felt sorry I'd insisted on an answer.

'Claudine did it on purpose. She knew I didn't want to be buried there. But the worst thing is, it's not me.'

In contrast, her reaction to the double-page spread in the *Weekend Australian* was nothing. I bought the paper at the bakery along with two croissants. She eyed the bag as I placed it on the table.

'A celebration.' I removed the coloured magazine from the newspaper and flipped it open.

MURIEL KEMP, OUR UNKNOWN GENIUS.

The headline topped a photo of Lexie Tanner, Director of the Muriel Kemp Foundation, alongside a reproduction of *The Girl on Riley Street*.

'Hmph.' Muriel pulled a croissant from the bag.

'I thought you'd be pleased.'

'It's taken fifty years and a lot of hype and money from Claudine.' She bit into the croissant and chewed slowly. 'Whereas you've only got a year.'

'A year?' I wiped crumbs from the table back into the paper bag.

'You'll have to approach Lexie Tanner. If you can't convince her, then burn them.'

I must have looked confused because she clicked her fingers in front of my eyes and hissed, 'The paintings.'

'Which ones?'

'All of them.'

'But it would be as if you were never here,' I protested. 'There'd be no point to a book.'

She wiped her hands, decided. 'Let them have the triptych but nothing else. You can tell them in the book what they've missed.'

•

In the final weeks of pregnancy, I waddled around to Muriel's house, overdue and overtired, and insisted that she take the cat back.

'The cat's yours. I don't want it.' Muriel had a bit of a cough and her eyes watered as she talked.

'I could go into labour at any minute; I need you to look after her. And go and see about that cough would you,' I snapped.

Muriel died in August as I lay spread-eagled in the labour ward giving birth.

'Do you want a mirror?' the midwife asked and, when I nodded, placed it at the end of the bed so I could see the baby's head as it crowned. Olivia tore her way out into the midwife's waiting hands.

'A girl,' she shouted. Howzat!

It was the cat, I was told later, who'd signalled for help. The cat, whose food had to be left under the eaves of the garage because it wouldn't come inside and who ran like the blazes every time Muriel approached, stood on the step in front of the screen door and yowled and scratched to get in. Mr Henley, fed up with the noise, entered the yard to investigate. There was no answer to his knock, but the door was unlocked. Mr Henley found Muriel on the floor in the kitchen. Not beside her paintings, which would have made a good ending, but alone on the lino, cold, stiff and gone.

The police came to see me in the hospital. Two of them, hats off, respectful. They entered the room as I was trying to manoeuvre my nipple, pushed flat by my milk-engorged breast, into Olivia's squawk of a mouth.

Muriel had left a note.

Please inform Jane Cooper, care of the maternity ward in Shellharbour Hospital, of my death.

Dead, dead, dead, dead, dead, dead, dead – the word left my brain in a stutter. It wouldn't stick. How could she have known? I'd seen enough death to realise how possible it was, but this was Muriel. My Muriel.

'When did you last see her?' one of the police officers asked.

'The day I was due. About a week and a half ago. She had a cough, that's all, a bit of a cough. I rang a few days later to see if she'd been to the doctor. She told me she had. *It's only a cold*, that's what she said to me. *Don't fuss and don't come over, I don't want you blaming me if you catch it.* I should have known. As if she'd care if I caught her cold.'

'She did go and see a doctor. The unfilled scripts were on the counter. Turned into pneumonia, they reckon.'

Olivia gurgled from the hospital's perspex crib. The officer looked down at the noise and smiled. 'The cat is at the neighbour's.'

I wept at that. My engorged breasts jiggled up and down. The young constable tried to hide his fascination then looked away, embarrassed, when I pulled up the sheet.

Three-day post baby blues. That's what a nurse called my tears. They fell in silent runnels that dripped from my face onto Olivia's head. We were both permanently damp.

'I heard about your old woman,' Annie said when she came to collect us.

I stared at her through red eyes and sniffed back another deluge.

'Let's get you out of here.'

Annie had parked the Laser in the pick-up bay near the exit. We put Olivia into the baby capsule, fitted in its reverse position behind the passenger seat. It was strange, to be allowed to leave with a baby.

I asked Annie to drive to Muriel's.

'Let me take you home first. I'll come back for the cat.'

But I insisted, surveying the surrounds from the car while Annie retrieved the cat. There was nothing to see. Muriel's house still looked like Muriel's house.

13.

The gap in the comb

August – November 1992

Annie dropped Olivia and me back at the flat, where the postman had delivered a letter from Muriel's solicitors offering me the use of Muriel's house, rent free with a weekly stipend that ceased at the end of two years. There was also a parcel from Dad and Lyn, which I left unopened on the table. I'd asked Annie to ring them about the baby while I was in the hospital and tried to forget what Mandy had said about their affair. But I saw it over and over, through tired gritty eyes. Lyn and Dad caught in an embrace by the hockey field sheds.

In that first week home with the baby Annie flitted in and out, bird-like, evasive. Then one day she knocked at the door, surprising me; usually she stomped in and called, 'It's me.'

'Sorry.' Annie's hair hung in tight corkscrews because of the weather. She didn't fill the kettle, chatter about fruit fly, the ear a straight guy wore his earring in, the latest asteroid or anything else. She just stood and watched as I undid the flap of my maternity bra and fed Olivia.

'I'm ready to head out,' she said, the same way she always said it.

'Where?' I thought it would be to see a band, to a lecture on astronomy or to sandbag her community garden.

'Western Australia to start. I leave next week.'

I fiddled with a button on my shirt, unable to look at her.

'You knew right? I mean I told you. Months ago.'

'It's just that we'd always planned to go together.'

Annie leaned over, kissed the top of my head and ran a hand over Olivia's scalp as she fed.

'I did think about postponing it, until you'd settled in.'

'You can't do that. Things have changed. It's not as easy as I thought, that's all.' I looked down at Olivia, trying to keep the resentment from my voice.

'It's only a year.' Annie mustered some enthusiasm. 'By the time I get back, you'll have fathomed your old woman's secrets and written a book and we'll be raising a glass to celebrate it.'

I laughed, not wanting her to go without me, but knowing that's how it would be.

I asked her to help me move into Muriel's before she left. 'It's the least you can do.' I tried to make light of the situation.

We fit everything into the back of a borrowed van and in our haste, dropped the TV and cracked the screen. We laughed and made jokes about it being on its last legs and Annie commented how Muriel's house was less cramped than the flat.

I slept in the double bed and there was room for the cradle, drying rack, nappy bucket and change table. I dined on sardines from the pantry and drank tea from Muriel's old teapot, swaddled in its cosy. Other than the electric typewriter, the kitchen table held documents and letters, a ream of A4 paper, the two recorders and Muriel's tapes. I was set.

Set? The first morning I found myself immobilised, siphoned of all energy and could have wept for an hour's unbroken sleep. Muriel's voice came to me, not as a taunt or an I told you so but as an infuriatingly neutral voice. *You won't get anywhere with a baby.* That's what got me out of bed and into the kitchen and as far as switching on the kettle, but the noise woke Olivia. Too tired to feel anything, I picked her up out of the cot.

I didn't want the stipend at first but accepted it after I got sick with mastitis. When that improved, I tried to return to work, but the childcare I'd organised fell through. My hours didn't suit anyone I was willing to trust with Olivia.

'What do you mean you don't trust anyone?' I held imaginary conversations with Annie. 'It would do you good to get out of the house, talk to other adults, be yourself for a while.'

But I couldn't hand Olivia over to just anybody. Not because of instinct or hormones or over protectiveness but because babies are vulnerable and can't fend for themselves. Wasn't that common sense? In the meantime, I felt the pressure of Muriel's story hanging over me and would wake at the death hour, or the 'blue hour' as Sylvia Plath called it, when the baby was still asleep and there was an hour to put pen to paper and what held me together, when my sodden brain couldn't absorb half a thought, was Muriel's certainty that I would fail. I needed to prove that it was possible, that I *could* do it.

Even so, I felt Muriel's absence and Annie's too. There *was* Mr Henley, who'd call to me from the dip in the paling fence when he had too many cabbages or carrots.

'If there's anything you need,' he'd tell me 'you know where I am.' We've bonded, Mr Henley and me, over the cat.

The tabby, at least, was happy to be in the house without Muriel. Each time I fed her I contemplated the package from Lyn and Dad that I'd stashed unopened in the cupboard beside tins of cat food. I missed Lyn but couldn't bring myself to ring her since I'd heard about the affair. As for Amanda, who worked Monday to Friday as an administrator at the University of New South Wales, she'd rung once since Olivia was born. And while I missed her less than the others, I had her direct number.

'Amanda.'

'Don't ask.'

'Ask what? Ask you to come down and visit me, bring a present for your new niece?'

There were voices in the background, quick steps, and someone said, 'Here it is.' Amanda said, 'Thanks.'

'All right.' I always gave in first. 'I just want to know that you're sure it was Dad and Lyn you saw at the hockey fields and that it was before the accident, not after.'

'Yes.' She was curt.

'Mum might have known about them then?'

'She might have.'

'How will I ever talk to Lyn again?'

'Your problem, not mine.' She hung up.

There was the gossip. What the neighbours said, the taunts in the playground. Amanda on a thrashing to nowhere as she retaliated and me, in hiding.

'Your mother was a slut. Took it up the arse in her Morris Minor. Got what she deserved.'

There were the letters Lyn gave me, addressed to Mum from an unknown man named Harry. There was Lyn in tears that first day she minded us because someone was a heartless bastard.

'They reckon she meant to kill the lot of us,' I'd said to Lyn.

Lyn, stony-faced, didn't defend Mum; neither did Dad. So I thought it must be true.

I took their package outside and threw it in the bin.

In my blue hour I saw visions. Mum flushed, flustered, as she says to me, 'Don't tell your father.' I go through each moment of the accident, but that's the only sentence I can find: 'Don't tell your father.' For weeks, in the sleepless early morning, that's all that comes to me. Finally, once I've given up, another memory surfaces, one that's not linked to the car or the accident. It's of a day I came home from school to find pots and pans pulled from the cupboards and cutlery piled on the bench in disarray. Mandy, who'd walked in the door behind me, shoved me out of the way.

'What's going on?'

'A surprise.' David raised a wooden spoon. 'A cake for Dad.'

'It's not his birthday.'

'That's why it's a surprise.'

It was a rush to bake the cake before he got home. Mum tied tea towels over our uniforms and melted the butter. I poured the flour and cocoa, Mandy the milk. We each had one egg to crack and David stirred.

'What colour icing do you think?'

I chose green but orange got more votes and the cake was perfect, with small silver balls and hundreds and thousands.

'Dad's late,' Mum said.

We ran to the window to look through the venetians then begged Mum for a sliver, just a taste of the cake before bedtime. Mum relented and raised the knife. Our backs were turned to the door so we didn't notice Dad at first.

'Surprise!' We made up for it with volume, glad we hadn't sliced through the cake yet.

Dad did look surprised, mouth open. His eyes swept from us to Mum. 'Teeny,' he said – her pet name. It came out like 'sorry'.

'Go to bed kids.' Mum's voice was low.

We scrambled between them, whined, begged. There was the cake.

Mum picked up the knife and slapped the flat of the blade through the icing. Bits flew everywhere. 'Go,' she said.

I looked at Dad but his eyes were on Mum.

In the morning Mum got up early and threw the cake in the garbage tin out the back. She put the lid on tight and looked towards the road, then back when she saw me watching. She hesitated, hands on her hips. 'Don't tell your father,' she said.

14.

The vanishing point

Summer 1933

Hang on, I might have missed . . . I want to rub that bit out . . .
This thing's not working.

•

*Biographer's note: Muriel tried to erase the first few minutes of this
tape (#9) but had trouble depressing the buttons on the recorder. The
first couple of sentences are intact. She begins by saying she will talk
about the summer of 1933. This is followed by static and some cursing.
The tape becomes indistinct for the next few minutes, although a few
words are discernible. She says 'muddy' more than once.*

*It's not clear if she changed her mind as to the date she wished to
talk about. Her original intent may have been to begin with 1933, but
some of the events she refers to occurred earlier, between 1930 and 1933.*

She mentions this period of her life again in tapes that follow, but not in any detail. Some correspondence from that period has survived. I've included what's available.

•

The Ridge
Southern Highlands

September 1931

My dear Muriel,

Your letter of the 12th reached us a few days ago and was as good as a cryptic crossword. I could barely make head nor tail of it. All your talk about the need to wear men's trousers and shirts. I understand if it keeps you out of strife, but if it gets you into fights then I can hardly see the point.

You don't tell us what part of the country you're in. The postmark was smudged, so no hints there. Tommy guesses Queensland, although he says they're pulling your leg about the plane. No such aircraft exists. Not yet anyway.

We've spent most of the winter in hibernation up here at the ridge. Father has gone hawk's eye on the assets and says he can do without my acumen for the present. He thinks I'm up here fixing the garden. It's very cold, being on the outer. Especially when the woodchopper can't keep pace (Tommy has grown as fat and sleek as a cat). On top of that, the fare is unvaried. Toast and jam, mostly.

My main task, in between toasting the bread and badgering Tommy to cut the wood, is to give out crusts and twists of tea to the stragglers that knock at our door. There's a regular line-up and ours is such a lonely old road. Tommy says they've marked the gate, but I guess people have to get what they can get, anywhere they can get it.

As for the garden, I've employed someone to fix that. It's all dirt at the moment but will be full of colour next time you're here.

We miss you, Muriel. Your letter didn't say much. As you seem intent on leaving us in the dark as to your whereabouts, I'll send this via Alice.

All our love.

PS The wattle is from Tommy.

PPS You are such a fiend, Moo, to up and leave the way you did.

I am not at

The Ridge

Southern Highlands

December 1931

My dearest Muriel,

Hip hip hooray! Back in the good books with Dad!

And while I'm assessing properties around the city, Tommy's flown off on one of his jaunts, to get away from everything. These bankruptcies really do favour us, Moo. Father says I have become quite greedy and I can only agree. So, no arguments from you please! It's just a few pounds and it gives me reason to feel pious.

I met an old friend of yours in the city. Do you remember Tozzi? I'm sure I've mentioned him before. He puts canvasses aside for me to look at. The best, or so he claims, but it's the same old dreary stuff. Nothing as good as yours. I give him a few coins to keep me in mind and he makes up the shortfall in gossip.

Anyway, I was in his studio last week when in walked a rather dashing figure. Your Adam Black. He swaggered in carrying the most atrocious cane I've ever seen! Tozzi introduced us. I must say, he's rather ill-mannered. Not that this will come as a surprise to you. He behaved very much as you said he does. Aloof; quite rude really. Barely nodded his head and left before I did, as if my presence was an inconvenience to him. Tozzi reveres the man, but then a little arrogance goes a long way with Tozzi.

Your story, by the way, the one about the blood tree and the blind dingo, is far too tall a tale to be believed. Although I do like the sketch that came with it.

I wish you'd come see us, Muriel, or tell us where you are so we can come and see you. Tommy and I rub along but it's not the same.

I won't say anymore but send all my love.

Write to me as soon as you can.

C

Claudine's father believed his daughter as good as any man, better than most. 'Shove it up their Khybers when I'm gone. Daft, pig-nosed bastards.' Which explains the money he left her and Tommy. I didn't hear too much said about the mother, other than she liked to play the piano, although she wasn't particularly accomplished at it.

Claudine and Tommy got married in the spring of 1932, six months after the Sydney Harbour Bridge opened. Claudine joked they'd name their first two kids Archie and Bridget in honour of it. News of the wedding was everywhere: in the papers, on the wireless and in people's conversations. I might have received an invitation – I guess I did. But it was Alice who had the yen to go and see it, not me.

'You'll come with me though, won't you? Just for a look.' I promised I would. Then Alice got sick and couldn't go.

'Come back and tell me about it. Every detail.' By then Alice had moved into a poky little ground-floor flat in Potts Point; if you stood on the tips of your toes and leaned out the window, you could catch a glimpse of the water. She still worked for Maggie. Business went on much as it had, despite the Depression, and Alice had the idea she'd take over once Maggie retired.

As for the wedding, it attracted a crowd. I was in among the spectators, pressed six feet deep between the church gardens and the road.

'Nothing like a spring wedding.'

'Did you see the motor? A Roller, Bert said.'

I pulled my hat low.

'Have you seen the bridesmaids?'

A girl shoved her way through the thick of everything. She scraped an elbow along my ribs, looked up, frowned, then nudged me a second time before she pushed forward to the road.

'Couldn't have ordered a better day.'

'Yes, just the weather for it.'

Perfect weather – if you focused on the northern half of the sky; but if you turned your head to the south you couldn't help but notice the dark clouds gathered on the horizon. The crowd surged left then craned their necks, waiting for something to happen.

'Seven.' Bridesmaids that is, each a different colour. They walked across the church lawn, the skirts of their dresses blown about like curtains in a sudden gust.

'That breeze has sprung up.'

'Bit of a relief. I'm sweltering.'

'You don't think it'll rain?'

A flower girl darted from behind a hedge like a bee, chasing the page boy. But where was the bride? Rumours started, buffeted by the rising wind.

The groom was a womaniser.

The bride wore trousers and smoked.

The groom was a war hero.

The bride had money and the groom was after it.

'And he'll get it all right, once that ring's on her finger.'

Bridesmaids fussed back and forth trying to get the flower girl out of the dirt and the page boy down from the tree. Claudine's mother emerged from the church briefly, a sure sign something was wrong. The sky changed. It became a thick, low mass that darkened as we watched.

Old man Worthington had put his foot down.

The groom was found in the wrong place with his trousers down.

No, it was the bride who'd done the dirty.

Either way, the wedding was off.

Hurrah! Someone raised their hat as a Bentley swung around the curve. Claudine, all smiles and framed by the window, cupped her hand and waved like royalty. The crowd nudged, nodded and I told you so'ed. The rain held off until the driver, now out of the Bentley, opened the rear door. Then it began, fat, smacking drops that broke like eggs. The bridesmaids rushed forward to the motorcar, then ran back without the bride, dragging the muddy page boy and the resisting flower girl into the church alcove.

There was a frenzy. A passing foot clipped my ankle as the mob bolted for trees and eaves and newspapers. Rain seeped through my hat, dripping from my hair and fingers. I pushed against a flow of stragglers, knocking hats and bodies askew. Alongside the Bentley, the driver opened an umbrella and held it high for the bride. Claudine floated from the car like mist.

It had been my intention to stay at a distance. Claudine and I had fought in the Southern Highlands and as far as I was concerned, nothing would be right between us again. Then I saw her in all her finery and thought how the price of a simple canvas was beyond me. There. I admit it. I darted forward and reached under the umbrella, grabbing a handful of ivory silk and beads and a piece of Claudine's flesh. The driver gripped my shoulder. I turned my dripping face towards him and he released me and grinned.

'Freddie.' I laughed like a maniac.

Claudine pulled my sodden frame beneath the umbrella. She clenched my hands between hers then bent and touched her lips to my knuckles.

'Where have you been?'

Rain gushed like a broken pipe from the edge of the black circle that Freddie held over us. Claudine took the handle while he fetched a fur-collared coat from the car. He passed it to her as water funnelled from his elbow. She draped it around my shoulders.

'I'll tell Tommy that you came.' She said it twice above the rain then beckoned with her finger. I bent my head and touched my lips to hers. Freddie looked away as she placed her hands around the back of my head. 'Oh, Moo. You know this is all for you.' Claudine kissed my lips and nose then shrugged and thrust the handle of the umbrella at me before she ran towards the bridesmaids, huddled in the alcove like a squashed rainbow. The outline of her body appeared through the wet silk of her dress before she reached them. What a sight for Tommy as she walked up the aisle. Freddie watched too until she was safely inside the church then offered to drop me wherever I wanted to go.

'I'll walk.'

I tried to return the coat and the umbrella but he held up his palms and shook his head. 'It's not worth my hide. She has a temper.' He looked towards the church and laughed as if he enjoyed her temper.

The hail started then. Small spiky dots that hit the ground with a ping and I was glad of the coat and umbrella.

When I got to Potts Point I was steaming beneath my layers. Alice opened the door, looking as healthy as I'd ever seen her. 'There's not a thing wrong with you, Miss Cooney,' I declared. 'Why didn't you come?'

She shrugged. 'It was you that needed to go, not me.' She helped me out of the coat and gave me a towel to dry my hair. 'You're for a bath.'

Alice dragged a metal tub across the floor and set a pan of water on the gas ring while I undressed, wrapping myself in the towel. I was lulled by the sound of the gas jet and the water coming to the boil and the rain beneath it all.

'We've put a gas bath heater in at Maggie's.' Alice poured the water into the tub, a bent stalk of grass. 'Takes all the work out of it.' She straightened, hand on her hip. 'Muriel!'

'I'm awake,' I said. Though I was more asleep than awake and felt shaky.

To keep myself going I told Alice the story of how I'd run from Claudine's house in the Southern Highlands the year before, out through the scrub and along the dirt track towards the railway station, asking myself at each step if Tommy and Claudine had noticed yet. Were they awake or still asleep? Were they wondering where I was?

I caught the overnight mail train to Central Station in Sydney, carrying the canvas bag that Tommy gave me the first day I flew with him, Constance Mawson's drawstring purse tucked inside it. She'd embroidered a four-leafed clover onto the calico and every time I saw clover after that, I thought of the feral dogs chomping on her fingers.

When I got to Central I bought a ticket to the North Coast.

'You could have come here.' Alice said.

'They would've found me.'

On the train I shared a compartment with a mother and child. The child – I couldn't tell whether it was a boy or a girl – mumbled something as I took my seat, then wailed as its mother slapped the travel blanket that covered their legs.

'But she *does*! She smells.' The child eyed me. A boy maybe. Though perhaps it was a girl.

'It's the turps,' I said.

The mother placed a finger on her lips and hissed at the child.

'I paint.'

They watched me through half-closed lids, then the child pinched their nose and flapped a hand, trying to wave away the smell. I stood, catching my balance against the motion of the train. The sound of another slap and wail followed me through the sliding doors. I lurched along the corridor until I found a seat in another compartment. Alone, I fished the rag from my pocket, stuck together with paint like a used handkerchief. It smelled of turps and the medium I used. I wondered if Claudine and Tommy had realised yet that I'd gone for good.

Steam rose as Alice mixed cold water into the hot. Her fingers dangled in the brew. 'Just right. Get in.' My skin prickled with goosebumps as I dropped the towel, stepped over the rim and kneeled tentatively. I wrung the washer out and placed it across the back of my neck.

'Are you going to talk to me, Muriel, or am I supposed to guess what's got your tongue?'

Waxy blobs receded into a line – the horizon. Vibrations rose through the seat of the train like bubbles then fanned along the window towards my cheek. The earth grew redder and the trees taller. 'I got out at Coffs Harbour,' I said as Alice topped the tub with more hot water.

The mother and her child were already on the platform. The mother scolded the child as they trundled its length. Sacks and crates were unloaded from one of the end carriages onto a trolley, lifted by workmen who tossed them high in the air, all efficiency and routine. I could have slipped in among them if I'd been wearing my trousers. A broad-shouldered woman with a plain hat got off the train in front of me. I followed her through the exit, past a sulky and a dray. 'Are you going anywhere near Bellingen?' I asked the sulky, the dray, then a man and a woman as they got into a motorcar. The man got out again and opened the door for me.

Coffs Harbour smelled of salt but the valley, when we reached it, carried the scent of the Bellinger River. Birds flew in and around the canopy, a multitude of greens and reds and watery hues. Everything a silent film beyond the rumbling motor.

The motorcar dislodged me, its engine running, below a sign that read SEFTON'S GUESTHOUSE. The house, set back from the main road about a mile or two outside of town, was fronted by a wide verandah, a scattering of chairs, a small round table and a bell beside a flyscreen door.

I got out of the tub and dried myself then lay down on Alice's bed.

'I can make you something to eat.' Alice said.

I meant to answer but must have fallen asleep. When I woke Alice was sitting in a chair beside the bed, her ear red as if it had been slapped.

'Get in.' I patted the space beside the wall. Alice extinguished the lamp then got under the covers beside me. We dozed, waking as my elbow clunked against Alice's knee.

'So that's all you have to tell me?' Alice said. 'There's nothing else?'

I rummaged through my memories and came across tea and fruitcake in the summer house at Sefton's. It was late, almost dark. Somewhere in the house a lullaby was being sung in a clear tenor voice. It stopped then started again from the beginning as the sun angled the last of its light across the Bellinger River, a deep crimson that fell on the still water. The same colour Claudine had daubed onto my canvas that last day in the Southern Highlands.

'There.' She'd leaned over my arm, reaching towards the canvas with her coarse brush. Then kissed my neck. 'That's all it needed.'

'Huh. Don't expect me to believe you ran away because Claudine altered a painting.' The blanket arced over Alice then resettled with a hmmph. 'You've had harsher critics than her.'

'We argued.'

'Yes, you said. But what about?'

I turned on my side and Alice put her arms around my waist. 'Muriel, there's nothing you can't tell me.'

The rain was tetchy against the window and the air was dark and fibrous like the coat of a horse. I tried to imagine painting what I wanted to say and saw blotches of deep crimson with patchy black centres.

'I fell pregnant and I promised to give her the baby.'

Alice's breath was warm against my shoulder. 'You're not the first woman to give her child away, Muriel, and for good reason.'

'But I lost it.'

'I'm sorry . . .'

'Don't be. I wasn't.'

'You didn't want Claudine to have it?'

'Someone else maybe, not Claudine.'

We listened to the drip of water outside the window then Alice asked, 'What now?'

'She wants to continue on as my patron.'

'It's not as if she hasn't got plenty to spare.' Weary, Alice rolled onto her back, nudging me across the narrow width of the bed until I was on its edge.

'You know how it'll be though.'

'There'll be a way around the parts of it you don't like.' Alice was with me for a few more seconds before she fell asleep. I couldn't close my eyes. I couldn't sleep. I listened to Alice's breathing for as long as I could bear it. Claudine's coat was nearby, draped over the back of the chair. Alice sighed in her dreams as I put it on, found the knob of the door and walked out onto the street. The rising sun a thumbprint, the colour of burning metal.

15.

A cricked neck and blurred vision

December 1992

I heard the knock on the door just as the cat appeared with a present that she placed near my feet. I was in the rocking chair nursing Olivia and couldn't see what it was, but the stench jolted me. Olivia startled, arms thrown wide, mouth full of milk as she unlatched from my nipple.

Using my toe, I prodded the unrecognisable lump of decomposed flesh deposited by the cat. A maggot emerged, then another. I pushed my way out of the rocking chair, one breast exposed, Olivia crying, the cat trying to wind its way around my legs as I stumbled towards the door.

By the time I reached it, the mercenary – I couldn't remember his name in my sleep-deprived state – was already inside, though

I thought the door had been locked. I hadn't seen him since the day he brought me fish and chips, and I didn't know how he'd found me now.

'Take her, take her.' I handed Olivia to him and ran to the kitchen for a plastic bag. I put the carcass the cat had left in it, and with toilet paper wrapped around my hand I scraped up the remaining maggots. Then I took the lot to the bin, waving a big cheery hello to Mr Henley the neighbour, who stuck his head above the palings then ducked out of sight again.

Back inside, Olivia was asleep in Matthew, Matty, Matt's arms. *Don't call him the mercenary*, I warned myself.

Matt opened his mouth to speak then closed it again.

'What?'

He pointed to my breast, still exposed by the unlatched maternity bra, my T-shirt rolled neatly above it like a blind.

'Bloody hell. I waved to Mr Henley.'

Matt looked down at Olivia as I tucked myself in. 'She's quiet.'

'Not usually,' I said, miffed by her sudden calmness.

'It's the smell of the breast milk; makes them restless.'

'How do you know that?'

'I read it.'

I hadn't read anything for ages.

'I can sit with her if you need to do something.' He looked around. 'Where's your TV?'

'Don't have one.'

He raised an eyebrow. 'I've got half an hour.'

'Before what?'

'Before I have to get back to work.'

What sort of work would a mercenary do on a sunny day in Shellharbour? I looked at his clothes, grimed at their edges but not with blood. There wasn't time to ask. I tossed the contents of the nappy bucket into the washing machine, refilled it with Napisan, water and the next lot of nappies that lay curled on the floor. I flicked the kettle on, thinking a cuppa would be good, walked outside while it boiled to the letterbox, which was empty. I made sandwiches out of half-stale crispbreads I found in the back of the cupboard. I handed one to Matthew in exchange for Olivia. Thirty minutes isn't long. Shorter than the cycle on the washing machine.

The next morning a TV appeared on the front step still in its box (along with a loaf of bread and carton of milk). Stolen, I was sure of it. So, I was now the receiver of stolen goods and too tired and too pleased to do anything about it.

Matt was back a week later. I was sorting out Muriel's paperwork at the time and was irritated when I heard the knock on the door.

'What are you doing here?'

He removed his boots and stepped into the hall in his red-and-white football socks.

'I'm working around the corner and,' he held up a carton of milk, 'I've brought my own.'

'I don't have time.'

'I'll make it.'

I flicked my hand towards the kettle and went back to the table. Not long after, a cup was placed at my elbow. I looked up to see Matt holding a grizzly Olivia.

'She was crying,' he said in response to my scowl.

I hadn't heard her. How was that possible? Had I been that absorbed?

'Has she got a teething ring?'

'In the fridge.'

Matt looked for it while I picked up the lukewarm tea and sipped – a neglectful mother.

He wiped Olivia's face with a washer, then handed her the teething ring. 'Pup's claiming that he could be this one's father,' he remarked.

'Pup's a dickhead.'

'Yeah, but that doesn't mean he shouldn't pay his way.'

'What else does he say? That I'm easy, so it could be anybody's? Do you think I'd want someone like him around even if he was the father?'

'You've given up your job?'

Olivia dropped the teething ring. Matt caught it and held on to it while she gnawed it.

'I've found another.'

'It's his money we're talking about, not him.'

'It's him *I'm* talking about. Besides, it's really none of your business.'

Matt put Olivia in the bouncer. 'She needs a change,' he said and left.

I knocked the dregs of the tea onto the floor with my elbow and bent to mop it up with a spare nappy, angry with myself. If I didn't watch out, Muriel, as dead as she was, would be the only friend I had left. At least the only one I could talk to.

I changed the nappy, ran a comb through my hair, washed my face, buckled Olivia into the Laser and drove to the shops, unbuckled Olivia, took her into the takeaway, bounced her up and down while we waited for the order, returned to the car and buckled her in. She was all gurgles and waving hands in the rear-view mirror. We spotted Matt on the next street, unloading plants from the tray of his ute onto a wheelbarrow. A mercenary landscaper?

By way of apology, I'd bought two takeaway coffees and, on the return, pulled in behind Matt's ute. I waggled the cup at him. He opened the front passenger door and looked at Olivia, rather than me.

'Get in,' I invited him.

'I'm sweaty.'

'I'm sorry about earlier.'

He folded himself into the car. 'I shouldn't have stuck my nose in.'

'If you like mashed banana and yoghurt, you should come over for dinner one night.' I put the key in the ignition and revved the engine. He took the hint and got out.

•

Annie rang from a payphone in Perth that night.

'I'm thinking of leaving,' she said.

'And going where?'

'Maybe Darwin.'

I told her about Matt dropping by. It turned out she was the one who'd given him my new address.

'He didn't tell you?'

No, there'd been no mention of it, nor that he'd met up with Annie before she left and they'd screwed.

'I thought you knew.'

'Why? Because I'm telepathic?'

'I thought I told you. I'm sure I told you.'

'I'd remember something like that.'

There was a clink as she dropped another coin into the slot. 'It was just before I left. I saw him at the pub, or maybe it was at the Workers' Club, and we talked. We were both pretty drunk. I'm surprised he remembered the address.'

'You just said you slept with him.'

'Oh yeah, that too. He's got a maths degree.'

I untangled the cord of the phone as she talked. 'Maths?'

'I think it was maths. Or maybe physics. Or phys ed. It could have been law. It's a bit of a blur. He was good in the sack. I remember that.' She paused. 'I didn't realise you were interested in him in that way.'

'I'm not. He's just an old friend.'

It wasn't their fling, that bothered me. It was the secrets. Lyn and Dad's affair, Muriel's supposed death and now Matt and Annie. All riddles to be solved.

'But you, you're supposed to tell me things like that.'

'I thought I had.'

16.

Call it what you want

January 1993

I'd listened to all of the tapes, gone through the correspondence and read everything I could find in the library, then stewed over Muriel's words. Convince Lexie Tanner of what? That the canvasses in the back room were painted by the real Muriel Kemp or something more – that the post 1936 Muriel Kemp was still a genius? I didn't see any of Muriel's work, other than the first two paintings of the triptych, until after she'd died and I'd moved into the house, wild passionate canvasses that stopped my breath. There was one I kept going back to, thickly painted and clawed in parts, almost threadbare. An old woman's face. Not Muriel, but someone else, or perhaps it was meant to be her in symbolic form. Either way, it was while standing in front of this painting in the first week of the new year that I planned my next move.

I rang Lexie Tanner, the director of the Muriel Kemp Foundation.

'I apologise for the intrusion,' I said, in a clipped professional voice. 'But I'm the executor of Muriel Kemp's will and it was her wish that I contact you. She left a package for you in my care.'

Lexie Tanner must have thought she had a nutter on the other end of the phone.

'Muriel Kemp? The only Muriel Kemp I know is deceased and I see no reason for any other Muriel Kemp to leave me a package.'

'The bequest is to the foundation, rather than to you personally.'

'I see. Are you able to tell me what the bequest is?'

'Paintings. A triptych she wanted to donate to your collection.'

'That's a very kind offer, Ms . . . ?'

'Cooper. Jane Cooper.'

'Ms Cooper. And while I appreciate her desire to donate to a foundation that bears her name, I'm afraid the Muriel Kemp Foundation only collects paintings by Muriel Kemp.'

The telephone buzzed down the receiver. A bad line. 'Yes, I understand that.'

'Are you saying the triptych is a Muriel Kemp?'

'It's not the whole triptych, just the first two paintings. I'd prefer to explain in person, if I could.'

Silence.

'They're original Muriel Kemps,' I insisted.

'Do you know when these paintings were purchased?'

'They weren't actually purchased.'

'They were a gift then?'

'Well, no.'

'Ms Cooper, I'm–'

'They are original Muriel Kemps, Ms Tanner. Muriel painted them.'

'You're not trying to imply your Muriel is *the* Muriel Kemp?'

'Let me expl–'

'Are you aware Ms Cooper, that Muriel Kemp, *the artist*, died in 1936.'

'Yes, look. I know that's what the history books say but–'

'Not just the history books Ms Cooper. There were witnesses to her death.'

'A witness, Ms Tanner. One. There is also proof that Muriel didn't die in that plane crash and when you see the paintings she left behind, you'll understand . . .'

There was a click as Lexie Tanner hung up. Who could blame her? Since Claudine's death, Lexie Tanner was considered the foremost authority on Muriel Kemp and her work – and as far as she knew, Muriel had died sixty-odd years ago.

•

Two weeks after Lexi Tanner hung up on me, I left the car near the railway station at Dunmore. Loaded with cooled boiled water, mashed banana, yogurt, teething gel, toys, nappies, pilchers, wipes, zinc cream, spare clothes, bunny rugs, the stench of sponged off vomit – on me not Olivia – and a cranky baby who'd slept in for the first time and had to be woken, I stumbled as I ran along the platform with the pram. I was frazzled, but we made it. The early-morning train rattled us to Central Station, where the fun began. I got the pram off the train okay, but the brakes kept jamming as I pushed it towards Surry Hills and the Muriel Kemp Foundation, located in the Worthington Museum on the corner of Campbell and Samuel streets.

The foundation was full of light: large glass windows, wooden floors and white-painted walls. It was a reprieve from the summer heat.

'Judith Greene,' I told the woman at reception. 'I have an appointment with Ms Tanner.'

'Of course, Mrs Greene. She shouldn't be too long.'

I sat on one of three black-and-chrome chairs arranged against the wall. Olivia was blissfully asleep, which gave me the chance to rehearse my lines. Except I dozed off.

'I remember what that was like.' The receptionist waited as I wiped the dribble from my mouth then led the way to a door. 'Mrs Greene.' She ushered me through.

Lexie Tanner looked too pleasant to be the person I'd talked to on the phone. 'Please, take a seat.' Her teeth were white, her smile warm. She seemed pleased to see me, if not overly glad to see a now awake and squawking Olivia.

'I understand you've brought something for me to look at?' She checked her notes. 'Your grandmother lived in Surry Hills at the same time as Muriel Kemp, is that right?' She raised her voice over the baby's noise.

'Great-grandmother,' I corrected her, holding a rattle for Olivia to chew on.

'Paintings or even sketches from that period are a rare find, Mrs Greene.' There was a glow to her smile. 'And while I'm happy to take a look, we shouldn't get our hopes up.'

'I didn't bring the painting, just photos.'

'Okay, but at some point I'll need to take a look at the work itself. To start with, though, perhaps you could tell me what you know of its history. How did your great-grandmother come to own it?'

Instead of replying, I handed her the photos and waited for her reaction. Surely, she would see something in them.

Lexie picked up the photos and flipped through them. 'So you have two paintings. Is that right?'

'Yes, there's two of them.'

Lexie's eyes slithered over the images then upward. She sighed, 'You're the one that rang a couple of weeks ago, about the triptych painted by some old woman you knew.'

'And as you can see—'

'No. Really, I can't.' She pushed the photos back across the table towards me.

'If you saw the canvasses themselves.'

'Unfortunately, you're not the first person to be convinced they had a genuine Kemp in their possession. I'm sorry to disappoint you.' She picked up a pen and lowered her head, dismissive.

'This is my address,' I persisted, placing a folded piece of paper on the desk. 'Muriel wanted the foundation to have the canvasses. I think you'll find they're worth the look.'

I rose abruptly and wheeled the pram from the room. I didn't look at the receptionist as I pushed Olivia through the foyer and out into the heat, deflated by Lexie's lack of interest. Maybe if I'd shown her the passports or the letters she would have been persuaded. But all of them were issued or written before 1936 and could have been acquired. What I needed was evidence, post 1936, to prove Muriel was still alive.

•

There was rain that night. It hit the bedroom window like blue metal, but it was Olivia who woke me with her grizzling. She eventually settled but I couldn't fall back asleep so I dragged the tape recorder out and listened to an early conversation between myself and Muriel.

'What would you have done, if I hadn't turned up?'

'You did turn up.'

'But what if I hadn't? Who would have written your story then?'

'I don't know. Somebody.'

'But you hadn't found somebody – before I turned up, I mean.'

There was a rustle on the tape; Muriel moving around in her chair, annoyed at my persistence.

'I didn't need anyone before you turned up.'

'But–'

'That's enough, Jane.'

'But–'

'No. No more on the subject. Not everything's your business.'

Claudine's death triggered this need in Muriel to have her story told. I'm sure of it.

But why, I longed to ask, *when for so many years you didn't care?*

I stayed awake listening to Muriel's tapes, playing one after the other. But the tapes contained only half the story. She'd narrated the beginning and I knew the end, but there was not enough of a middle to determine what happened to her after the plane accident. Not long before dawn, sick of Muriel, I crawled into bed, just as Olivia woke once more, ready to be fed and changed.

After the feed, I took her into the garden, perched on my hip, and pointed to the birds as they fled from the cat's tinkling bell, and then to a dog that wandered along the nature strip past an expensive car parked in front of the house. A maroon BMW.

'Shit,' I said to Olivia. 'It's Lexie Tanner for sure.' I ran into the house and strapped her into the bouncer. I moved the nappies from the bathroom into the laundry out the back. I turned the tap on over a sink full of dishes, brushed cat hair off the lounge, smelled the milk – on the turn, but it would do, wiped surfaces in the bathroom, took a quick shower and got out of the trackies I'd worn for far too many days without washing. To put on what? I didn't fit into most of my non-maternity clothes and Olivia had vomited on the dress I'd worn to Sydney the day before. I picked out an elastic-waisted skirt and a swing top. They would have to do.

'Fuck. Fuck it, Olivia.'

I looked through the venetian blinds that faced the road. There was no sign of movement, no signs of a body occupying the car. Maybe it wasn't her at all. It might be someone visiting Mr Henley next door, I reasoned.

I switched on the TV, changed channels to the ABC and fiddled with the aerial to minimise the static.

I sang along to *Bananas in Pyjamas*; Olivia was captivated. It was only when I stopped, that I heard the knocking.

'Fuck.'

It was her at the door. Lexie. There was no smile, no greeting, just: 'I heard you up and about.'

Her clothes – mossy green skirt with matching jacket, cream shirt and shoes – looked slept in. Her face was immaculate above the rumple. As was the rest of her. Designer sunglasses pushed back from her forehead, gold jewellery, hair in a French roll.

'I've decided to accept your invitation to see the paintings.'

'Take them,' I said. 'They're yours. The foundation's.'

She drilled me with a stare. Olivia gurgled in the background. There was a sting as my milk let down.

'First things first. Let me take a look at them.'

I opened the screen door. The edge of it scraped against the moss green of her outfit. She ignored the dirty line, removed her sunglasses and squinted as she stepped over the threshold into the gloom of the corridor. The corridor opened onto the combined living area and kitchen. Lexie glanced at Olivia, strapped into her bouncer.

'Tea, coffee?' I offered.

She looked at her watch. 'I have to get back.'

I led her into the kitchen, where I pointed out the two canvasses tilted against the wall. She glanced at them. 'The light, would you mind?'

I switched it on.

She picked up the first canvas and bent her neck over it.

'It's well done, but . . .' She shook her head.

'What?'

'It's not the real thing.'

'You've barely looked at it,' I protested. 'Surely these days, with the forensic testing that's available . . .'

'Ms Cooper.'

'Jane.'

'Ms Cooper, Muriel Kemp did indeed paint a triptych similar in its narrative to this one. The third piece of that triptych is already

215

in the possession of the Muriel Kemp Foundation and the first two canvasses are indeed missing. So, you can understand the necessity of my coming here this morning to ascertain whether these are indeed the ones we've been looking for.

'The two canvasses in question disappeared during the thirties. The only information we have on those canvasses is the detailed descriptions written when they were catalogued. Those descriptions do not match the compositions of these two canvasses.'

I threw my hands in the air. 'How accurate is the catalogue?'

'The description was written by Claudine Worthington herself.'

Claudine again. It was my turn to shake my head. 'Couldn't these two be part of a different triptych?'

'It's possible, but unlikely. As I said, they're well done – and you're right, we'd need to undertake further testing and analysis to be completely sure. But I have to tell you, Ms Cooper, I was warned that these paintings might turn up at some point.'

'Warned? That these two exact paintings might turn up?' That didn't seem possible.

'I'm afraid so. They turned up once before, in the fifties. That was before my time, of course, but there are records of the assessment and descriptions of the paintings.'

'Who was the artist?'

'A woman called Muriel Rose. Perhaps that's who your Muriel is, Ms Cooper.'

•

That afternoon I curled around Olivia on the bed and slept. There was no relief in either the sleep or Lexie's assertions. My Muriel – a fraud. I woke knowing that I had to at least consider Lexie's implications; forger, delusional old woman, imposter? Muriel hadn't made things easy by omitting years – decades, when she recorded the sequence that made up her life.

Restless, I took Olivia into the back room and crouched in front of the painting of the pregnant Madonna wading in the night surf with her friend. The Annie in the painting glowed like a beacon. She looked out from the canvas, her gaze directed through me, rather than at me. In contrast, the Madonna gazed over her shoulder, away from the surf, towards the shore. The glow of moonlight oozing from her hair like an ill-fitting halo.

I didn't buy it. Lexie's certainty that my Muriel wasn't who she said she was or her story about the descriptions of the two missing paintings in the catalogue – something didn't fit. Besides, it wasn't only those two paintings my old woman wanted recognised. It was all the paintings in the back room. Original paintings, nothing like the earlier work produced by the historical Muriel Kemp but just as brilliant. I cursed Muriel. If only she'd told me everything.

17.

The eyes and teeth of it

Summer 1936

The Old Farmhouse
Gerringong

September 1935

Dearest Muriel,
 You have to come. It's all greens and blues and briny air and it's
been arranged.
 Yours always,
 Claudine

●

The old farmhouse in Gerringong was a haven at first. Endless skies,
hills and ocean. When I conjure it nowadays I fly in, dropping my
speed to sixty mph as I circle the stubbled paddocks, no stumps or

holes, no boggy patches. No obstacles. I hover a few feet above the ground then rise for one last circuit before landing into the wind.

A woman dressed in a man's shirt and trousers, hair tied back in a scarf, waves a bright red handkerchief at me. No, no, no, that's not right. Because I'd be the woman dressed in a man's shirt and trousers, waving a red cloth and here I am – flying the plane.

I cut the engine. Summer seeps beneath my jacket and leather helmet as I push my goggles back, glide over the cockpit and out of the Moth. Grass swelters, flies cling and there's the sound of a cow calling for her calf as I chock the wheels. Cattle like the taste of the dope painted on the fabric of the wings and can cause a lot of damage. I look around but the nearby paddocks are empty.

A lot will be made of the work that I painted in Gerringong. *The lost paintings*, Claudine called them once they were retrieved and made ready for the 1982 retrospective. They were nothing compared to what I painted afterwards. In 1981 I sent her a small canvas with a note: *From the other side of the Styx.* I wanted her to acknowledge what she'd really lost.

•

I went to the retrospective uninvited. It had been decades since I'd seen Claudine other than in the pages of the papers. She was well-groomed in an expensive way. But, in her attempt to look more youthful than she was, she looked reined in, unnatural. In comparison, I resembled Mallee scrub. Still, she recognised me. Even without the red hair.

'What are you doing here?' Champagne sloshed over my sleeve as she dragged me through a side door to the back of the building. 'You can't stay.'

'The painting I sent you, that last one. It's not here.'

'Of course it's not here.' Her well-drawn eyes glistened. 'How could it be?'

'It's better than anything else you've hung.'

'This is *your* work you're talking about.'

But it wasn't. Not anymore. She put her hands around the back of my head and pushed her face into mine. 'I warned you you'd get nowhere without me.'

I lashed out – slapped her face. 'You'd rather I failed than succeed without you.'

'You couldn't succeed without me,' she hissed as she cooled her burning cheek against the rings on her hand. 'You've proven that.'

•

Back at the farmhouse, that future was a long way off. I ascended the steps and paced the length of the verandah, past the meat safe swaying from its horizontal beam. A buzz of blowflies rose then resettled as I opened the farmhouse door and moved into the pools of harsh, concentrated light that poured in from its northern angles. That was Claudine's work – the light. She'd had skylights put in, and extra windows.

I saw the woman standing at an easel on the other side of a cluttered table, her back to me, hands and fingernails in the paint. Sniffing like a dog, I nudged my nose into the crook of her neck then down the back of her shirt, my tongue beneath its cloth licking, my hands on her hips, digging into her flesh while she continued to fingerpaint like a child.

I dragged her away from the canvas, mopped her hands with a rag then led her to the door, where we exchanged the pungent odour of the room for the clear muggy air outside. Clanging against each other like coat hangers, we walked across the grass. She helped me unclip and fold back the wings of the Moth before we wheeled the machine into the barn and parked it beside a dark green Dodge Tourer.

You see how I mix things up? I'm Tommy as well as myself. Or perhaps it's not Tommy but Alice I'm thinking of. Tommy was a bastard when it came to Alice. They were too similar to really like each other. 'She drags you down; you're better off without her,' he told me. She said the same about him.

What else do I remember about the old farmhouse? Cracked grey linoleum decorated with yellow and purple bouquets, their long green stems tied in dark pink ribbons. And the furniture, what there was of it. A sink and bench, a Metters wood stove, the icebox in the corner, the table at the centre of the room stacked with palettes, paints, brushes, trowels, glass jars, squeezed-out tubes of paint, feathers, seed pods, dried-out grasses tied with string, a small branch from a tree, roughly torn squares of hessian and pieces of scattered masonite. Flat surfaces were layered with thick corrugations of paint, mixtures that had dried in peaks like an escarpment. Books sat in piles on chairs and on the floor. An anatomy and physiology book with coloured plates lay open on top of a listing hill. The place smelled of turps and paint and ashes from the wood stove and sometimes the flesh of a model that had rotted before I'd finished with it.

There were two bedrooms off a short hall. The second bedroom was smaller than the first, with a single cast-iron bed, lumpy mattress and a packing case covered with a doily that served as a side table.

Everything was smeared with greasy dust. The first bedroom was much the same but larger.

There was the noise of blowflies, mosquitos, cicadas and frogs, especially around the water tank, and there was the scuttle of skinks and blue tongues everywhere. A big red-bellied black snake made its way into the house in the summer. I didn't notice until it skimmed past my foot as I stood in front of the easel. By then it was on its way out. I picked leeches off my shins and ticks from warm moist crevices and small black beetles from my hair.

'It's too much,' I said the first week, scratching and pulling and shooing, but then there was the sound of the ocean and the rain and the soft dark flesh of the sky, dimpled by stars and the clear grey moon and Claudine's offer of an exhibition to be held in 1936. And there was Tommy and his interest in racing cars along the compact sand of nearby Seven Mile Beach, a location previously used as a runway by Kingsford Smith in his record flight to New Zealand, and by Wizard Smith, who broke the land speed record there in 1929. You'll have to change your name to Smith. Before I got a chance to say that, Tommy arrived at the farm in a red-and-white Ford V-8 – a standard model that he'd modified. I was going to tell you that I hadn't seen Tommy since I'd escaped the Southern Highlands, but that would be a lie. I'd seen him all right, more than I'd wanted to.

In *The Last Man*, Adam Black referred to Tommy as 'the Drunken Lover'. Adam hadn't met him and never would, but Sydney was a small place and stories got around. In his book Adam recounted how Tommy had flown over a charity picnic organised by Claudine. He flew in low, skittling the sparkling burgundy from some of Sydney's finest hands, then landed lopsided, one wing removed by a eucalypt that got in the way. As the crowd ran towards the biplane, he rose from the cockpit stark naked and offered to auction himself to the highest bidder. Adam told this story alongside the rumour that Tommy preferred the company of a renowned Campbell Street whore to his own wife. Adam meant me, not Alice.

In retaliation, I sketched a headless nude of Tommy, my lips and tongue brushing the fine line of hair that spiralled downwards from his belly button. Adam was in the sketch too – a shadowy background smudge, watching on. I posted it to him along with the typewritten title, *Kisses For My Lover the Drunk*. What could he say? I was long dead.

Tommy was a problem though. Even I had to admit it. He sought out Alice when I couldn't be found. He'd front up to her Potts Point flat or turn up at Campbell Street drunk and unruly, pissing on the front door, punching one of the customers, shouting obscenities until he was dragged away by one of the brothel's guards, who beat him within an arse crack of his life. He didn't care and went back for more. I was called upon to settle things before Alice lost her livelihood.

Where was I? Oh yes: Tommy arrived at the farm in his modified Ford V-8, a beautiful machine, tooting his horn, kicking up stones. I burst from the house. The screen door slapped like a shotgun blast as I ran across the verandah and jumped. 'Catch me!'

Tommy toppled backwards as we hit the ground. A tangle of limbs and hair. He was pinned beneath me. 'Try and get out of that.' I manoeuvred my elbow into his sternum. He twisted sideways. A patch of grey whiskers caught the light. I wedged a hand beneath his shirt and followed with my lips, but Tommy didn't like to lose, not to me. He struggled, righting himself before lifting me off the ground. Staggering beneath my writhing weight, he tried to raise me to the sky, but lost his grip and dropped me. I rubbed the dirt and grass from my hands onto his shirt. I laughed as he pushed me against the door of the Ford and nuzzled my ear and neck.

'Get in. I'll show you how well I manage a fast machine.'

Before we set off in the Ford, I have to describe the landscape. Have to – because if you look at the paintings from the retrospective, you'll see the landscape was part of everything. When Lloyd Rees painted *The Road to Berry* he tamped down its greenness but kept its curves. So did Brett Whiteley in his eighties homage to Rees. I loved the green but agreed with Lloyd: you couldn't paint it like that. I rolled its lushness in crusts of salt and textured it with the winds that blew over the hills, much like Tommy in his red-and-white Ford. 'That's how you manage it,' I would say as I scratched a stick through a gob of thick paint that was meant to be him.

We drove to the southern end of Werri Beach and the wonder of the tidal pool. Holidaymakers swam and babies were dangled, the tips of their toes dipped in cool froth then pulled back from its nibble. Bathers sat on the sand, shadowed by hats, while families set up picnics further back where the shore turned into grass. The V-8 was an attraction.

'Do you race it, mister?' the smallest of a group of boys asked.

'Not me. It's Miss Kemp's motor. She's the racer.'

There was a general look of scepticism. The boy ran his hand over the paintwork. Tommy lifted him into the car for a 'test ride' and I got in beside him, hands on the wheel. I started the engine and there was a scrambling of arms and legs as bodies packed onto the running board and clung to the doors. Unable to lose any of them, I accelerated over the bumps and beeped the horn, encouraging them to yell.

A couple of fathers were talking to Tommy on our return. He introduced me as Miss Kemp, saying, 'She works as a driver for Movietone.' The men shook their heads and laughed.

Afterwards, we found a patch of grass overlooking Seven Mile Beach and Crooked River. Tommy spread a blanket on the ground then reclined, swigging from a flask without offering me any.

'We could go north.' His gaze swept the view then he turned to face me, his vivid eyes scrunched against the glare.

'But . . .'

'Listen to me. Listen.' He leaned in, filling the space between us with his urgency. 'I've put money into a separate account. Not enough that she'll complain. But enough.'

'What about the exhibition?'

'You can still paint.'

'For who?'

Tommy leaned back and drew breath. His shoulders dropped from his ears. 'For yourself. I thought that was the point.'

I shook my head. 'You said you'd wait.'

'I said a lot of things.' He spoke in a low voice, the urgency gone. He turned his gaze back to the view and took another swig from his flask.

'You're angry.'

'I'm not.' He lay back on the blanket, shutting his eyes against further talk. He slept, twitching like a dog as he dreamed. Sometimes I wonder 'what if?' – but then what's the point of that?

Tommy let me drive the Ford back to the farmhouse, where I was comforted by the odour of turps and paint and the brewing smell of something as it festered. I sought out my unfinished canvas. Tommy came in the door behind me, saying – I don't know what he was saying, his voice was a background murmur, like birdsong. His hand on my shoulder stopped me from getting to my brush and palette.

I must have frowned. Is that what did it, the frown? It couldn't have been. I replaced the frown with an action. Unbuttoning my shirt, I removed it. Surely that was enough? I'd give him what he wanted. All the while my thoughts were on one corner of the canvas. A noise broke my reverie. A glass jar was smashed. Tommy picked up another and threw it towards the canvas, missing. He slammed through the door, gunned the Ford and left. I suppose he left. I didn't check, but swept the broken glass into a corner and reached for my palette and brush.

It was late before I looked for him. I'd lit the lamp hours before and guessed it was after midnight. My tongue was dry and sticking to my mouth and I needed some water. That's when I felt the squelch on the linoleum and noticed the red marbling. A sliver of glass had lodged in my foot. Once I saw it, I felt the sting. I took a mug of water to the verandah, limping now, feeling the pain each time I put my foot on the ground. It was cooler outside. I sipped under the full moon, aware that the Ford was there but parked in a different spot. Tommy had returned and I hadn't noticed. I hobbled over to the car, stubbing the toe of my uninjured foot on an unseen obstacle. Tommy lay beside the car. I lowered myself onto his torso, smelling the grog and the fuel and the heat of his salty skin.

'You'd be better off if you forgot about me, Tommy.' I lay my head near his.

'Hmmph.' He laughed, low in his chest. It felt like a purr. 'I think it's the other way around.'

I was shirtless, not having bothered to dress earlier. Tommy ran a hand over my shoulders and neck then rolled me onto the ground.

'You smell worse than I do.' He wrinkled his nose as if I were rancid.

'Impossible.' I slid my hand under his shirt.

After a long stretch of painting I'd feel elated or sometimes depleted. Tommy called me greedy because it didn't matter which way I felt, I'd want to touch every part of him.

'What do you do when I'm not here?'

'I keep painting.'

'There are other ways.'

'I do that too.'

Art is aggressive. Lowering horizons, sliding hills one way or another, shifting trees, bending faces and bodies to suit. I liked the resistance of Tommy's flesh and his unpredictability and the fact that he wasn't always there. Even now, at eighty-eight, I shiver when I think how fast he was with his tongue and how soft with his hands. He could take my weight, all of it – he was the perfect fit. And when I hated him, I made him suffer. Getting out of bed as soon as he'd come, sometimes *while* he was coming, to stand at my work naked. I did this even when Claudine watched. Perched on the edge of her chair, smoking a cigarette, one leg propped on the edge of the bed while Tommy and I worked our way through miles and miles of flesh, never forgetting she was there.

'You could have waited until he'd finished,' she said to me once.

Claudine did join in on occasion – usually when I'd taunted her about Tommy's silver screen dick and his sac full of gold and about the women who'd lick his arse just for a whiff. Claudine had an insatiable taste for my Surry Hills talk. She liked it fast and darting in her ear like a moist tongue. It lubricated her.

There you've heard it. All the trashy secrets. I could have stayed working at Maggie's but Claudine's rates were better and there was also the exhibition.

'You're mine,' Tommy claimed that night beside the car.

'I'm nobody's, Tommy.' To be fair, he took anything I'd give him. Our nights together, in whatever form, thinned down his nightmares. There were periods when he didn't dream at all, or so he said. I was as good as a bottle of rum. Although he'd take the rum as well, if he could get it.

'I can't give up everything just so you can sleep.'

'I'm not asking you to.'

But of course he was.

•

— do what you want. I'm just saying Potts Point is here if you need it and going to waste since I took over from Maggie. What a mess. She had two sets of books and now I've had a look at the both of them together, I'm not sure if I'll get more than a couple of years out of the place. The old bitch. I'll have to work ten times as hard as I ever did if I want to keep the business afloat.

The resumptions? They've got rid of the riff but not the raff. And talking about that, the girls have got me marked. To think they once begged for a bit of housekeeping and never gave a toss where I got the money.

As for those old coots, they never saw any worth in a canvas they weren't good enough to paint themselves. It's the same in here. A girl

will work up a sweat bringing a man to his peak and you'd think
he'd done the deed himself.

Come and visit, I could use a good laugh.

Yours always,

Alice

•

Tommy bought me a pale green teacup and saucer, rimmed in gold
and decorated with a delicate floral spray, white petals edged in
blue with pink at their centres. I'd never seen flowers like it.

'It's meant to be good to drink from.' The porcelain was so thin,
my lips felt as if they met.

'I'd rather look at it.' I placed the set at eye level on the shelf
above the icebox.

He brought me other gifts too. A knotted piece of wire, butterfly
wings, feathers, a copy of *The Australian Women's Weekly* with a
picture of the recently deceased King George on the cover, a stick-
figured self-portrait – his own sketch – framed in silver, a curled
leaf, a milk bottle filled with oddly textured stones that took him
months to collect, a ring made from a shilling, a piece of metal
roughened by rust, a hand-carved spike to gauge my paint.

His visits were brief flings. A few hours, the occasional night.

'What have you brought me?' My impatience made him smile.

'Why would I bring you anything? . . . It's on the front seat of
the car . . . I've left it in the cockpit . . . I've only got an hour, they're
racing down at Seven Mile . . . I'll bring something next time.'

He'd tell stories, describing colours and shapes as he went along. 'The skin on his arms was blue right up to the elbows as if he'd dunked them in a vat of ink and they were permanently stained.'

Afterwards I'd paint my version of his tale.

'That's it,' he'd say, watching me paint. 'That's just how I remember it.'

Then:

'Cunt, cunt, cunt.'

I couldn't touch him or let him hear my voice.

'What did you say? What did you fucking say?'

Best to stay silent, not answer his questions.

'You don't give a fuck, do you? *Do you?*' He'd clench his fists and the veins would pop on his neck.

'Tommy . . .'

'You fucking, fucking serpent cunt. I wish I'd never laid eyes on you.'

He'd walk away, then turn and point his finger. 'It's finished between us. Dead like you, you cunt. You won't hear from me again.'

Always the same. A repetition. A chorus in my head. He'd leave for good then return, in the Gipsy Moth or the V-8, hours, a day, several days, a week later, on his knees, arms around my thighs, sorry. Fluid seeping from his eyes and his mouth, buckets of it, seeping through the cloth of my trousers. I'd prise his fingers from my hips, still hating him, but he'd clench them harder. 'I'm sorry, I'm sorry.' His sobs the pitch of a squealing pig, louder than the fretful cow searching for her calf. 'Please, please, please. I can't live, I can't live.'

'Come inside, Tommy.' Still angry, always angry with him now.

'We'll go anywhere. You choose. Not Claudine, just you and me, and Alice if you want. Anywhere.'

I painted him in wild furious strokes, harsher and more eroding than the fierce Gerringong winds, his war medals pinned to his naked flesh, the face of the artist, me, reflected in their surfaces. He slid his arms around my waist, nose pressed to the nape of my neck. 'I'll bring you something back, anything you like.' Then he'd reach for the bottle.

'Don't.' My voice was abrasive.

'What's wrong with you?' His fists clenched and it became my fault again. Cunt, cunt, cunt.

That's when the dream began; it turned up every time I slept. A southerly tailed me all the way up the coast to Mascot. I landed, ahead of dark gathering clouds and squalling wind, and there was Alice, an outline against the grain of the storm, signalling me in. She helped me tie down then cover the machine as raindrops, big and as hard as gumnuts, broke on the ground around us. That's as far as the dream ever got. I'd wake sweating, shivering, not sure why it was a nightmare.

There was the nightmare and then there was the exhibition. Between them I couldn't sleep. For nights on end I'd work, dozing on my feet, waking to finish what I'd started. It was all in the 82 retrospective. My lack of sleep, the dream, Tommy, the landscape. *Genius*, Claudine said, until the word was echoed elsewhere. She told her friends she had an artist tucked away in a little place down on the south coast.

Claudine rarely came to see me though and never brought her friends. Instead she sent scribbled love notes via Tommy. *I promise, my sweet, the exhibition will be a real exhibition. You'll have your very own screen star to squire you around, and that'll be the least of it.*

She arrived in the February of 1936 to confer on the final details. The entrepreneur. But she didn't discuss a thing. Only told me how it was going be, 'You're an investment my love.'

Claudine had shown samples of my art to critics whom she knew would despise it, and despise it publicly. 'The old guard,' she called them. Sentinels protecting the gate.

'You could have dunked a spoon in their outrage and supped. There'll be articles written damning the whole thing. And not just cursing you, Miss Kemp – I'll get a mention too. A carnival, Norman said. A great flabby spectacle. I hope so, I told him. People will flock to see it.'

'Come on, you two.' Tommy, waiting, tooted the horn of the Ford. Claudine picked up her sunhat. I followed her through the door and across the verandah. 'I've brought a good bottle of hock to celebrate.'

Tommy drove south to Seven Mile Beach then along the fore-shore, howling like a shot dog as he accelerated. I shut my eyes against the blast of sand and felt Claudine's hand anchor itself on mine. Tommy accelerated again, then braked, skidding into a halt that turned the car around. We got out.

'What a noisy beast. We really must get you something better than this, Tommy.'

'Something noisier.' Tommy laughed. 'That would be better.'

Claudine ignored his jibe, pirouetting between the blue of the sky and the blue of the water. 'It's picture perfect.'

'Not my kind of picture.'

'No, of course not, too sentimental to be worth the paint. But good for swimming.'

Tommy lit a cigarette between his cupped hands then strolled in the direction of the dunes.

'Oh, come on, Tommy. Come in for a swim.'

He dismissed her with a raised hand, eyes on me.

'Looks like you and me, Moo.' Claudine pulled her dress over her head, stepped out of her peach knickers, shed her camisole and ran into the breakers. The water was glary, harsh on my dry, sleepless eyes. Tommy sat between two dunes, cigarette dangling, watching.

'Come on, Muriel, it's beautiful in.'

I undressed and joined her, diving under the first decent wave.

We lay in the shallows after that, two floating pieces of seaweed, tangling and untangling in the sun-laced water.

'We'll get burnt if we're not careful.' Claudine stood, pushing her hair back from her face, raising her hands skywards. 'I had a friend,' she said, as we forced clothing over damp rubbery skin, 'who went shirtless at a picnic. He got burned to a deep crimson with blisters on top of that and was so ill he almost died. His suspenders crossed over his heart. Right here.' She touched my heart. 'The doctor said that's what saved him. Mind you, he died the following winter. Jumped into a creek and got double pneumonia.'

The drive back dried our hair and reddened our faces. Scratchy with salt, we jumped out of the motorcar as Tommy slowed to a halt. Claudine raced ahead and called over her shoulder, 'The bottle of hock, Tommy? Do you know where it is?' We walked past the meat safe, flipping flies from our nose and eyes as Tommy went back to the car to fetch it.

Claudine pushed me through the door and against the wall, licking drops of salt water from the edge of my shirt then sucking my nipples through the cloth until Tommy's footsteps approached along the verandah. I straightened my shirt.

'It's warm.' Tommy held up the bottle.

Claudine winked at me then went to the cupboard to look for glasses. I was tired of them both and wanted to get back to work. I placed a small primed canvas on the easel and let my thoughts drift from my knotted hair to knots of seaweed to Claudine and me floating naked on our backs. A glass was placed in my hand. I moved some objects on the table and positioned the drink next to a thick dribble of paint, spilled when I'd worked on the rabbit canvas. I'd given the painting to Paul, the son of the Quinlans, who lived over the hill in the new farmhouse.

Paul, who must have been eleven or twelve, left the occasional rabbit, skinned and gutted, on the verandah. He was the type of kid who was always around but you never quite saw. I might not have noticed him at all, if I hadn't been out walking one day and spotted him as he peered through my open door, craning his neck, rifle propped against the wall beside him.

'Go in and have a look,' I called from beyond the verandah.

He sprung back, stammering an apology.

'It's okay – go ahead. They're meant to be looked at.' He stepped through the doorway, nervous until the rabbit painting caught his eye. He crept towards it. Rabbits surged in from the left-hand corner of the canvas, swarming over the far-too-green hill towards a Moreton Bay Fig.

'Is that you?' Amid the crawling mob of fur overlapping fur and outstretched paws and pinned-back ears was the half-hidden face of a lone rabbit looking directly at the viewer.

'Why do you ask?'

'It's on its own.' His voice broke between the first and third words, veering from a high to a low pitch. That was the end of the conversation. He came back though, with his own composition. A squashed, hairy cylinder. Meant to be a dog, I think. I didn't mind him hanging around. I gave him an old sketchbook to work in and showed him a few tricks. He was killed a few years later, in the war. I'd like to say it was a shame, but I can't after what happened.

'Muriel, you haven't touched your hock. If you don't make a start Tommy will claim it.'

I picked up the glass and sipped. The farmhouse was too quiet for Claudine. Or vice versa. She liked to sharpen her wit against another's, and Tommy and I were too dull for her on that score. Tommy picked up the hock, sculled the remains of the bottle, then went in search of more supplies.

'He keeps a stash under the tarp by the water tank.'

Claudine talked over me as if she hadn't heard. 'You know, you've never painted me. And I should be painted. Don't you think?' She turned to Tommy as he pushed through the door with a bottle of what looked like whisky, the neck of it already gone.

'Don't you think that I should be painted, Tommy?'

'She could paint us together. The happy couple.'

'Are we happy?'

'I am.' He toasted her with the bottle, then took a drink.

'The happy couple then.' She raised her glass in return. 'The official portrait.'

That painting should have stayed missing. Overdone, the critics would say nowadays. Remiss of the sitters to let me pose them that way. They were naked. Claudine's idea, not mine. I had Tommy lie on the floor on his back, an easy position to maintain in his almost unconscious state. I got Claudine to sit side on, her backside on his chest, her feet on the floor by his ribs.

'Here. This is the closest thing I can find.' I gave her a frypan and told her to look into it.

'What's it meant to be?'

'A mirror.'

Claudine laughed so much she peed. A portion of it filled Tommy's bellybutton and was still there when he woke in the early hours.

'God, the people I'll show this too,' she said, before I'd even lifted a brush.

'It won't be you in your best light.'

'No, it won't.' More laughs rolled out of her; big, rumbling belly laughs. When I think of moments like that, I wish I'd liked her more.

I didn't bother with preliminary sketches, not even on the canvas, but painted what I saw. Tommy's prop was the bottle at the end of his outstretched arm, balanced on the tips of his fingers. It was empty, but I painted it with a small amount of liquid in it, like shallows rolling in to the shore. 'You could call it *Sloth and Pride*,' quipped Claudine. 'Or *Soused and Cooking*.' It went on like this for hours: me painting, Claudine witting, Tommy snoring. Tommy never said afterwards what he thought of the work. He got up the next morning, glanced at the canvas, then looked for his lighter and fags.

I haven't told you how the canvasses for the exhibition were stored. This is important. Claudine organised storage in the city and Tommy transported the canvasses from the farmhouse to the site. Claudine didn't trust anyone else to do it. Later that day, Tommy loaded my finished canvasses into the Ford, including *The Happy Couple*.

'It's not dry,' I protested, 'and I haven't finished it yet. Leave it for next time.'

'It's finished,' he said. 'And this will be the last lot I transport before the exhibition – ask the boss.'

Claudine shrugged. 'It's finished, Muriel, and so are you for now. Take a little holiday.'

I stood beside Claudine on the verandah and waved Tommy off. He was due to fly back at the end of the week. It was strange that Claudine wanted to stay and odd that Tommy insisted on taking *The Happy Couple* with him. I should have noticed but I was distracted by the pressure of the exhibition and it's always easier to see the signs in hindsight.

Claudine linked her arm through mine as Tommy drove over the rutted track towards the first gate. 'He's bringing you a surprise when he comes back. Don't ask me what, he wouldn't tell; he thinks I can't keep a secret.'

Tommy opened the gate, drove through and got out again to close it. He threaded the chain over the hook and glanced up but didn't wave. I wanted to run after him and tell him to forget about the surprise, just to come back. Ridiculous. I was being ridiculous.

'You really need to sleep, Moo. You can't even walk straight'.

•

I heard they have a piece of the propeller from Tommy's Gipsy Moth in the local museum at Gerringong. I don't know if that's true.

•

The day that Tommy returned there was almost no wind, and only the odd cloud or two scuttling over the sun. White and fluffy or thinly scraped. Not a drop of rain in them.

'Here he comes.' I heard Tommy before I saw him and moved to the front of the farmhouse in my trousers with my red handkerchief on the ready. Claudine stood on the verandah behind me. The drone of the Moth was faint, a buzzing fly. It flew in from the north then veered west towards us but barely above speed. We watched Tommy's progress with increasing concern.

'Could be a mechanical,' Claudine said.

That's what I thought too, until the Moth picked up speed and flew in an even line towards us, dipping a wing once it was overhead. Tommy waved from the rear cockpit. A second arm rose and waved from the front.

Claudine brimmed her eyes with her hands. 'I hope he hasn't brought that new girl of his, not here.'

Tommy flew away from the farmhouse, then circled back again. Picking up speed he climbed vertically, gaining altitude.

'He's going to stall it.'

The plane stuttered. Tommy turned the nose down, accelerating towards the ground. We waited for him to pull out of the dive, but he didn't. The impact was less than you might imagine. A thump, yes. But there was more disintegration than thump. The cloth and plywood that made up the Moth crumpled, dislocating as it speared through the fence, jettisoning fragments over the paddock.

'Muriel,' Claudine said, but it was on the intake of a breath, a delicate whisper.

We stood, ossified. Then we ran.

There was no fire only wreckage and bodies. Tommy was thrown clear of the fuselage, a crushed pulp, his head partially severed, his face untouched. Claudine was on my left beside the other body. She picked up a shoe then put it down. It was a common enough brand. It could have belonged to anybody.

'Don't look.' Claudine held up a hand as I approached. 'Her face – it's gone.'

The shoe was shaped by the foot that had worn it and was as familiar to me as my own.

'I'll go for help,' I said.

'It's too late.' Claudine was the colour of ash. But she was thinking, organising – I didn't know what. 'You can't think why he did it, Muriel. Try not to think of anything.' She had her arm around my shoulders, leading me away.

I remember asking, 'Are you sure it's her?' I moved out of Claudine's hold and back to the shoe, following the point of its toe. Alice's face was unrecognisable, torn from the skull. But the hands were hers and the ring was the one she wore. I must have taken it, because I found it later, on my finger. I stared at the debris of the bodies and the wrecked plane, and I said to myself over and over, *Claudine planned this.*

'It had nothing to do with me.' She stood next to Alice's body, arms behind her back. She kicked at a piece of debris when I accused her, and the debris landed on Alice's chest. I hated Claudine then and I hated Tommy too.

I went back to the farmhouse and collected my canvas bag. Claudine watched as I stowed it in the Dodge. I must have told her I was going for good. I don't remember saying it but I remember her response. 'You'll get nowhere, not without me.' But I was as good as anybody ever was and didn't believe she could change that. I have to admit now, I was wrong.

Somewhere in all that Claudine got the idea to tell the police that one of the bodies was mine. She'd lost me either way and the publicity wouldn't do her or the paintings any harm.

'Go ahead,' I said. 'Do what you want.' I was angry, in shock, and wanted to be free of her.

As I drove down the track towards the road, I saw Paul Quinlan, the farmer's son, running across the paddocks, waving. I didn't return the wave and I didn't slow down, but he stopped and watched me go, close enough to see that although I may not have been well, I was very much alive.

PART III

PART III

18.

Too sweet for me

February 1993

I heard the phone but let it go through to the answering machine. Lyn and Sean sang, 'Happy birthday to you, happy birthday to you, happy birthday, dear Jane . . .'

Thirty-one.

I waited till Lyn was at work before I called back.

'Hi, Dad. How's the Gold Coast?'

'Yeah, great.'

'And Lyn?'

'At work. Listen, I'm about to take Sean to cricket.'

'What's he now – under tens?'

'Under twelves. How's um . . .'

'Olivia.'

'Olivia, that's right . . . Coming,' he called to somebody in the background.

'Teething.'

'Look, I have to run.'

'Say hello to Lyn, would you, and thank her for the present.'

I put the phone down. Olivia banged on her highchair table with a red plastic hammer. It was like a drumroll.

I picked up the receiver again.

'Amanda, its me.'

'Me who?'

'Your sister. What's wrong? You don't sound well.'

'You wouldn't sound too good either, if you'd just been woken up after a big night out. What's that noise? Is it you?'

'The baby, banging on the table.'

'You're not after a loan, are you? Lyn said you'd given up your job.'

'When have I ever asked you for money?'

Amanda covered the receiver. 'Hang on, babe.' Then, too loud in my ear, 'I have to go.'

'I hope you're using condoms.'

She laughed. 'You should talk.'

'Olivia was planned. Besides, it's AIDS I'm worried about.'

'Bullshit and bullshit.' She hung up.

The phone rang as I put it down. She must have remembered my birthday after all.

'I thought you'd forgotten.'

'Ms Cooper?'

'Excuse me?'

'It's Lexie Tanner, Ms Cooper. I'm calling in regard to your two paintings.'

I unwound the telephone and moved as far as I could down the hall, away from Olivia's noise.

'Are you there, Ms Cooper?'

It had been nearly three weeks since she'd been to look at the paintings. 'I didn't expect to hear from you again.'

'This is just a follow-up call.'

'Go ahead.'

'After our previous discussion, I went back and searched the original documents on Kemp's two missing paintings from the triptych.'

'That's conscientious.'

'I wanted to ensure there would be no misunderstandings.' Lexie cleared her throat. 'It might interest you to learn that the triptych in question first appeared in a catalogue from 1936, under the title, *The Mothers*.'

'I see.'

'It was part of Kemp's *Gerringong* series. A postscript in the catalogue notes that the first two paintings from the triptych were promised to Alice Cooney, a childhood friend of the artist. This was why they were stored separately from the rest of the collection. As you know, the third painting remained with Claudine Worthington.'

'The triptych was split between two people?'

'That's right.'

But it didn't sound right. None of it sounded right.

'And you haven't been able to trace Alice Cooney or the paintings.'

'The paintings may have been destroyed, sold, passed on or even taken out of the country, but they were never publicly exhibited. No more than a handful of people ever saw them. Thus, the importance of the catalogue description. It's all we have.'

'Muriel, *my* Muriel identified her canvasses, the ones that she painted, as being the missing two from the triptych. Surely, if her aim was simply to fool you, she would have matched the paintings to the catalogue description.'

Olivia bang, bang, banged. I stuck a finger in my ear to hear the reply.

'I don't know who your Muriel was, Ms Cooper, and I have no idea about her aims, but I can tell you the catalogue has not been made available to the public. She may not have even known it existed.'

'I have her passport, Ms Tanner, and letters she exchanged with Claudine Worthington.'

'Collector's items, Ms Cooper. The foundation would be interested in those, if they're genuine.'

'You think I've been taken in.'

'Who ever painted those canvasses, Ms Cooper, was an artist, but they weren't Muriel Kemp.' She rung off and I was left to think about it.

It made sense and it didn't. The paintings were fake and the real Muriel Kemp died in 1936. Bullshit and bullshit.

Olivia had thrown her hammer on the floor and wanted out of the highchair. I put her in the pram and walked in the direction of the harbour, where there was plenty to look at but where I could think it through.

As soon as Claudine, the only woman who could have identified her, dies, along comes my Muriel, claiming to be the real Muriel Kemp. But that didn't explain her motive or, despite what Lexie Tanner said, the correspondence, the passports or any of the new paintings. It also didn't explain Lexie Tanner's reaction. If it was so obvious the two paintings weren't genuine because they differed in their composition from the catalogue description, why didn't she say that when I'd visited her at the foundation with the photos? Instead, she'd driven all the way to Shellharbour to view them in person. Then there was today's call, unnecessary, unless she was trying to convince herself that the paintings were not Kemp's. The more I thought about it the more I thought there was something wrong with Lexie's vigilance.

I pointed out birds and boats and butterflies to Olivia. We watched a group of boys in Billabong board shorts dive off the rocks into the surf at the back of the pool.

It also didn't account for Muriel's meeting with Adam Black in the sixties. That's if it really happened, of course . . .

I released the pram's brakes and sprinted back the way I'd come. An old guy with dark sunnies and a tatty length of hair down his back cheered me on, yelling, 'You can do it!' Olivia gurgled and laughed.

I fed her banana mashed in yoghurt and changed her nappy. She was sleepy after the outing and went down with less fuss than usual.

I searched through the tapes until I found the one I was looking for and inserted it in the tape deck. I fast forwarded to the section I wanted then rewound and listened to it again, then one more time to be certain. Muriel's meeting with Adam Black. That was the key. I was back on track or I would be, if I could obtain the right information.

•

It was hours since I'd rung Amanda. She acted as if it had only been five minutes ago.

'I was asleep,' she complained.

'It's three o'clock in the afternoon.'

'So?'

'I know what I want for my birthday.'

There was a clatter on her end of the line. Something dropped, it sounded like a book, maybe her diary. There was a flutter of pages. 'Oh, your birthday.'

'It's good that you forgot, because I know exactly what I want.'

I had to tell her about the business of Muriel and the book. It was the only way to get her to do what I wanted. She was interested, nosy. Told me where I'd gone wrong. I got off the phone before it disintegrated into a fight. There wasn't much I could do before the information arrived. So I went through the tapes one more time.

19.

Jetsam

February 1993

Amanda called a week after my birthday. 'I've sent your birthday package as requested.'

The package, she explained, consisted of photocopied articles from the library at the Muriel Kemp Foundation. Magazine stories, biographical information, excerpts from dissertations. Useful background research for the book.

'Nothing that questions Kemp's death. Although –' she tapped her nail against the phone '– I did have a conversation with one gentleman that might interest you.'

'Gentleman?'

'A volunteer who's been with the foundation for years.'

Amanda is six foot one. Unmissable and striking, people are drawn to her. I'm thankful she's on my side for this project.

'I brought up Adam Black.'

'Go on.'

'You're right. He claimed he saw Kemp in the early sixties. The foundation's take on it is that he was more interested in notoriety than in the truth. It seems he had some financial problems and they believe he wanted to trade on the story.' Her nails clicked, there was a shuffle, the sound of a seat as it scraped along the floor.

'He and Kemp were a bit of an item in their younger years, apparently. One of the foundation members interviewed him in the seventies. He made the same claim then: Kemp was alive and had come to see him in the sixties. There's a transcript. But it's restricted access.'

'I'd love to get hold of that.'

'You will. I've sent you a photocopy of it. Don't ask.'

I almost purred. Perhaps I did, because Amanda added, 'I can tell you something even better than that. Adam Black is still alive.'

'No! He'd be . . .' I counted the decades on my fingers.

'Ninety-one and still causing mayhem. He has a portrait that Kemp did of him. The foundation want to get their hands on it but he won't sell.'

'I think I know the one.'

'His address is in the parcel. Happy birthday, big sister.'

•

The package arrived in the middle of a Monday morning. I heard the postie's bike and went out to collect it then sorted the contents into piles. Research, the transcript and two articles that didn't relate in any way to Muriel Kemp. The latter were newspaper stories, written in 1969, one in January and the other in July. The first told the story of a family from Victoria whose eleven-year-old daughter had gone missing during an outing to the beach. The second detailed the finding of a body six months later in bushland eighty miles to the north. It was believed to be that of the missing girl. Amanda had underlined the name of the girl and her younger brother in the first story. Fiona and Matthew Vittore. I was angry. Amanda should have warned me.

I pushed the newspaper clipping aside to deal with later and distracted myself from the Vittore's by re-reading the interview transcript with Adam Black. Along with his contact details it was the most useful piece of information in the package. The next day I contacted Adam Black to arrange a meeting. He was an absolute charmer, much like my sister. Be warned, I told myself.

•

In the meantime, I read about the abducted and murdered Fiona Vittore. Clipped articles that speculated on how and why Fiona had ended up in a shallow bushland grave. A creeping feeling of guilt took over – I should have known. Not that me knowing would have helped Matt any, not as a kid. I looked at the black and white photo of Fiona in her school uniform. One more unexplained riddle to think about. I felt a dull empty ache in my stomach and an urge to talk to family. Well, to Lyn at any rate.

'Hello Lyn, it's me.'

'Long time no hear.'

'Yes. It's been a while.'

'It's difficult with a new baby. I get it.'

Olivia was asleep and the cat was curled on the lounge. It would be a short conversation. That's what I thought.

'It's not that, Lyn.'

'Well, go on. Don't be shy. There's nothing you can't say to me.'

I took a deep breath. There was a tremble in my throat. 'I know you and Dad had an affair.'

'Everyone knows that, sweetheart. Sean's proof of it.'

'Not then. When Mum was around. Before the accident.'

There was a splutter, then Lyn's voice rasped, 'What on earth makes you think that?'

'Amanda told me she saw you and Dad down by the hockey fields just before the accident.'

'That bloody sister of yours. Sweetheart, I had a miscarriage about the time of your mother's funeral. Before that I was hospitalised and in bed for weeks trying to hold on to it. You know that. It's the reason I was so mad with Chevo for volunteering me to help your dad. Even if I'd wanted to have an affair, which I didn't, I wouldn't have been capable of it.'

Fuck, I thought to myself. Fuck. I did know that. 'But you did have an affair?'

'Years later. When it was obvious that it was over with Chevo. You should have said something earlier. I could have set you straight.'

•

'Amanda, it's me.'

'What time—'

'You fucking liar.'

She placed her hand over the receiver. 'Sorry, babe, I need to take this.'

'Don't bother with your bullshit.' How many times had she pretended that someone was in her bed in order to dodge my calls?

A male voice answered her. 'I have to go anyway.'

'What's this about?' Amanda said to me with a sigh.

'I've just accused Lyn of having an affair with Dad while Mum was alive. And she reminded me that she was in hospital trying to prevent a miscarriage until after the accident.'

'What's that got to do with me?'

'You said you saw them together at the hockey fields. Dad and Lyn. From Minta's house.'

There was a pause followed by the familiar scrape of Amanda's nails against the phone.

'I didn't say it was Lyn.'

'You swore to me that it was Lyn.'

'I would never have said that. I didn't see the woman's face.'

It wasn't the first time she'd lied to me or the first time I'd wanted to tear her apart. Something wasn't right between me and my sister.

The word *burst* popped into my head. I was about to burst. I slowed my speech so that each word left my throat in a clear growl.

'You said it was her. That you saw her. When I asked you how I'd ever talk to Lyn again, you said it wasn't your problem.'

'How ridiculous. I know you're stressed with the baby and all, but it was your choice to have her. Don't take it out on me.'

That phone call was the beginning of a new rift between us. Amanda rang Dad the following week and said I'd told her he and Lyn were having an affair while Mum was still alive. I phoned him in return and refuted her claims, citing Amanda's original story. She contacted the Muriel Kemp Foundation after that, to alert them to the fact I'd got hold of inaccessible documents and was out to cause trouble. Tit for tat.

No more, I decided. We'd been caught up in this contest since the whole sordid shemozzle of the escape in the Morris Minor. We'd absorbed every spiteful story that said Mum deserved what she got. And, instead of uniting against the muck, we'd equivocated – and acted as if punishing each other elevated us somehow, made us the good one.

Blood is not thicker than water, Annie would have tried to set me straight.

And you can always choose your friends.

Good advice. Matt must have felt it too. That same cinching of shame or guilt. I dialled his number.

'Matt. Do you want to come over for dinner?'

'When?'

'How 'bout tonight?'

'Okay but you've got Olivia and the book to worry about. I'll bring dinner.'

•

He turned up with a roast chicken, some bread rolls and a tub of tabouleh. We sat in the backyard with Olivia on a blanket and talked about plants and birds as we ate. 'Some cats immobilise the bells on their collars while they stalk.' We watched the tabby for a while, but if she'd learned that trick she knew enough to hide it from us.

I told him about Amanda.

'I remember her being like that as a kid, always pointing the finger. And you–' He said.

'What?'

'–biting at everything she said.'

I laughed. 'Nothing's changed.' There was that strange familiarity that came with having known someone when you were a child.

'She sent me a couple of newspaper clippings about your sister.'

'What, you're trying to work out my life now are you?' Matt threw a piece of bread on the grass for the birds.

'I didn't know about Fiona.'

'No,' he said. 'I didn't talk about Fiona and you didn't talk about your mother or brother.'

The magpies started singing. One of them swooped, probably the one that Muriel used to feed.

'I guess that was a fair swap.'

'Yes,' he said, but didn't look at me. 'Still is.' I put the lid back on the tabouleh assuming he meant that even now he wouldn't talk about Fiona and I wouldn't talk about the accident, but then he started telling her story, in jagged spurts at first, as if responding to an interrogation.

'It was a promise.' His eyes were on Olivia who'd fallen asleep on the blanket. 'The outing to the beach. Ice cream, fish and chips for lunch. Dad had promised. Mum said, "Don't hold your breath."'

Matt held up the bottle of wine he'd brought. 'Want any?' I shook my head and he poured some into a plastic cup for himself.

'It was a hot day. Not heatwave hot, but warm enough, and I'd got a surf mat for Christmas which I shoved between me and Fiona in the back of the car . . .'

He was eight again and telling the story as if he was there.

'Get it off me! Mum, tell him to get it off me.'

'Move it over to your side, Matt.'

'There's not enough room.'

'Move it off your sister or we'll pull over and leave it at the side of the road.'

I grabbed my sister's wrist and gave her a Chinese burn.

'Ow, Mum make him stop.'

'That's enough,' Dad said.

'But he–'

'No more.'

I pulled a face and made pincers of my fingers, snapping them at her like a crab. Fiona shrieked. I was a bastard of a kid.

'Enough, Fiona, or we'll turn around and go home,' Dad thundered. 'Is that what you want?'

'Steve . . .' Mum said.

'Is that what you want, Fiona? To turn around and go home?'

My sister met Dad's eyes in the rear-view mirror and shook her head.

'Steve . . .' Mum said again.

'You're too soft on her, Narelle,' Dad snapped.

When the police asked about that day I told them how Mum and Dad had fought. Dad reached out and clipped me around the ear right in front of the policeman. 'Don't tell stories, boy,' he warned. But it was true. They'd argued as we rumbled out of the car, across the grass and down the track to the beach. Later, when I walked out of the surf, they'd set up on the sand, my towel between theirs.

'Do you want a drink?' Mum held up a frozen bottle of cordial she'd wrapped in a tea towel.

'No.' I dumped the surf mat on the sand and went past them.

'Where are you going?'

'Toilet.'

'Why didn't you go while you were in there?'

'Not that, the other.'

'Hang on, I'll come.' Mum stood and wiped the sand from her dress.

'Let him go on his own.' Dad sucked his cigarette through to its end and stubbed it out in the sand. 'He's not a baby.'

'He's eight.' Then, in a lower voice, she whispered something about the Beaumont children.

'They caught the bus on their own. He's just going to the bog. Don't fuss.'

'He can come with me,' Fiona said. 'I've got to go anyway.'

I went to the men's and Fiona went to the women's. When I was done I sat and waited on the retaining wall beside the toilet block. When she didn't show up after a few minutes I went back alone.

'Where's your sister?' Mum asked.

I shrugged. Dad rolled onto his side to read his paper and I drank from the frozen bottle of cordial. Mum waited five minutes then went to look for Fiona.

'At first Dad called her a spoiled bitch, said Mum had spoiled her. He thought she'd run off.'

'Were there any witnesses?' I asked.

'She was seen with a man. Blond hair, white T-shirt, blue swimming trunks. She wouldn't go with a stranger, Mum reckoned. Not willingly.' He took a swig of the wine. 'We moved up here to get away from everything.'

'Your parents still together?'

'Split up not long after the move.'

'Is that why you came to talk to me in the library that day?'

'What do you mean?' He poured some more wine into his cup.

'You know, on the lookout for a substitute sister.'

It was the first time I'd heard him laugh. 'If I was I wouldn't have picked you. I don't think I'd ever seen a kid who looked as miserable.'

'And you weren't?'

'No.' He shook his head. 'That didn't happen until later for me.'

I thought of the dead-eyed look of twelve months ago. It had softened, was hardly there at the moment.

Whatever was happening between Matt and me – it wasn't a romance. That's what Muriel would say if she were telling this story. I watched Matt brush a leaf from Olivia's face before he lay back on the grass and looked up into the tree.

'Your turn,' he said.

'What? Now?'

'Don't think you're getting out of it.'

I heard the first mosquito buzz of the evening and picked up Olivia and the blanket. Matt must have heard it too and began to collect the plates and food and we carried everything inside. I made a cuppa while Matt put the dishes in the sink, then, not wanting to get out of it, I told him about the accident.

20.

The good mistake

March 1993

Adam Black differed so much from Muriel's descriptions that he puzzled me at first.

'I'm like a lit match.' He shook my hand. 'Lots of flame but goes out quickly.'

Adam Black at ninety-one was nothing short of a bonfire in his Mambo T-shirt. The one of the farting dog. Tall, lean and funny. He greeted me at the door of his goddaughter's unit in Potts Point and we sat in the front room, which overlooked the water.

'Does she walk yet?' he asked as I sat Olivia on a bunny rug and handed her a rattle.

'Not quite. She crawls and has started to pull herself up on the furniture.'

'Gives you a run for your money, I bet.' *That smile! False teeth and all.* 'So, Muriel sent you,' he prompted.

'You didn't seem surprised when I rang.'

'Surprised no one's been before this.'

The room was light and airy, the furniture scant: two wingback chairs upholstered in cream fabric, a restored fireplace and Adam, seated beneath his portrait. *The First Man.*

'The original. Worth a fortune these days.' Two sets of eyes, one vivid, one almost vivid watched me.

'I understand the Muriel Kemp Foundation is keen to get their hands on it,' I said.

'They've got no chance. Not while I'm alive. Not even when I'm dead.'

'Can I ask why?'

'You can ask anything you like.' He lifted a hand in the air. 'I might even give you an answer before we're done.' He lowered his hand.

'Do you mind if I record our conversation?'

'Go ahead.'

I set the tape deck on a small side table near his chair and crouched over it. 'Conversation with Adam Black in his goddaughter's home in Potts Point. The sixth of March 1993, at –' I glanced at my watch '– ten forty-seven a.m.' I returned to my seat.

'Everyone believes Muriel Kemp died in 1936,' I began.

'Ha! Who's everyone?'

'Biographers, historians, the experts. You implied it yourself in your book, *The Last Man.*'

He grimaced as if in pain. 'People believe it because Claudine Worthington said it happened.'

'Why would she lie?'

Adam leaned forward in his chair. 'Muriel didn't tell you? Claudine Worthington got exactly what she wanted, when she wanted it. In the early days, we called her a spoiled girl with too much money. If she decided a green sky was the thing, you'd paint a green sky because you knew if you painted a blue one she wouldn't buy it. Somewhere along the line, people came to believe she knew something about art.'

'You think she was wrong about Muriel's ability?'

'No, I agreed with her on that one.' He ran a hand through his hair and turned to look at his portrait. 'Back in '39, the *Herald* sponsored an exhibition of French and British art to come to Australia: Picasso, Modigliani, Cézanne, Matisse, Van Gogh, Max Ernst. I saw the exhibition in David Jones, along with everybody else who flocked to it because it couldn't get a showing in the Art Gallery. The director called them reprobates, perverts, degenerates. Muriel's work would have matched the best of them.'

'Mr Black . . .'

'Call me Adam.'

'Adam, why are you so sure Muriel didn't die in that plane crash?'

'I thought she did. It wasn't until I looked for Alice after the accident – actually, it wasn't until I saw Muriel herself that I put things together.'

'You were friendly with Alice?'

'No. We didn't get on.'

Adam rose from his chair unsteadily. For a moment I thought he'd changed his mind about the interview.

'We don't have to do this today,' I said. 'I can always come back.'

'No certainty in that. Not at my age.'

We both laughed. In the replay, it sounded like a dry scrape followed by a gap where he walked to the window and stood in front of it.

'Let's get this over with.' He turned to face me.

'You said you looked for Alice, after the accident.'

Settling into his chair once more, he nodded. 'When I first heard Muriel and Tommy were dead, I didn't believe it. Tommy yes, but not Muriel. It had to be wrong or some kind of stunt. I got on the tram to go and see Alice, because if anyone knew the truth it'd be her. You know about the brothel she ran in Campbell Street?'

I nodded.

'I don't know what you've heard about Alice, but I can tell you she was fond of the horses and of cocaine. That's how she paid her girls – in cocaine. To earn a living, they had to sell it on to the clients and the coppers. I didn't know at the time that she'd stopped paying the girls altogether and owed money all over the place, but I soon worked it out.

'The place in Campbell Street looked deserted when I got there. The ex-boxer who ran her security was gone. The front door was off its hinges and minus a brass knob.' Adam's focus wasn't on me as he spoke but on that day in 1936.

•

I found one of the girls in the old office. Last time I'd been there was to see a couple of Muriel's paintings that had been hung in that room. They were gone now. The room was bare other than a desk pushed against the wall with a bit of a girl sitting on top of it.

'Where's Alice?'

'It ain't Alice you want, mister.' She swung her leg over the edge of the table provocatively.

'I'm not a customer,' I told her. The air in the dim room was rank with lard, sweat and the smell of mould. 'It's Alice I want.'

She raised an eyebrow and shrugged. 'You and everyone else.'

'I need to see her about a friend of ours who's died.'

She scowled and half laughed. 'I'm not that stupid.'

There was a movement in the corner, and I realised that what I'd taken for a pile of rags was bedding. A voice groaned, 'Lizzie, I'm trying to sleep.'

I pulled a pound note from the back of my shoe and held it up. Lizzie made a grab for it but I held on tight. It was the only one I had. 'I promised to get word to her.'

'Not the painter?' She slumped back against the table.

'You know her?'

'It's the painter who was going to give her the money. That old drunk was going to fly her there to get it.'

'Tommy?'

'I'm warning you, Lizzie.' The bedding lurched upward and a pair of dark eyes glared at us.

Lizzie beckoned me into the hall. From there she moved into a room that held pots and pans and a gas ring. She opened a pantry door and pointed to an old newspaper clipping stuck to the back of it. Tommy, younger and fitter, arms raised above his head, face turned to the camera as he stretched forward to dive into a pool.

'God Almighty, that ruins it.' Lizzie frowned. 'Most of the others have gone. We only hung on because she said she'd pay us the minute she got back.'

I gave her the pound note.

Next, I tried the Cooneys' place in Riley Street. Mrs Cooney remembered me. I didn't mention Muriel's death, just asked if she knew where Alice was.

'I haven't seen Alice for months.' She talked through a slit in the door. 'You have to understand, Mr Black, my husband won't have her here.' She looked over her shoulder into the house. 'But if you see her, say her mum asked after her.'

•

My gaze drifted to *The First Man* on the wall. There was something crude and unformed about the way it was painted that compelled me to look. 'Do you think it was Alice who was in the plane when it crashed?'

'I didn't just think it – I knew it, once I saw Muriel.'

I glanced at my notepad. 'There are a couple of things I can't work out.'

'Fire away.'

'Muriel said the two of you fell out when she worked as James Dennison's assistant, and she didn't see you again after that.'

'Muriel and I were always falling out. Didn't talk for months sometimes. But once that old souse moved into hers, she had me over there wiping his arse and cleaning up after him. What a bastard. If she hadn't spiked him, I might have done it for her. I didn't see her for a couple of years while the warrant was out for her arrest, but after that I saw her every few months and she wrote. Her last letter came just before the plane accident. I'll show you before you go.'

He sat up in his chair and repositioned himself. 'Muriel hated Claudine with a vengeance. Did she mention that? Said that when Claudine waved her magic wand the hangers-on recited,

"Muriel's got talent."' He laughed. 'As if the talent didn't exist before they said it.'

'Muriel described the plane crash as if it was intentional.'

'She was better off without him and Alice. Tommy knew it.'

We fell silent. I contemplated my next question – the one I thought most important.

'If Muriel didn't die in that crash, then what happened to all that ambition? It doesn't fit that she stopped painting for so long and that she left a room full of canvasses that nobody but me has seen.'

Adam shook his head. 'There's no answer to that. Nothing would have stopped the Muriel I knew. Maybe she just couldn't get people interested.'

As the interview progressed, Adam's voice grew slower and quavered with hesitation, but when I suggested he might like to rest he shook his head. 'No, no,' he said. 'Let's finish it.'

'Did you ever hear anything about Muriel having a baby, a little girl?' I asked.

'What? Tommy's?'

'I don't know. Muriel talked about having a miscarriage in 1931. She also mentioned painting a child in the third part of a triptych.'

'The one that Claudine owned?'

'Yes – the baby being held by the two women. She said it was hers and she'd given it to Claudine. I wished I'd asked her about it at the time. I thought she'd go into more detail on the tapes.'

Adam shook his head. 'So you don't know what happened to it?'

'I did a search of Births, Deaths and Marriages and there was no child registered under the surname of Hasluck, Worthington, Kemp or Rose, an alias of Muriel's. She doesn't mention being pregnant for a second time anywhere and all sources indicate that Claudine didn't raise any children.'

'Hmmph, another puzzle.'

'Can we move on to when you saw Muriel in the sixties?'

'It was 1962. Four years after I wrote *The Last Man*.'

Adam leaned forward, his eyes droopy, his false teeth a little too loose. 'I knew it was Muriel camped out in the Greasy Spoon. I sensed it. Then I saw her. Faded – her hair, I mean – and bunched at the back of her head, but with that same unmistakable profile. She was bent over I don't know what; a newspaper, I guess, or a cup of tea. She was never good at discretion.

'I went to the shops and when I came back there she was, peering through the window as if I couldn't see her. I decided to wait her out. It took her three days to cross the road and shove that sketch under the door. I chased her across the landing to the top of the stairs and called out, "Muriel!" She turned around.'

He leaned back in his chair, eyes half closed. 'That was it.'

•

Playing the tape back later, I could just make out Adam's sigh before it was drowned out by the sound of the postie's motorbike. I stopped the tape, picked up Olivia from the playpen and carried her outside.

There was no mail. I'd been hoping for something from Annie.

I wondered what she'd make of Adam's ten-second sighting of Muriel in the sixties, and what she'd say about my reclusive old woman and the gaps in her story?

Back at the table I went through the pile of photocopies Amanda had sent. I read a double-page feature from 1981. It discussed the

Kemp paintings stolen prior to the 1936 exhibition, which had since been recovered and were to be unveiled for the 1982 retrospective.

Claudine explained to the journalist that the paintings hadn't in fact been stolen. Her husband, Tommy Hasluck, had rented storage space in the loft of a nearby barn. Tommy died in an aviation accident and the elderly farmer forgot about the lease and had no idea paintings had been stored in the attic of his old hayshed. It was his granddaughter who found them years later and recognised the name of the artist.

An immaculately groomed Claudine Worthington stared out at me from her home in Sydney's northern beaches. The photo had been cropped so that Claudine took up most of the image, but above her head and to the left I could see a section of a framed canvas. I peered at it, then looked at it again through a magnifying glass. It looked similar to some of the paintings in Muriel's back room.

I scrambled through the box of tapes until I found the spot where Muriel explained how she'd sent Claudine one of her new paintings not long before the retrospective was held.

21.

The dispersal

April 1993

'I don't have time for this, Jane.' Lexie Tanner was terse.

'You can spare me one minute, surely.' I fiddled with the cord of the phone, nervous.

'One minute, but that's all.'

I picked up my writing pad and read over my notes. 'I came across an article in the *Sydney Morning Herald* written in 1981. It's a double-page spread with a photo of Claudine Worthington taken in her home. There's a canvas behind her that was painted in 1980 and given to Claudine the following year by my Muriel.'

Lexie gave an exaggerated sigh. 'Ms Worthington was gifted a lot of paintings.'

'You think she'd hang a fake Kemp in her home?'

'If she liked it, yes. I imagine it would amuse her. That's it, Jane. Your minute is up.'

Despite her nonchalance, I knew Lexie would track down the article and check out the canvas for herself. My own misgivings about Muriel's story centred on those paintings in the back room. They were so unlike Kemp's earlier work that I'd begun to doubt they'd been executed by the same artist. Lexie would know, composition aside, if she ever deigned to look at them.

I'd come to a dead end with Adam Black. Two weeks after our interview I'd rung him as agreed, to ask any follow up questions. His goddaughter answered the phone with the news that Adam had suffered a major stroke.

'I'm so sorry. Would it be possible to visit him?'

'He's not expected to last the week. It's close friends only.'

He'd had a series of TIAs or mini strokes, leading up to the major one, she explained. 'He knew it was on the cards.' She said this as a kindness, I thought, so I wouldn't worry that my interview had played some part. Sometime after the funeral, I read she'd sold *The First Man* to the Muriel Kemp Foundation for what was described as 'an undisclosed sum'. Adam had told me she'd been as keen as he was to keep it from their clutches.

My next move after interviewing Adam had been to get in touch with a relative of Alice Cooney. I managed to find a niece, Grace Townsend, one of Marie's daughters. She and her parents had moved to Newcastle from Surry Hills after the war.

'Anyone with a connection to Surry Hills has heard of Muriel Kemp. Mum said the family knew her, but I didn't realise how well.'

'She considered Alice her best friend. Do you know much about your aunt?'

'Only that she was the black sheep. Got in with the wrong crowd.'

'Did she owe money, perhaps?' I thought of Adam's story about cocaine and gambling, which hadn't quite rung true for me.

'Not that anyone said. If she'd owed money then left, you'd think they'd have come after the family. To be honest, Mum and her sisters rarely talked about her. Not in front of us, at any rate. Mum said she disappeared before the war and nobody heard from her again. To start a new life is what I always thought. After Mum died I found a postcard from the Gold Coast among her things, signed with Alice's name and two crosses. It was postmarked 1970. Aunt Edna, the youngest of the sisters, was still alive back then, but she reckoned she knew nothing about it. She didn't know Alice as well as the others.'

'Do you still have the postcard?'

'No. I threw it out.'

•

'We might never know the answers,' I said to Olivia as I changed her nappy.

She gurgled and rolled onto her belly, crawled to the coffee table and pulled herself up, then took two wobbly steps from the edge of the coffee table into my arms.

•

While Olivia napped, I scoured the back room yet again. Other searches had produced sketches and notes (*paint the cat the colour of the sun*), blank postcards, broken ornaments and various bits and pieces buried under tubes of paint, tucked behind canvasses, tossed on top of the wardrobe. This search produced nothing more than frustration. I lay on the floor and closed my eyes. There were no secret compartments or riddles to solve, no encrypted messages written on rice paper. Besides, if Muriel had wanted me to know something she would have placed it somewhere obvious, not hidden it so that it was impossible to find.

Still on the floor, I drifted off for a moment. A good night's sleep was long overdue. I forced myself out of that sinking feeling that comes before sleep and pushed up onto my elbows. And that's when I saw it: a blurred glimpse of something on the underside of Muriel's work table. A muddy stain that turned into a sketch of a horse's rear end, legs pulled up ready to kick. I crawled beneath for a closer look.

I'd like to write about this moment in detail, for posterity, but I'll be buggered if I can remember it all that clearly. I kept thinking to myself, *This is it,* as I crawled forward and reached up. Taped next to the drawing of the horse's hind legs was a manila envelope, a honey-coloured rectangle barely darker than the raw wood of the table's underside. I don't remember peeling off the tape or opening the envelope, which I did at the kitchen table. I got there from the back room by magic, or sleight of hand, take your pick. I tipped the envelope upside down and two items fell out. A page of writing – no, two pages; the writing covered both sides of the sheet of paper. I recognised the hand as Claudine Worthington's, but there was no signature at the bottom nor greeting and address at the top. The middle page, then, of a letter. The other item was a list whose content and meaning I didn't understand at first.

I'll start with the letter. It was to Muriel, from Claudine. The paper was fragile after so many years and was unlike any other correspondence I'd read between the two women. In it, Claudine pleaded for what she said was hers. She sounded bitter, resentful about their relationship. I put the page down then picked it up and re-read it.

– promised me that baby. I shouldn't need to remind you. You ran screaming to me, remember, when I pulled up in the car. Blood-soaked paint rags jammed between your legs, your face powdery white. We argued about a doctor; I wanted to fetch one, but you insisted, you didn't need one. Tommy claims you lost the baby because I refused to get the doctor. Why would you tell him that? The baby was meant to be mine. You knew how much I wanted it. But I lay on the bed next to you, stroked your arm and told you it was all right, and that we'd get a doctor as soon as you were ready.

The bedding was not the catastrophe you said I'd made it out to be. Yes, it was ruined and so was the mattress, but I only said it would have to be burned when you told me to leave. And yes, I admit I said it was too late, that the baby was gone, but I was frightened and wanted to get help. You say you don't remember it, but I brought you a basin of warm water and a cup of tea, neither of which you wanted. I did not leave you alone. I went into the next room, stoked the stove and mopped the blood from the floor. I did not disappear.

Your violence, Muriel, the way you dig into your palette with your hands and nails and smear your work with your spit – you treat me the same way. When you came into the room behind me I did not ignore you. I was absorbed. There was blood on the canvas, the one on the easel, and when I looked at it I asked myself if I loved the woman or just her art.

When I saw you there I didn't tell you to paint, I told you to go and lie down. It was you who swapped the canvas from the easel with a second one, smeared it with the rag that staunched the blood, then wiped my hand between your legs and rubbed it over a third surface and said, That one's for you. We both know you promised it to me, not the whole triptych, just that one canvas, and I will have it. As for Tommy, he believed everything you said, but you and I both know the –

The baby Muriel had given Claudine. It was the baby painted over the blood from the miscarriage – the canvas itself. I paced the room, agitated. An expert could assess the handwriting. I didn't know whether that would persuade Lexie and the foundation, but it was enough for me. They must have fallen out, like lovers. But why? Because Muriel believed she'd be a success on her own and Claudine maintained she'd get nowhere without her. Not just maintained but made sure of it, falsifying the description of the triptych in the catalogue and alerting Lexie to an alternative painted by an artist known as Muriel Rose. Revenge or hate?

I took a deep breath. No more conjecture, I chided, reminding myself of Muriel's rules. Two years in the house with a stipend in order to write the book, but only one year in which to convince Lexie and the foundation the paintings were genuine. The end of that first year was not far off. But who'd know that I'd agreed to burn the paintings? I'd know. That was the problem. The decision was Muriel's, whether I agreed to it or not.

Only then did I look at the list that had come with the letter. I spread its pages over the kitchen table and for a good ten minutes couldn't work any of it out. I don't know why. It was straightforward enough. The pages were a record of paintings. Each entry was written in tiny print that included the work's title, the date it was completed and the price it had sold for. Although few were sold. Some had 'destroyed' written beside them or 'painted over', 'given to the neighbour's daughter for her treehouse', 'left in Dalton Herd Park'. Then came a section with an explanatory note about a group of canvasses being held in storage. Those were the ones in the back room, I presumed. That's when I understood what I should have known from the start: Muriel had not stopped painting after Alice's death. I was holding a list of every painting she had completed from 1936 until her death.

I placed my head in my hands, knocking the envelope to the floor. Claudine was right. Muriel hadn't been able to succeed without her. Nobody had been interested in the work of an unknown and unsponsored female artist. These two documents were the evidence I'd been looking for, but with no signatures and no dates, they didn't prove a thing.

The cat entered my side vision, commando crawling across the floor as she prepared to pounce on the fallen envelope. I kicked at it with my foot. The tabby leaped onto her prey then scooted it across the floor towards the kitchen. I watched for a moment, amused by her antics then rescued the envelope before it got damaged. As I stood my chair toppled behind me. The cat hissed at the noise and unsheathed her claws. I bent to pick up the envelope, the visible edge of something protruding above the seal. I pushed at its sides so that the top opened like a mouth, revealing a smaller, tea-coloured envelope gummed to the bottom by its sticky edge. Clasped by the same thread of glue were two rectangles of paper. I prised all of it free.

The envelope was addressed to:

Miss Muriel Rose
c/o Sefton House
Bellingen

It contained the missing pages of the letter I had just read, and the last page was signed – *Claudine.* It talked of little other than the third canvas in the triptych and how it belonged to her. Claudine demanded Muriel return the painting and threatened to pursue her for the money Tommy had stolen and expose her for faking her own death if she didn't comply.

The envelope had been franked in Bowral and postmarked 12 December 1936 – a good ten months after Muriel's official death.

I lifted the cat to my chin and felt her purr vibrate through my jaw. 'Proof,' I said. 'I've got the proof.' As soon as I'd uttered the words the cat squirmed and tried to jump free of my arms. I set her down on the floor.

There was a crash and a howl from the bedroom and all thoughts of Muriel left me as I rushed to investigate. Olivia's near-bald head was marked by a vivid red welt as if she'd bashed her head against the bars of the cot. She was inconsolable as I carried her around the house on my hip.

The cat yowled at the screen door, muted beneath the baby crying. I opened the door and the cat scuttled over the fence towards Mr Henley's, her plump belly scraping the top of the palings. Olivia's wail turned into a broken sob.

'My name never mattered,' Muriel had said to me. 'Claudine didn't matter either. The work was the proof. Nothing else will ever matter.'

If Muriel believed her genius would out itself, that it would take her death to unveil it, then why insist her paintings be burned at all, even after a year? It could take longer than that to prove what they were.

I kissed the welt on Olivia's head, then wiped her scalp and face with a cool washer. She chewed on the cloth, still emitting the occasional sob. I put the washer to one side and sat with her on my knee. 'Why, why, why?' I clapped her hands in rhythm.

Olivia gave one last sob then laughed as I pulled a face and stuck out my tongue. Bloody Muriel. I wished she was here so I could tell her; I *will* find you out – baby and all.

22.

Claudine

Summer 1936

Muriel stood as she always did in front of the farmhouse. I'd come to hate her as much as I hated the red handkerchief she held, ready to wave Tommy in. We both watched the sky. The Gipsy Moth was small, a dragonfly in the distance. I said, 'I hope Tommy doesn't bring his latest girlfriend.' She didn't answer. We both knew he was bringing Alice; that was his big surprise.

The drone of the engine reached us as the Moth turned inland from the coast. I scanned Muriel's face but she gave nothing away. She and Tommy intended to start a new life together after the exhibition. Tommy had stolen sums of money from me and thought I didn't know. The plane, not far away now, stuttered and lost height before righting itself. 'Engine trouble.' I shaded my eyes with my hand. The Moth flew like an erratic bee. We both stepped forward as the plane dipped above us and tilted a wing. Alice waved a hand from the front cockpit.

Tommy circled the paddock then ascended vertically. 'What's he doing? He'll stall.'

I turned to Muriel, who was rigid, eyes fixed on the biplane.

The Moth continued to climb, then Tommy turned and flew it deliberately towards the ground. There was nothing we could do but we ran anyway, skirting the paddock where the plane would crash. Muriel screamed Alice's name, I screamed Tommy's. The noise was a shudder of wood and cloth as the machine jarred against the ground and skidded through a fence.

I reached Alice first. Her face was unrecognisable, peeled back from its bones. She gasped as I kneeled beside her, clenched my hand, then was gone. 'Stay back,' I warned Muriel as she ran towards us. But she leaned over and called, 'Lissy!' as if she could wake her friend. I wrested the ring from Alice's finger and gave it to Muriel, then dodged the debris to find Tommy. His head was tilted at an angle, partially removed from his neck. I didn't feel as sad about this as I might have. That was my only thought when Muriel put her hand on my shoulder and shoved me.

'You made him do this.'

'As if he still listened to *me*.' I took a step backwards as she swung a punch. She didn't miss. Floored, I shook off a cluster of lights as she pinned me down with her body and crushed my throat with her forearm. I didn't defend myself. Perhaps that's what stopped her. I gasped, turned over on all fours and vomited. 'This was not my doing, Muriel.' My voice was a croak. 'Tommy wanted what was best for you and must have thought this was it.' Muriel threw herself on the ground somewhere between the two bodies.

I could have kicked her or picked up a bit of wood and belted her with it, but that would have started something I couldn't win. There were other ways.

'You want to be free of me? Take the money Tommy stole and go. I'll say it was you in the plane.' I sneered as I said it, knowing she wouldn't leave me; she'd be done as an artist if she did.

Muriel sat up, wiped the grass from her trousers and headed towards the house. Five minutes later she came out again and walked towards the barn with that old flying bag of hers in one hand and a couple of canvasses under her other arm.

She drove the Dodge to the first gate and got out to open it.

'You'll get nowhere,' I yelled.

She looked up and blew me a kiss, then drove through the gate and closed it behind her as if she didn't have a thing to lose.

23.

What you can't have

February 1936

I drove to the house in the Southern Highlands while the police were in the paddock inspecting the corpse that was meant to be me. A fog descended as I drove over Macquarie Pass. It seemed impossible on such a warm, cloudless, summer day, but the mist seeped through my skin until I felt part of its chill. 'Whacko-the-diddle-oh!' I shouted. If I had a voice, I reasoned, then I couldn't be dead in the paddock among the debris.

What I remember next is standing in front of an easel in the large back room of Claudine's house. The easel held a canvas of Alice painted in blues, mauves and sharp-edged whites. She was looking at her reflection in an oval shaped mirror. I was in the composition too, watching on like a shadow. When I turned, I saw the room was full of portraits of Alice with her acid mouth, dark hair and limestone skin.

There was one of her as a six-year-old, splinters for legs, running down the narrow street towards the Chinese grocer. A day I'd not forgotten. Alice, familiar with the counter, the abacus, the glass jars filled with dried leaves and gristle, ran her finger over every object in the shop, including the Chinese grandfather who sat behind a partition, blanket over his knees, pipe in his mouth. She kneeled at his feet. The grandfather's hands rose like spiders and ran over her scalp, palpating its bumps and rivets. 'You –' he prodded her forehead with his knuckle '– are too clever to run around like a lost cat.' He read my head too. I remember the smell of the resin from his pipe and the feel of his disinterested fingers. I was not special; Alice was the one. I looked around the room again. I must have painted them all.

Poor dead Alice. Who would tell Mrs Cooney? I imagined fronting her, my face contorted in sympathy for her loss as she asked what would become of Alice's money, and decided it wouldn't be me who told her. As for her portraits, I left Alice in the Southern Highlands. Claudine would not destroy them, I thought at the time.

After that everything went silent.

•

Adam Black and that blasted book of his, that's what started me again. *The Last Man*. Huh! They used the portrait on the front cover of his book, censored with a vine. Can you imagine that? A bit of climbing ivy stuck to his groin as if I'd painted it.

There was a photo of him on the back flyleaf of the book above a blurb that said he lived in Kings Cross. I looked up his exact address in the phone book. That would've been in '62, I think; maybe '63.

The great Adam Black. I sat opposite his flat in a greasy little coffee shop and waited for a glimpse of him. He would have enjoyed the idea of that. It was a cheap place with strong coffee and generous servings of food: spaghetti bolognaise, vegetable soup, mixed grills. We ate a lot of mixed grills back then. I sat among the other artists, hunched over a sketchbook, drawing what I saw through the fly specked window. But I wasn't like the other artists. I shook like a drunk when I tried to draw. (The sketchbook is in the pile in the back room, Jane. See for yourself how little control I had. It had been so long.)

I finally saw Adam scuttling down the road like a curled-up leaf, drab in his funereal clothes. Easy to spot alongside the thigh-high shifts and psychedelic shirts. He fumbled for his keys then turned towards the cafe, staring through the window as if he knew I was there.

I waited until the cafe closed then, under the cover of grey light, I crossed the road, climbed a set of stairs and stuffed one of my sketches under his door, confident that it would scare the bejesus out of him.

•

Back to the Southern Highlands. I can't tell you much about my first days there, although I have a memory of Freddie arriving to fetch the Dodge. I must have talked to him before he drove it away, because how else would I know that young Paul Quinlan had proved to be problematic? He told the police he'd seen me drive away from the plane crash in the Dodge. Old man Worthington, when questioned, stated the Dodge had been garaged at his North Shore property in Sydney at the time, so couldn't have been on the south coast as the boy had claimed. Paul maintained he was no liar.

I'd raised my hand as he ran across the paddock towards Claudine and the remains of the Gipsy Moth. Claudine declared him a nasty prankster and advised the police the boy had stolen a painting from the house, one of rabbits, and she'd threatened to report him for it.

'I didn't steal it. Muriel gave it to me. Ask her. She's alive – I saw her.'

Paul died in the war. So did Freddie. But they knew too much and I didn't regret their deaths.

Here's a fact I don't like: Claudine summoned my father, Lionel, and had him identify my body. She must have paid the old rogue. I read about it in a month-old newspaper I found on the train. I thought of my father running his filthy eyes over Alice's body and slammed my hand in the door to stop the rage that buzzed under my skin. There was another passenger in the carriage, an old woman, corsetted in a dark scalloped dress decades out of fashion. 'Come and sit beside me, dear.' She patted the seat next to her as if we were two friends in the school playground. I never did as I was told, but I sat where her thick, knotted fingers indicated and rested my head on her shoulder.

Before any of that, Claudine arrived in the Southern Highlands, driving the Dodge she'd picked up from her father's property on the North Shore, where Freddie had delivered it. By the time she got to me she was irritable from the hindrances (Paul) and the realisation she'd made a mistake.

'We'll report to the nearest police station,' she decided. 'Tell them it was a dreadful misunderstanding. You were here the whole time and knew nothing about the accident. Stop painting, Muriel! Talk to me.'

I hadn't slept since the crash and I'm still not sure if my conversation with Claudine was real or imagined. Nan often heard voices in our flat at Surry Hills. They'd argue with her sometimes and try to get her do things she didn't want to do. Perhaps I'd inherited them from her.

Alice stared out at me from the canvas. The mouth wasn't right. I wiped a dribble of paint with a cloth.

'You can't paint if you're dead, Muriel,' Claudine said.

I looked at Claudine, or the vision of her. 'But I'm not dead.'

'You know what I mean.' Claudine faded in and out.

I came to believe my head was flyblown. Filled with maggoty thoughts that came from painting anything that wasn't Alice. Eventually I couldn't even paint Alice. I'd always been grateful for the art; I thought life would have been a liability without it. But now I wasn't sure. I packed the small canvas bag Tommy had given me and took the triptych, stored separately to the exhibition canvasses, and then left the Southern Highlands.

•

This is where my fortune and my misfortune starts. First, my fortune. I caught a train where I found a newspaper and read an article about my death and my body being identified by my grief-stricken father. My calico carry bag contained personal belongings, along with a few shillings and five one-pound notes for emergencies. It also contained a passport in the name of Muriel Rose, a bank account, investment papers and the key to a safety box. Tommy's legacy.

My misfortune. Twelve months later I returned to the Southern Highlands. I'd wired Claudine to meet me but I got there first. Claudine sought me out in the airy back room. She kept her distance, sniffing the air. 'You smell awful.'

I looked over her shoulder for Tommy, then shifted my gaze back to her. She looked robust enough, red-cheeked. Her hair was glossy and as black as a crow's wing. She hadn't noticed the bulk I held beneath the flap of my coat.

'You heard about the exhibition?' she said.

I tilted my head sideways, unsure what she was talking about.

'I haven't heard anything.'

She raised an eyebrow. 'We couldn't find them – the paintings. I had to cancel the exhibition.'

Tommy's doing.

'I don't paint anymore,' I said.

'It wouldn't matter if you did.'

I opened the flap of my coat to show her what I'd been concealing. She stepped forward and held out her arms. I handed her the baby then left.

●

Biographer's note: The following is a transcript of the last tape Muriel recorded. Muriel's pneumonia was at an advanced stage by then. Her breathing was laboured throughout and she talked with difficulty. At times she was incoherent, possibly delirious, and moved between topics at a rapid pace, making transcription difficult.

●

There's [so much?] still to tell you, Jane, and not much time to tell it.

[First few words indiscernible] Muriel Kemp retrospective in the eighties. Out the back of the exhibition, Claudine and I argued until a man in a white shirt and black trousers came looking for her.

'I'm coming. I'm coming.' She shooed him away, then hissed at me, 'It's all too late. You can't come back.'

'That's nothing –' I waved a hand towards the gallery '– compared to what I paint now.'

'You made your choice.'

•

[Adam Black's?] Kings Cross flat, must've been 62. After I shoved the sketch under the door and walked away, I heard the door open behind me. I didn't turn, but I could sense him watching.

'I know it's you.'

If I could have talked to anyone it would have been to Adam. But what was the point? There was nothing he could do to help me. I ran down the stairs.

'Muriel! Please. Come back.'

•

Sefton's guesthouse 1940 – no, before the war . . . 1938, I think. The second time I was there. I was in the summer house for fruitcake and tea. The sky looked . . . I was going to say burnished, but that's not right. It was streaked with amber, pale pinks and crimsons like a scraped knee. Somebody sang a lullaby in a tenor voice. When the song stopped, the singer came out to the summer house and sat beside me.

'Hold my hand would you, Clive?' I said as a joke, because he already clasped my hand in his.

'Muriel Rose.' He kissed my fingertips and placed his nose against my hair. 'Why don't you stay?'

'If I could think of something to stay for, I would. But there's nothing here to interest me.'

'Ha! What a lie. I saw you out on the track today. I know it's you sculpting the rocks down by the river. We could have a life. The two of us together.'

'I already have a life.'

•

Tommy yelled, 'Follow me!' in his sleep. Cursing the Hun, the guns that jammed, the dilapidated planes with their lack of speed and the novices for their too few hours of training. He crashed and tried to beat the flames out with his hands then tried to beat the flames from his burning flesh, screaming the whole time because of the pain. When he opened his eyes and saw it was me, he whispered, 'You fucking whore.' Then he yelled, 'A fucking cunt of a whore, who'd open her legs to a mangy dog.'

Sometimes the trick was to say nothing. At other times no trick worked. He'd lash out with his hand or fist or grab a handful of hair, thigh or breast. It was best to stay still but I always fought back.

•

What was that boy's name? David. [Duane?] On the Gold Coast. I told him not to bother coming back for the lessons. 'You're a waste of your parents' money.'

'My mum will make me come anyway. Not that Dad cares. He's seen your paintings and reckons he wouldn't pay two bob for any of them.'

'Your dad can kiss my arse.'

•

Sydney, 1919. I kicked Karl James's arse right below the ARTIST FOR HIRE sign his mug mates had taped to his back. He yelled then took off. I ran after him through a scatter of his friends who stood and watched as I tanned his hide.

'Please, Muriel, at least let me stand up.' There were tears on his cheeks and his lower lip trembled.

'Embarrassed?' I rubbed his face into the shitty dirt. 'You'll be more embarrassed when I tell your cobbers you passed one of my paintings off as your own.'

•

Alice and I laughed. Scrunched up, gut tight, eyes watering, unable to breathe. She raised her head to point at the glue coming from my nose and shrieked, 'Your porridge,' and that started us again. Have I mentioned Alice before?

[Long coughing fit.]

The thing is, Jane, if I don't tell my story, someone will do it for me.

•

Biographer's note: The tape continued to record after Muriel stopped speaking and her breathing was no longer audible. After ten minutes or so there was the sound of the cat yowling and scratching at the door. The tape ended at that point.

Acknowledgements

Thank you might not be the right word, but if I hadn't been hit by a B-double truck while driving between Wollongong and Campbelltown for work some years ago, I may not have quit my job to write this book. I appreciate the nudge.

A big and definite thank you goes to my generous family and friends. You have supported me – and continue to do so – in your conversations, knowledge, feedback, advice, time, your nods, laughter, hugs and in sharing your lives. All of it has meant something to me and I'm grateful to every one of you.

In particular I'd like to thank my parents, Maxine and Barry Keys – the source of my determination – for your stories and your love.

Likewise, I'm grateful to Olena Cullen a constant friend, you have pointed me in the right direction many times; Professor Catherine Cole for your invaluable support and encouragement;

my agent Sarah McKenzie for your enthusiasm and championing this novel; Madeleine Kelly for talking to me about art and letting me sit in on your class; and The Friday Writers Group – Donna Waters, Chloe Higgins, Helena Fox and Hayley Scrivenor – for your wisdom.

Thanks to my wonderful publisher, Robert Watkins, and the team at Hachette: Brigid Mullane, Ali Lavau, Erin Stutchbury, Jenny Topham, Lydia Tasker, Kelly Jenkins, Fiona Hazard and Louise Sherwin-Stark for your insights and attention; and to designer Christa Moffitt for capturing the essence of the story in the cover (it's just right).

The book (and me) greatly benefitted from a two-week Varuna residency courtesy of a Litlink fellowship and from the careful reading and feedback provided by Mark Tredinnick during this stay.

Greatest thanks go to my family – Elwyn Asgill, Sam Keys-Asgill and Noah Keys-Asgill – for your sledging, constant questioning, debates, reassurance, love, and for valuing what I do. You have inspired me more than you know. Special thanks go to Molly for making sure I walk each day.

The impetus for this book has been the creative women who came before me, who were not acknowledged for their art, written out of history and denied both acclaim and prestige, along with the current and future generations of women as they continue to advocate for parity.

Julie Keys lives in Illawarra on the NSW south coast. Her short stories have been published across a range of Australian journals.

Julie has worked as a tutor, a Registered Nurse, a youth worker and as a clinical trials coordinator. She is now studying a PhD in Creative Arts at the University of Wollongong and writing full-time. Her debut novel, *The Artist's Portrait*, was shortlisted for The Richell Prize for Emerging Writers in 2017.

THE RICHELL PRIZE

Hachette Australia, along with the Richell family, established The Richell Prize for Emerging Writers in partnership with The Guardian Australia and The Emerging Writers' Festival (EWF). The Prize was launched in 2015 in memory of Hachette Australia's former CEO, Matt Richell, who died suddenly in July 2014.

Throughout his publishing career, Matt Richell was a passionate advocate for writers and believed investment and support of new voices to be vital for the future of great literature. The Richell Prize has been established to continue Matt's work in encouraging emerging writers in Australia. It is a prize for unpublished writers who are serious about their craft and aspire to commence a professional writing career.

The Prize has also been made possible through the support of Simpsons Solicitors and Joy.

For more information about
how to enter The Richell Prize, please head to

hachette.com.au

If you would like to find out more about Hachette Australia,
our authors, upcoming events and new releases you can visit
our website or our social media channels:

hachette.com.au

 HachetteAustralia

HachetteAus